I can't help feeling angry sometimes at a system that locks so many people out. Everything seems designed to make the rich get richer and the poor poorer, while the young especially are ignored or patronized. But in *Payback* we find a group of young people fighting back, taking expensive, privileged objects and selling them to give the money to the poor. But what's the power behind the Robin Hood slogans and social media sensation? And what happens to those caught up in the movement? This is a gripping adventure that makes you think as well as gasp – a thriller of soul and importance.

BARRY CUNNINGHAM
Publisher
Chicken House

PAYBACK
M.A. GRIFFIN

Chicken
House

2 Palmer Street, Frome, Somerset BA11 1DS
chickenhousebooks.com

Text © M.A. Griffin 2018

First published in Great Britain in 2018
Chicken House
2 Palmer Street
Frome, Somerset BA11 1DS
United Kingdom
www.chickenhousebooks.com

Cover and interior design by Helen Crawford-White
Typeset by Dorchester Typesetting Group Ltd
Printed and bound in Great Britain by CPI Group (UK) Ltd, Croydon CR0 4YY

'Everybody Knows' by Leonard Cohen. Copyright © 1993,
Leonard Cohen and Leonard Cohen Stranger Music, Inc,
used by permission of The Wylie Agency (UK) Limited.

The paper used in this Chicken House book is made from
wood grown in sustainable forests.

1 3 5 7 9 10 8 6 4 2

British Library Cataloguing in Publication data available.

PB ISBN 978-1-911077-81-7
eISBN 978-1-911490-43-2

For Saffiyah Khan,
Juan Manuel Sanchez Gordillo
and of course for Robin Hood

Also by M.A. Griffin

Lifers

Everybody knows the fight was fixed
The poor stay poor, the rich get rich
That's how it goes
Everybody knows

Leonard Cohen, 'Everybody Knows'

1

The Night of the Jaguars

'**E**verybody know their roles?'

We all nodded. We'd been through it a hundred times.

Satisfied, Gedge slipped his mask down and we followed suit. Now we were a gang of four anonymous identical foxes; red, lean faces, high ears and dark noses. Kallie adjusted her mask, loosened her stance and stretched. Coke went through a final check of the camcorder, panning it across the darkened car park. These guys were real pros. Me? It was my first ever steal. I was fizzing with terror.

We dipped our phone torches and moved off, skirting the walls and following Coke's CCTV map to ensure we stayed off-camera. Gedge made short work of a locked door and led us through into the dark, deserted shopping mall. It extended, vast and silent, towards the glittering glass roof of the central dome. Above us was the first floor – two wide balconies with brass balustrades. That's where we were headed. We stuck to the shopfronts and doorways.

'The night guy swiped in at ten p.m., just like normal,' Gedge whispered, 'but right now he could be anywhere. First rule – don't get yourselves caught before we reach the cars or it's all off.'

My breath felt hot and damp against the plastic mask. I followed Kallie and Gedge, high with panic. Coke brought up the rear, filming. He'd be uploading the footage once we were home and dry. We skirted a silent fountain, its glassy water still, and squatted against the shuttered hut of an ice cream vendor. No sign of the night guy. Gedge made a bunch of incomprehensible SWAT-team hand signals – mostly for the camera, I guessed – and I nodded, pretending I knew what the hell he was on about.

Mostly adrenaline and fear kept my mind on the job but now and again terrifying thoughts surfaced. *What if we get caught? What if the cops are waiting for us? Imagine if Dad finds out...* I'd be kissing goodbye to my cushy allowance, for one. I wouldn't be enjoying the luxury of the sixth-form dorms come September either. The thought sent stabs of shame through me. I was jumpy as a bag of caffeinated puppies and my Zen breathing trick – in through the nose, out through the mouth, count the breaths with your eyes on the mile of shadowy shops ahead – wasn't working.

The Westwater Mall is basically two giant wings extending from a central atrium designed to look like the deck of an ocean liner. In the domed hall hangs the world's largest chandelier. There are Egyptian columns, acres of Italian marble, statues of lions, griffins and angels. And that summer, two elegant Jaguars. Top spec, high performance, the works. They were due to be there until the end of August. But we had other plans.

We'd be liberating them, breaking them into bits, and selling them online.

The first of the Jags looked like a silver bullet with a red leather interior. Gedge and I tucked ourselves in against it. Kallie and Coke continued along to the second car. I checked the mall again. A grey-blue emptiness punctuated by low lines of safety lights. Maybe the night guy was taking it easy in an office somewhere. Gedge hopped into the open-top car and used his phone torch to illuminate his work. He plugged in some tricksy gizmo that could disable immobilizers and tracking devices. Nothing happened. He leant in close, cursing.

'Hold my phone. I need both hands.'

I jumped in alongside him. The car was incredible – sleek dash, dials and data screen, bucket seats in soft leather and that unmistakable fragrance of the new and the beautiful. I felt a rush of pleasure. 'Rendall!' Gedge hissed.

In a daze, I'd begun taking my gloves off to run my hands along the surfaces. I stopped myself. 'Sorry.'

Gedge fiddled and cursed in the torch beam, and something made me look up.

A sound.

Gedge killed the torch and we sat next to each other, two breathless thieves, statue-still in our badass masks. There was someone approaching. The passageway ahead was a high-ceilinged space designed to look like an oriental street market – cafes, noodle bars and conveyor-belt sushi places crowding either side of a marble walkway. Whoever it was moved cautiously. If they had a torch, they weren't using it. The two of us instinctively slid down in our seats.

It was our night guy. By his chunky silhouette, I'd have guessed he was middle-aged. He held his guard's cap under one arm and he was creeping through the dark like a pantomime villain. He hadn't seen us yet; an advertising hoarding obscured the front of the car. But he was in our way.

The food hall was our escape route. Gedge set to work again. His hands weren't as steady as before.

The engine exploded into life.

The roar echoed up the mall. The headlights came on and the night guy shouted 'Hey!', shielding his eyes and dropping his cap. Gedge crunched the gears with a desperate series of jerks and released the clutch. We were off. I was petrified Gedge was going to mow the night guy down, but he reversed, thank God, and we crashed backwards through a display board, wheels squealing on the polished floor. He swung the Jag to the left, hit the brakes, spun the wheel right, and we shot off along the upper floor of the mall. I saw the night guy running after us, his jacket open and his shirt untucked over a swaying belly. He was already knackered. We hit maybe forty miles an hour, the engine wailing in third gear, and I winced and flinched as the balustrade flew past on one side and the store windows on the other. The car's dash was beeping a shrill seatbelt warning.

Gedge hit the horn a couple of times. Ahead, Coke and Kallie in the second Jag were still struggling with Yate's gadget. And they were in our way.

'C'mon, C'mon!' Gedge yelled, accelerating towards them.

I found myself stamping on an imaginary brake. Kallie had the video camera on us, and even through her mask I could see her eyes widen from behind the viewfinder as we closed in.

Then I heard a guttural roar as their engine sprang to life and the Jag's lights came on full beam, dazzling us as Coke reversed wildly, leaving us a sliver of space. We screeched between the storefront of a jeweller's and the car, swung a sharp left and tore towards the food hall, smashing a sand-wich board aside as we went. Coke and Kallie followed, their engine bellowing. I got the blurred impression of a thousand cafe seats whizzing past in the dark as we screeched between marble pillars.

'This is it! Hold on!'

The stairs – that's right, the actual designed-for-pedestrians stairs – that took us down to the exits felt steeper than I'd imagined. We both screamed as the Jag tipped forward, its tyres hammering down the marble steps. We crashed noisily against the ground floor, braked hard and skidded to a stand-still, leaving space for Coke to pull up alongside. As I leapt from the car and ran for the doors I could hear his extended howl as he followed us down, his headlights pitched towards us like an aircraft coming into land.

Ferg had disabled the alarms on the main doors. They were built to concertina open, so all we had to do was push them apart. We kept the engines running. Gedge and I shouldered the left-hand doors, Kallie and Coke the right.

'Enough!' Gedge yelled. 'Let's go!'

I held my breath as we edged through, wincing as Gedge smacked a wing mirror, but we were out.

The night air was warm, the sky a pale purple underlit by the sodium-yellow of London. We hit the gas and roared across the painted grids of the empty car park making a crow-flies line for the exits, howling wolf-whoops under a crescent moon.

Gedge threw his head back and bawled, 'Smashin' the system every damn day!' as behind us mall lights exploded into life and an alarm blared. Ferg had hacked security so the police would get a delayed signal, allowing us time to vanish into the night. Gedge put the radio on and we both gave a roar of celebration at the opening of 'Carjack', a Kiss FM fave that name-checked us in a chorus that went, 'Crown Heights carjack, ass on the tarmac. I'll make you holler, shake your dollar like Payback.' We roared the words out between gales of laughter, chanted them back to each other when the track was over.

Weird to think that only a month ago I'd started as a porter at the Midland Hotel back in Manchester, helping out Mr Ruiz. It was how I first met Payback. How all this madness began.

But for now I was sixteen, Payback was famous and it all felt good.

I wasn't thinking about Ruiz.

2
Thief in a Palace

When the top floor of the Midland Hotel was quiet I'd ride the corridors on a laundry trolley, pushing hard from the lifts, throwing myself on to my stomach like a surfer and swishing along past the double doors of the penthouse suite, two sharp rights, steering with my trailing leg and back around to where I began. I'd set a personal best for the circuit one Saturday night in early July, despite clipping the plasterwork near the stairs and tearing a gash in the fancy wallpaper, so I was preparing myself for further greatness the night the whole Payback thing started.

I was up there delivering whisky. Edison Ruiz, I'd discovered, loved his whisky. I'd first met him, along with his associate Mr Gonzalez, when I'd dragged their bags across the lobby a few days earlier. He was just in from New Mexico, staying in Manchester for two weeks of business negotiations, and had brought enough luggage to crush an Olympic weightlifter. I'd dropped his briefcase – Mr Ruiz had it actually chained to wrist when he arrived – and ensured he was settled in his suite of penthouse rooms. It had felt good to be useful. I'd decided to celebrate by taking a laundry trolley for a spin before heading back to the lobby.

Then the old man's door had opened again. 'Bellboy,' he'd said. He had grey-green eyes and held one of the hotel's crystal decanters in liver-spotted hands. 'I'll be needing different whisky.'

I raised an eyebrow. The booze was on the house. 'Is there a problem, sir?'

Mr Ruiz gave a nod. 'This is a blend, not a single malt.' He unstoppered it and held it out in demonstration. All whisky looks the same, right? I examined it, pretending I knew what I was looking for. 'No, Bellboy. You smell it.'

'Right. I knew that.' My stomach lurched at the scent of the stuff. Last term I'd tried a few shots of a sixth-former's stash in the dorms after lights out. Aside from drama productions one of the only benefits of boarding school was getting to experiment with smuggled goods. The whisky, though, had been a bad experience. I'd spent the bulk of the night making a close inspection of the inside of the seniors' upstairs toilet. I battled to keep the memory from my face as I sniffed the Scotch.

'See?' Mr Ruiz said, replacing the glass stopper and handing the amber-coloured liquid over. 'Ask for a single malt. Aged for twenty years, preferably more. Understood?'

Downstairs in the bar, I'd gazed hopelessly at the wall of gleaming bottles while a guy in a hotel waistcoat polished glasses. I repeated Mr Ruiz's instructions.

That's when Mr Gonzalez set aside his newspaper and gave a clinical smile. 'He's got you swapping the whisky, huh?' He laughed, one of those joy-free sub-zero laughs, and shook his head. He had a square face, a long nose and dark hair. 'That one,' he suggested, pointing out a bottle.

'Thanks.'

Gonzalez sipped his coffee and grinned. His teeth were American-bright. He straightened his canary-yellow tie. Despite the suit, he had a boxer's build and hands. His knuckles were bruised. 'Any time,' he'd said.

In the next few days I'd refilled Mr Ruiz's supply twice. We'd swapped phone numbers; he'd text when he ran out and quickly got used to me arriving with a fresh bottle wrapped in a napkin and refilling his decanter while he flicked through paperwork at the coffee table, his precious laptop in the briefcase between his legs.

That night, though, I'd knocked and got no response.

I waited and tried again, weighing my options. I had a keycard for all top-floor rooms, it felt good to help out and I didn't want to anger the old man. Those steely eyes, immaculately pressed white shirts, that briefcase cuffed to his wrist, those polished shoes – they all belonged to a guy used to getting things his way. *If he returned from a meeting to find he was out of whisky . . .*

I swiped the door open and slipped inside.

The penthouse suite was a run of three connected rooms; a plush bedroom, a bathroom and a lounge with carpet so thick you could swim in it. I felt like a thief in a palace.

'Hello?'

I waited. The lights were off. The place felt empty. I'd never been beyond the sideboard where the drinks cabinet was. I decanted the whisky then stood scoping out the suite, fighting the temptation to have a quick look around. Temptation, as always, won. I took a turn through Mr Ruiz's sleeping quarters. I checked out the huge claw-footed bath and the gold taps. I padded across the fireplace rug and spent a few minutes goofing around on the cross trainer. Then I headed to the sliding glass doors to check out the roof garden and pool.

And that, in a way, is where everything started. The small thing that snowballed.

The doors to the roof garden were open a crack.

I stood on the threshold, feeling certain someone like Mr Ruiz would have left the place secure. I scanned the terrace, my pulse a quickening thud. The swimming pool lights made the water look milky. A towel lay on the cushion of an oak sun lounger, one of its edges lifting and dropping in the breeze. I looked for wet footprints on the decking, imagining that potential thieves might stop for a swim then leave handy tracks. Turns out they don't. The air was still warm and somewhere below a late tram hooted its passengers home. I took a few steps out into the night before I heard the noise. Someone shifting position out there in the dark.

A sharp note of fear sang in my chest. I wasn't alone.

I ran back inside, drew the doors shut and stopped for a quick panic. One noise on the terrace and I'd transformed into nervous-breakdown-boy. Mr Ruiz was being burgled. I couldn't just run away, could I? *I need to help in some way. Demonstrate some backbone for once.*

Then I heard more movement. This time coming from the bedroom. Someone had got inside.

Screw backbone. I did what any terrified sixteen-year-old hotel porter would do. I hid behind the sofa.

I was reversing arse-first towards the shadows gathered at the fireplace when I realized there was a torch beam scanning the room. I curled up as light swept the wall above my hiding place. While I was thinking through my options, I realized the beam had changed. The torch was on the floor now,

10

balanced on its base and projecting a pale moon on the ceiling. I heard someone prise open a door and rummage.

'Gedge?' said the intruder. Footsteps padded towards the glass doors. 'It's not here.'

Was there someone else in the room? I moved further back and found myself pressed hard against something. It was Mr Ruiz's briefcase, tucked in against the side of the sofa. The voice, sibilant and young, continued, 'That's right. Nothing.' I realized he must be talking on a phone or using one of those fancy earpieces. I gathered the case slowly into my arms. Since old man Ruiz had it handcuffed to his wrist when he'd first arrived I could at least rescue it, right? I peered around the sofa at the burglar's thin silhouette. He had a mask pushed up into his hair so he could talk. 'The combination is academic, isn't it? Like I said – no case.' He punctured a carton of juice with a straw and took a long suck. *The case was what they'd come for.* 'What about Kallie?' There was a pause. I looked across to the front door of Ruiz's suite. I'd left it open. The intruder, finishing his juice as he leant against a doorframe, had his back turned. 'Well I seriously doubt that's necessary. But I can check,' he was saying.

I had a once-in-a-lifetime chance to get the hell out. I'd done my bit, right? Now it was time for the cops to swoop in and save the day.

I swallowed hard, my muscles rigid. Then I made my move.

3

Tom, Keep Your Clothes On

I broke cover fast, leapt over the back of the sofa, then crashed through the door of the suite and out into the corridor. Behind me, someone was following, steps drumming down the hall carpet. I took the stairs three at a time.

I think I came off at the third floor and barrelled into the corridor towards the lifts. I swerved to avoid a cleaner with a trolley of laundry. There was a ruckus behind me – I heard the trolley tumble over and angry shouts – and I ended up taking the west stairs, using the banister for balance as I swung around the corners, the briefcase clattering. I virtually fell down the final flight to the ground floor. I was about to head to reception when a thought struck. If I went charging across the lobby with a guest's private possessions, I'd be the one who looked like a thief. Michelle, the night manager, was prickly at the best of times. She'd go ballistic.

I needed to be far more discreet. I shuttled low into the kitchens, heading for the service doors at the back of the hotel. Once outside, I put the case on the floor between my feet and leant on my knees trying to catch my breath, wondering whether I should join a gym. I heard the door click shut behind me and realized I was locked out. No problem, I could use the side door. Better that than circling the building to the guest entrance carrying Mr Ruiz's case.

I rested in the delivery bay where the vans reversed in. The night air was delicious. I'd be asking Ruiz for a reward, I decided as I descended the concrete ramp on unsteady legs, crossing the cobbles to the side door. There was an electronic combination lock that I only half-remembered. I stooped at the keypad, prodding hopelessly.

Then, a yell – a voice giving a roar like a tennis player – and something belting me big-time across the back of the head. I staggered, spinning the case across the cobbles. I managed to straighten. My neck glowed with pain. I spun woozily and fended off a second blow with a raised arm.

Someone in a fox mask was hitting me with a broomstick.

I knew that mask.

They came again and I dodged a blow and tried to throw a punch. Not being the fighting type, I swung and missed but found myself grappling the guy's shoulder and pulling at the mask. It came free with an elastic snap. The broom we'd been fighting over broke in two and I fell backwards and struck the floor. I remember the rainwater between the cobbles against my cheek as I rolled. I could taste blood. I looked up. The kid had scooped Ruiz's case under an arm and was replacing the mask hurriedly. It wasn't a guy, it was a girl. I didn't see much except dark skin, a bob of black hair and wide, amazed eyes. She turned and bolted for the gates and the street beyond, impossibly quick.

I don't know how long I lay there but by the time I'd shuffled, bleary-eyed, into the lobby there was already a cop car in the turning circle and a crew of uniformed officers at the revolving doors.

Michelle waved me over. She was on the phone, one hand over the receiver. 'There you are Tom! I'm afraid there's been a theft.' She clocked my crumpled uniform and bleeding lip. 'What happened to you?' Before I could answer, she was back to her call. 'I know, Mrs Hollander,' she cooed. 'It's not acceptable. Let me make a note. You saw a hotel staff member riding a laundry trolley like a go-kart. I'll review the CCTV footage immediately.' She put her pen down and placed a hand over the mouthpiece. 'Could you speak to the DCI please Tom? I believe Mr Ruiz from the penthouse suite has asked for you.'

My head ached as I crossed the lobby towards the officers.

A woman in a grey suit looked up as I approached and held out a hand. 'DCI Sinclair,' she smiled. 'You're the night porter? You've been in the wars, eh? If you wouldn't mind . . .' she indicated the bar. 'Just a few questions Thomas.' She was brisk and cheerful like a primary school teacher. She sat me down, produced a notebook, then considered the barroom's polished brass and chandeliers with a soft whistle. 'Nice place! Have you worked here long?'

We went through the basics – shift hours, recent whereabouts – until I mentioned refilling Mr Ruiz's whisky. The DCI said, 'This might be a good time to speak to you both together.' She nodded to an officer and sipped her water. I cringed inwardly and waited. A few moments later a cop accompanied the old man to the table. Mr Ruiz pulled out a chair and sat. I thought he might be mad but to my relief he placed a sympathetic hand on my shoulder before smiling at the DCI . She covered a few things quickly, asking after his business here, date of arrival, associates. Then she queried our working relationship.

'So you made an arrangement about accessing the room?' she asked us both.

Edison Ruiz straightened his cuffs. He seemed totally unruffled. By contrast, I was big-time ruffled. I'd let the old man down. 'Mr Rendall is a trustworthy young man,' Ruiz said. 'And he knows which whisky I like. I was happy with him performing that service.'

'So you were in the penthouse suite when it happened?' The DCI's gaze skewered me.

I stammered out an account of the roof garden, the noises, my escape. 'I ended up at the side entrance' I said. 'That's when I got hit.'

Sinclair tapped her teeth with the end of her pen. 'Could you describe your attacker, Thomas?'

I felt hot and itchy. I paused, maybe a touch too long. 'No. I'm afraid not.'

Sinclair smiled. Her eyes thinned. 'You remember *nothing* about your attacker's appearance?' She took a super-casual sip of water.

No way was I mentioning the mask. That was something I'd be following up myself. 'They were just a figure in the dark.'

Rather than write my answer down she took a long unblinking look at me. I managed to hold myself together. 'Height? Build? Gender?'

I tried to loosen my bone-dry throat and croaked, 'Male, I think. Difficult to tell, it happened so fast.' My smile, I'm pretty sure, came out guilty and wrong.

The DCI watched me. 'Thanks,' she said eventually. 'We'll be in touch.'

*

Slipping back into the lobby, I began to relax. I needn't have bothered. The night still hadn't delivered its knockout blow.

'Thomas?' Michelle was hunched over her monitor as I passed. 'Do you mind having a quick look at this footage?'

It's too painful to tell the next bit in detail. The short version: I had to stand next to my boss, twisting with embarrassment as we watched grainy CCTV pictures of some juvenile lunatic executing a 360 spin on a laundry trolley and scaring the hell out of a guest's dog. Then we both agreed it looked startlingly like me. We watched the same person body-boarding the same trolley down a wide corridor, backwards and at high speed. Again, we discussed the uncanny similarities between the perpetrator on the video and the Midland Hotel's current night porter.

I was asked to clear out my locker.

'I'll need your uniform,' Michelle pointed out afterwards as I handed over my badge.

I got the wrong end of the stick and fumed, 'You want me to walk home *in my pants*?'

Michelle gave a weary sigh. 'No Tom, keep your clothes on. I'll need you to bring them in tomorrow.'

'Right,' I said with a nod. 'I knew that.'

Outside, the night air was still warm. I walked through town feeling sorry for myself. It's not like I needed the cash but I'd enjoyed working at the Midland. With Dad chasing the corporate dollar on his never-ending business trip – he was the uptight CEO of a fracking company – and Chris at uni, school holidays tended to be me rattling around at home checking social to see what the boarding-school crew were up to. Night-portering had been a happy distraction. I wondered what the hell I was going to do now I'd blown the gig.

Waiting for the late bus on Oxford Street I noticed the new graffiti under the arch of the railway line:
Payback: Changing the world one steal at a time.
I thought of the girl in the mask and felt my spirits lift.

4
Unmasked

It was close to three in the morning by the time I made it out to the suburbs but I was too wired for bed. I let myself in quietly. Chris had been back from uni a fortnight but was still sleeping off the end-of-term parties. He'd left strict instructions not to be disturbed. I shucked off my shoes, swapped my uniform for a pair of Kylo Ren pyjamas and padded into the kitchen. Despite owning two fridges, we never had anything interesting to eat. A glance in both confirmed this. Dad had never got his head around supermarkets – it'd been Mum's thing. I made a bowl of cereal at the island and dug out my tablet. I kept the kitchen lights low, drew the curtains across the French windows, brought up my favourites and got started. First up, as always: Payback.

I was their biggest fanboy; a T-shirt wearing, forum-chatting, fully geeked-out Payback fanatic. My obsession had started a couple of years ago; a kid at my boarding school had found out about them from his cousin who'd taken a gap year to live in a tree and protest about sea levels. They'd only had the bare bones of a website to start with, a white on black banner-heading. *Payback*, it had said in the beginning. *The Second Coming . . . of Robin Hood*. They began uploading videos a year or so after that and my whole school went crazy for them. Everything was shot at night with those special cameras that bleach people white against a pitch-black backdrop and soon I knew every jumpy, torchlit frame by heart. They robbed betting shops, broke into golf clubs, did over company offices and here's the thing: the text across the screen would give you this lesson on how bad these guys were – they exploited workers or didn't pay tax – then you'd see their stuff taken. In the closing shots, Payback would hand out the money they'd made, giving cash away in packets to people who needed it the most. It was real-life rob-the-rich stuff. I loved the drama of it.

There were no new posts or videos so I decided to re-watch a few old faves, starting with the JSR Casino steal. I'd seen that rooftop break-in dozens of times; you get a pretty good look at the gang as they speed confidently across a pitched roof, leaping from guttering to fire escape, then move to a pyramid of raised skylights where they use a glass cutter to make a perfect incision before lowering themselves inside. There were five of them in total; one behind the camera, four in shot, all anonymous behind their masks. They'd started out wearing kids' Robin Hood masks for each video (you know the grinning cartoon fox with a feather in a Lincoln green hat) but last summer they'd switched to proper wild-looking urban fox masks. Despite the disguises I felt I knew them. I'd often daydream of a world without school in which these guys were my friends. My family, even.

I rolled my shoulders, feeling my bruises ache, and re-focused on the video. Payback's leader was a big guy with cropped blond hair who wore black hoodies with 'New World Order' written on them. He was out in front as they scampered low across the roof. Following was the tall guy, the slightly awkward one with the long coat. You could tell from their build and voices that the two following were girls, and it was these figures I watched silhouetted against the pale triangle of illuminated glass as they forced their way in. I paused, scrolled back, watched again, then jumped to the closing scenes. Each Payback video ended with a shot of the gang dropping the money off as a donation or giving it out to crowds. A metallic voiceover always finished by saying, 'This film is dedicated to victims of the system. Ninety-five per cent of what we take is given away to those in need.' Then, after a pause, 'Payback. The redistribution solution.' In this video they were pushing packets of cash through letterboxes, running fast along a dilapidated row of terraced houses somewhere, whooping delightedly. The girl I was studying got caught out as a resident opened their door. She handed the cash over to the surprised woman in a dressing gown and slippers, bobbed a neat curtsey and ran.

I stretched my legs, searched the fridge again and ate an apple while I scanned the Payback discussion boards. I was always first in the queue when national newspapers ran 'Who are Payback?' stories or published cool infographics, each crew member a silhouette with a question mark for a face. Every website in the land ran pieces speculating about its members. Payback were all public-school educated Oxbridge undergrads; Payback were selected by a secret anti-government agency; Payback were a fake-news conspiracy; one member was a drug addict, one was the renegade son of a high-ranking diplomat, one used to be in a boy band, one was Banksy.

That night there'd been a link to a recent newspaper piece

called, 'Crusades, Charades and Midnight Raids: The Rise of Direct-Action Pressure Groups' which mostly went over my head, and afterwards the usual comments suggesting who Payback might hit next and a collection of pro-Payback graffiti, including a cool mural on the side of a bank in south London that read, *Robin Hood is back . . . and this time there are five of him.*

I logged off and climbed the stairs, creeping past Chris's room just in case, then hauled myself up to my attic room and lay on my bed, wincing at my bruised shoulders.

After everything that had happened I expected to sleep easy and long, but that first night, every time I closed my eyes I saw the wide-eyed girl unmasked.

Next morning, I folded my uniform and used some of the cash Dad had left me to taxi myself back into town. My body ached as I crossed St Peter's Square towards the hotel. A queue of guests was checking out in the lobby so I decided to wait before dropping off my kit. Someone had abandoned their copy of the *Telegraph* and I flicked through it in a seat by the window, looking for Payback stories.

I'm not the brightest but here's what I'd been thinking all night: there was a chance I'd just been given a battering by *actual Payback*. There'd been plenty of copycat activity – like those naff tribute bands with a name that's nearly but not quite right – gangs had been acting like they were the real thing. I'd read all about them. Pretenders were mostly small-time: a group spray-painting graffiti; someone vandalizing the offices of a dodgy loan company. Knowing everything about Payback, I could easily spot an amateur crew pretending to be big-time. And the more I thought about it, the more last night's theft looked like the real deal. There'd been a few of them – the kid up in Mr Ruiz's room, the person he was speaking to, the girl in the mask who'd hit me – and they'd all had earpiece communication with each other. Plus they'd broken into a top-floor suite of rooms and they'd actually stolen something.

I'd been staring blankly at the newspaper but my eyes suddenly popped into focus. I was looking at an article with the headline PAYBACK ON THE MOVE AS THEFTS PROLIFERATE. I wasn't familiar with *proliferate* but I got the gist. *After high-profile thefts in London and Oxford, Payback appear to have moved north. The direct-action pressure group, who have become famous for stealing high-value items in order to re-distribute earnings amongst those considered less fortunate, may be connected to recent burglaries in Birmingham and Manchester.* I felt my skin prickle. I devoured the rest of the article and finding nothing I didn't already know, stared out of the window, grinning at my own reflection. It *had* been them last night.

I'd been assaulted by my actual heroes. I'd never felt so proud.

A few minutes later I was beginning to grasp what this actually meant. They'd stolen Mr Ruiz's case. Payback never took anything from an innocent victim; they did their research, they targeted the bad guys and they exacted the kind of justice beyond the reach of law or government. So if it really *was* Payback last night, Edison Ruiz must deserve it. The thought sent a sharp chill through my gut.

I folded the paper, watched passing pedestrians and thought: *Payback could still be in town, right?*

5
That Thing with the Balloon

Scattered among the crowds of suits outside were little explosions of colour and life. That guy with the skateboard and multicolour high-tops . . . could he be a Payback member?

That art student with the goth backpack?

A girl was pushing an older guy in a wheelchair and they were laughing and singing something together. Maybe they were involved.

Three black kids with killer Afros were sharing a bench at the tram stop – they looked the right age and build.

Across the street there was a little girl whose helium balloon had drifted out of her grasp and snagged under the high entrance to the library. A crowd had gathered and it took me a moment to clock why. Someone was shinning their way up one of the columns to get the balloon, and passers-by were stopping to watch their progress.

It'd be *so* Payback to spend your spare time rescuing kids' balloons, I thought.

I grinned as I watched. It was a girl. She was amazing – spanning the gap between two columns to climb, strong hands gripping the sheer stone. There was a gasping crowd below her, phones uplifted to capture the moment she grabbed the string of the balloon and worked her way back down with it in her teeth. A cheer went up as she handed it back to the girl, whose amazed mum was giving her a hug of thanks. The climber did a little comic curtsey.

Something about the gesture struck me.

The JSR Casino drop. *It's her.* I'd seen enough videos to be sure. *It's actually her.* I left my porter's uniform on the table by the window and headed outside.

It took me a moment to find her in the crowds heading down Peter Street. I followed on the far pavement. She was young and athletic, walked fast on long legs; black jeans and a hoodie, dark bobbed hair, brown skin. She turned right on to Deansgate and I crossed, my heart tight and jumpy.

'Hey!' I called. 'Hi, wait.' She turned, gave me a glance, walked on. 'Wait a sec. That was amazing!' I drew alongside. I had to jog to match her. 'That thing with the balloon. Fantastic. Where did you learn to do that?'

The girl shrugged, uninterested.

I kept up my scamper. 'I got robbed last night,' I said, which was at least a memorably random thing to say.

'Yeah. Listen, I'm in a bit of a hurry.' She found another gear and strode forward, head down.

I had to swerve through a crowd then run to catch up. 'My name's Tom. I got done over at the Midland Hotel.' She was a stride ahead. 'I think you hit me with a broom.'

She raised her head, laughed, and slowed. This time she actually looked at me. Being a pretty good liar myself, I reckon I've got a sense for when I'm being played. I swear she waited a split second too long before giving me the brush-off. 'Are you nuts? Go away.'

She recognized me. 'Wait. I'm a huge Payback fan. Massive.'

At that she opened her stride and left me for dead. 'Get lost or I'll call the police.'

I got trapped at a crossing and she disappeared into the crowds. After that I had to run just to keep her in sight. That little curtsey was pure Payback. She was for real and she was heading for Victoria Station. She looked back and I had to duck behind a posse of skaters. The crowds thinned beyond Exchange Square so I loitered near a tattoo place, watching from a distance.

Near Victoria Station the railway arches are numerous and deep, big brick-ceilinged holes punched under the city. Dad had told me about these places – ancient offices and docking stations that used to be for old steamers and packet-ships using the river. Now they were converted into lock-ups and garages or hipster breweries and sourdough bakeries. She was heading for a series of arches used as an underground car park. I hung back, weaving between vehicles as I followed her into a vast twilight space. Cars were packed in, and around the edges were further arches under humming strip-lights. *Arches 1–5*, indicated a painted sign with an arrow. *Arches 6–11*, said another. Each arch had a huge metal shutter, most dragged open on runners, and each space beyond was occupied by a business. Revolution Media had one. Banks Audio-Visual and Riverborn Gin Distillers had others. Three couriers at *Arch 11: Pedal Power Bikes* were pushing off to begin their days' work.

The girl was crossing the parking lots towards the rumble of a spotlit workshop where disassembled cars were raised on rotary lifts. Blokes in greasy overalls lay beneath them. Tools clanged, a radio played Bon Jovi and a guy with a blowtorch sent an arc of sparks bouncing. I felt my blood thud. I watched as the girl waved at the welder, who raised his mask and returned the greeting. She passed through the workshop – *Arch 16: Maxi's AutoService*, the sign said – then took a sharp right up a set of steps into a brick passage. I moved quickly, keeping her in sight and caught a glimpse of her dragging aside an interior metal door that squealed on its runners. She slipped beyond.

An arch within an arch.

I kept my distance, scuffing my trainers nervously under a crew of cooing pigeons. I was sufficiently alert to wonder what the hell I was doing. Maybe they were all inside that secret place – the whole gang. My first thought was to get in, snap a selfie and hashtag it all over social. But I hesitated. No one knew I was here. Dad was hundreds of miles away as usual, I hadn't told Chris, I'd left the hotel without handing my uniform over and I was loitering in an underground world I hadn't known existed. I might vanish and never return.

On the other hand . . . I steeled myself and crossed the cobbles. The welder looked up as I approached. I decided I'd unleash one of my killer accents. Manc – not one of my best, despite living here. I sloped towards him and said, 'Hi. I'm meeting with Payback.'

The guy narrowed his eyes and took his gloves off slowly. He was Caribbean-looking, a wide face pockmarked with scars, a gold tooth. Maxi Johnson, I'd learn later, was shrewd, clever and super-loyal. He plunged a hand into the pocket of his oily overalls, produced a phone and turned away from me. I didn't hear what he said. The conversation didn't last long.

Maxi ambled back to me and shrugged. 'Nah'dea what you

mean man.'

'I saw her go in. I just want a few minutes.'

'Like I said,' Maxi scowled. 'Talking nonsense, boy.'

I tried again. Maxi wouldn't budge. 'Please,' I said. 'I just want to talk to her.'

Eventually it was the girl herself who emerged from the arch. Turns out she'd been watching. 'Thanks Maxi,' she said. 'I'll deal with him.'

She beckoned. I followed her in.

Beyond the workshop and through the door was another space, its interior on two levels. Upstairs, three people around a table watched a film projected on the wall. They were sitting under a shaft in the roof, which illuminated their workspace with pale daylight. The talk was raucous. A dog scampered between their ankles, barking happily. A roar of laughter rose as they watched the video. On the lower level where I stood there were rucksacks, climbing gear, waterproofs. Suspended from the underside of the upper floor was a sign. *Payback* it said, white letters on a green background, *Stickin' it to the Rich, 24/7.* My heart pistoned.

This was real.

6
Arch 17

A set of wooden stairs hugged the far wall. I swallowed back nerves and followed the girl up to the noise of the mezzanine. The video was a rough cut of last night's grab. Three people, backs to me, were guffawing at a handheld shot of my arse disappearing down the hotel stairs. They'd filmed my cack-handed escape attempt. I watched myself vanishing into the kitchens. Then there was a cut. Now I saw the girl, complete with fox mask, clutching the case and executing a smart victory dance. Gales of laughter at that.

In the centre of the table was Ruiz's briefcase.

The girl motioned for the movie to stop and the frame froze. A second girl spun away from her laptop and considered me. Two guys looked my way. Four of them, I thought. If this was Payback, they were one short.

'You again,' said the figure at the head of the table, a broad-shouldered blond-haired guy with a beard. He wore a black hoodie and he was running a hand through his hair. His build and manner were just like the Payback leader guy. That's because he *was* the Payback leader guy.

The others looked at me through narrow eyes. The girl I'd

followed pointed at a spare seat. I took it. The dog, a little black thing with beady eyes, growled at me.

'He followed me from the hotel. I know, I know,' said the girl as the others winced. 'Hassled Maxi downstairs, been pretty persistent. Thought it might be good to find out why.'

A thin lad in a neatly ironed designer polo-shirt pursed his lips in disapproval and said, in a voice I recognized, 'This complicates things.'

The big guy spoke. 'Nice run last night.' He had a soft Irish accent and was older than the others, maybe early twenties. He put a baseball cap on and rotated it so it faced backwards. Against all known laws of science and nature, he managed to make it look cool. 'I'm Gedge.'

The other lad's jaw dropped at this display of trust. I'm pretty sure mine did too. Real-name terms with Payback was like a dream.

'Tom Rendall,' I said, before finding a way to wreck the camaraderie. 'Listen. That case belongs to someone else.'

'You sure about that?' asked Gedge.

'Yeah, I'm sure.'

Gedge twisted the ring-pull on a drink can. 'Ownership is kind of a slippery idea, isn't it?'

Ownership is a slippery idea. Such a Payback thing to say. I wasn't totally sure what it meant and I couldn't think of a good answer. 'Mr Ruiz is . . .'

Gedge ignored me, skimming the briefcase across to the neatly dressed, skinny kid, who set aside a carton of apple juice, reserving the straw to chew, and fastidiously smoothed the front of his shirt. 'Coke, why don't we see what's in the case?'

The guy called Coke – the slim one from the videos, the one often behind the camera, I realized – barely needed to examine the combination locks. 'Three barrels,' he said, chewing his straw. 'That's a thousand possible combinations. I'll do it in three. Any takers?'

'That'll get me into trouble,' I said.

The whole table laughed and I realized how pathetic it sounded. To my right, the girl I'd followed regarded me with amused dark eyes; to her left, the girl at the laptop, maybe fourteen, was picking at her fingernails, her mousy hair chopped into spikes. No one looked ready to help me out.

Coke sighed and paused to polish his Tom Ford glasses with a monogrammed handkerchief. 'No one bets against me these days,' he said, tucking his hankie into the pocket of his razor-sharp chinos as he set to work. He chose his sequence and pressed the catches. Nothing.

'One,' said Gedge with a grin.

Coke raised his eyebrows. 'Unusual. OK, let's try . . .' he rolled again. 'Statistically speaking,' he explained in his sing-song voice, 'this is highly likely to . . .' He pressed. The catches popped open. Coke grinned.

'Two. That wasn't so bad,' Gedge said. He turned to me. 'Right. Let's see what you've been guarding, shall we?'

The four of them crowded around the open case. I stood to get a better look.

Inside were two bottles and two neat packages of cash, each sealed in a red paper band that said '£2,000'. The queen stared up at me from the top of the stack.

'How much is this worth, Ferg?' Gedge levered one of the bottles out. It had no label, but traced into the glass were the words 'Michter's Celebration Sour Mash Whiskey'.

The quiet girl with the crazy hair prodded her phone. 'Three thousand six hundred pounds and seven pence per bottle,' she said.

It sounded a hell of a lot to me but Coke's forehead was creased as he said, 'That's it?'

Gedge unpacked the remainder of the case. Two newspapers, a cardboard folder, glasses case, pen drive, cigarettes. He lined it all up neatly, opened the folder, slid out the contents and leafed through the papers, carelessly at first, then with a sudden and intense focus.

He studied a few pages. Then he swallowed back a grin and folded them shut. I'm no shrink but even I could tell the guy had seen something magnificent. Whatever it was, he kept it to himself.

He set the papers aside and stared at the money.

'Gedge?' Coke prompted.

The big guy ran a distracted hand across his face, then cleared his throat. 'Yeah. Right. What have we got here?' He counted the cash, big fingers moving swiftly. 'Turns out your Mr Ruiz isn't so squeaky clean. This,' he fanned the twenties, 'is one of his gifts. He's very generous with his gifts. I mean, as the CEO of a private equity firm he can afford to be, particularly when he's looking to acquire certain . . . financial advantages.'

I'd half-figured out Ruiz might be corrupt. It was weird to have it confirmed. 'Are you sure?'

'We do a lot of research,' Coke said in a bored voice, examining his fingernails.

'Well, Ferg does,' corrected Gedge, raising his chin at the girl on her phone. 'Becky Ferguson, our 414 and hacker supremo.'

'It's the most expensive American whisky in the world,' said Ferg in a neat, nasal voice, studying her screen. 'Second is Old Fitzgerald Bourbon. Third is Parker's Heritage Collection Number 2. Fourth is A. R. Hirsch's sixteen-year reserve. Fifth is—'

'Thanks Ferg,' said the girl who'd hit me the night before. 'Becky loves her lists.' She seemed to think for a moment. Then she smiled. 'I'm Kalima.'

I raised a hand, going for cool and ironic, still not quite believing I was doing introductions with *actual Payback*. I had their logo as my screensaver. I had two Payback T-shirts in case one was in the wash. This was my one shot, I figured. I had to take it.

'Listen,' I said. The damn dog growled again, skittering around my feet under the table. 'I could help out. I kept the police off your back. I love your work. Just give me a chance.'

Coke gave me a pitying grin. 'We're not looking for a hotel porter.'

It stung but I pushed on. 'I'm an actor,' I said. That much was true. Back in my junior-school-nativity days I'd been the wise-man-bearing-gifts five years on the bounce. By boarding school I'd started getting proper parts. Peter Pan, the Scarecrow from *Wizard of Oz*, the fat guy from *Bugsy Malone*. Mum was always in the front row. She used to save my write-ups. *Thomas Rendall's performance was a triumph of enthusiasm over technique,* says one about *Technicolour Dreamcoat. Rendall was obviously enjoying himself tremendously!* says a piece about my Long John Silver in *Treasure Island*. (I remember asking Mum, 'Is that good?' and she laughed and said it was.) '. . . And I'm good with people,' I continued. 'They trust me – it's how I ended up in his hotel room.'

'Tell me about the police,' said Gedge.

I sensed a crack in the door and jammed my foot in. 'DCI Sinclair,' I said. Gedge gave a nod to Ferg, who turned back to her laptop to begin an immediate search. I continued, 'Pretty old, maybe five foot ten, short greying hair. I stayed vague, pretended I hadn't seen anything . . .' Ferg showed me her screen. 'Yes. That's her.'

Becky Ferguson read aloud. 'Amelia Sinclair joined Greater Manchester Police in 2008 . . . started her career in Staffordshire . . . variety of uniformed roles . . .' she scanned further. 'Firearms officer . . . strategic on-the-ground role in serious crime, counterterrorism and public protection . . . prior to this, Head of Crime for Northumbria.'

Gedge held a hand up. 'She's a major player. We could have some problems.'

'I think she liked me,' I said. 'I can help.'

'We don't need this,' Coke pointed out. He was brushing his hair into a neat parting with a little comb he kept in the breast pocket of his top.

I'm not proud of this next bit. 'You're one person short,' I pointed out. 'If you've lost a member, I could step in. Plus, I know your names, I know what you look like . . .' I was wincing even as I made this feeble threat. Coke shot me a look I thoroughly deserved. I fought back a blush. 'Sorry, I just *really* want to help.'

'OK. How about this.' Gedge straightened. Kalima sat forward. 'We give you a trial run. First, we'll need this case returning to Mr Ruiz. Minus the booze and cash.'

Coke looked up. 'You want to return the case? Why bother?'

Gedge shrugged. 'A test for our friend Rendall. And if that goes well,' he added, turning to me, 'One grab. That's it.'

'Excellent!' I boomed, clapping. 'Excellent! Really excellent.' It was embarrassing; I said excellent a few more times, adding swear words for extra emphasis.

'Calm down,' Kalima laughed. The dog yapped happily.

'Drop the case back this afternoon. Then you'll need to be available tomorrow night,' Gedge said. 'All night. We're in London.'

I nodded eagerly. 'No problem. What are we doing?'

Gedge grinned. 'Stealing a pair of Jaguars,' he said.

7

Strictly Summer Operation

So that's how it happened. I threw Ruiz's cigarettes, pen drive and newspapers into the case and that afternoon wandered back across town to the hotel. My porter's uniform was still where I left it, folded on a coffee table in the reception lounge. Michelle only worked nights, thank God, so I dropped the uniform at reception then used a napkin to wipe the case clean of prints – Gedge had been insistent on that point – and left it at the lost and found. That night I rode down to London in the back of Gedge's van, listening to Kalima laughing up front with Coke.

After that fabulous Jaguar grab, I never expected Payback to call. I'd had my brush with glamour and now it was back to the treadmill of normality, right?

Wrong. Gedge phoned the night after. Turns out I'd passed the test. 'Rendall,' he said. 'Everyone's here. We've got work to do.'

My crazy summer was just getting started.

The next morning I made the trip beneath the arches. It was a walk I'd get to know well: through the underground car park, past the distilleries, the lock-ups and small businesses huddled in the shadows, over to Maxi's AutoService where the radio echoed Green Day across the gutted shells of picked-apart cars, the coffee machine hissed and Maxi wiped his oily hands on a rag. He'd nod and stand aside, giving access to the secret interior beyond.

On that morning Gedge was sitting on a fold-down bed downstairs amongst piles of books and papers, pulling on a pair of sneakers, smiling at the dog as it rolled around with a punctured ball.

'That's Marx,' Gedge grinned, putting on his baseball cap – backwards, as before.

'I assumed it was yours. Who's Mark?'

Gedge laughed, rubbing the dog's ears affectionately as it fired off a volley of yaps. 'Not "Mark's" – *Marx*. Karl Marx.'

I'd never heard of Karl Marx but I styled it out with an expert change of subject. 'You *sleep* here?' I'd honestly figured they were loaded. How many hundreds of thousands of pounds must have passed through the Payback machine? As I stared at Gedge's makeshift accommodation, I fully accepted for the first time that this gang really were redistributing ninety-five per cent of the money they made.

Gedge shrugged. 'We're on the move a lot,' he said. The warm nights helped I guessed, but he'd freeze over winter. I said so and he laughed. 'We won't be here by winter. For a start, Payback's strictly a summer operation. When these guys go back to school,' he jerked a thumb in the direction of upstairs, 'we'll shut down until next year. We're never about for long – keeps the cops off our back.' He watched Marx scuttle off under his bed. 'C'mon.'

We headed up the stairs. Around the table under the light well, Coke was swiping through a website on his phone, Ferg seemed to be colour-coding flash drives and Kalima was rifling through a bag of climbing gear; those flexible shoes, ropes and crampons, hip-bags for chalk. Her hair was pulled back into a ponytail.

'You always make it complicated,' she was saying to Coke. 'It's like we can never just hand the stuff out, y'know? You think Robin Hood arsed about checking the whatever-it-is?'

'The World Bank Development Indicators,' Coke said. He looked up as Gedge and I arrived. 'Kallie Shah got her political education via Disney,' he said to us both. 'All we have to do, apparently, is find a handy peasant village and distribute the Jaguar money.'

'Shut it, Databoy,' Kallie objected. 'I'm just saying we waste time on websites.'

Coke held his phone up and flapped at it with a delicate hand. 'Look. We should be routing funds abroad. Poverty is relative. This money belongs in a developing nation.'

'Help me out Gedge,' said Kallie.

The big lad smiled but when he talked his voice was full of fierce authority. Those books by his bed weren't just for decoration. 'The richest one per cent of this country's population own nine and a half trillion in property,' he said. 'Five billionaire families own as much as twenty per cent of the rest of us put together. One in nine households now own a second home. By contrast the poorest fifty per cent of the UK control only nine per cent of its wealth.' Gedge held up a hand as Coke looked to interject. Coke must have heard all this before – he'd probably put the copy on the website – this speech was for me. 'If the government of this country doesn't redistribute wealth fairly, Payback has to. We've got five weeks until we close down. Time for three more takes.

37

You've got a point, Aidy, but we're not in a position to change this year.'

'You said that last summer,' Aidy Coke said. 'I'll wager you said it the summer before. This is why Jay left.' Ferg turned away at this, crossing her arms, her head down.

Gedge placed his hands on the table and spread his fingers. 'That's not true and you know it. Jay left because of the Lucille Deutsch Investments con. Nothing else.'

The what? I didn't know the Lucille Deutsch con – it hadn't ended up online. *Not every job gets filmed? They do secret stuff too? Whoa.*

'Anyway, we may well have our Jay replacement now, mightn't we?' Gedge continued, pulling a chair out for me.

'Come on,' Aidy Coke laughed. 'Rendall's no actor.'

That was a cheek. 'I am,' I objected. 'I've done the genie in *Aladdin*.' (Basically dressed in a nappy, painted blue and belting out 'Never Had a Friend Like Me', but I wasn't about to point that out.) 'I've done *Peter Pan*,' I was counting them off on my fingers now. '*Our Day Out, Blood Brothers . . .*' I thought about mentioning my Shakespeare but decided against it. A snarky local paper had murdered me in *A Midsummer Night's Dream. Rendall may deliver with gusto,* it grumbled, *but it's clear he has no idea what his lines actually mean.* I thought that was harsh. It's Shakespeare, folks. *No one* knows what their lines mean. 'And *The Sound of Music*,' I added, praying there wasn't any surviving footage of that particular car crash.

'Quality productions, I'll wager,' Coke sneered, tidying the tassels on his tan-coloured loafers. Ferg, satisfied with the gaudy symmetry of her flash-drive collection, picked up her laptop.

'We're always like this,' Kallie pointed out, packing her climbing gear away. She stuck her tongue out at Coke, who rolled his eyes.

Ferg put her hand up like a schoolkid. 'Actually, we're not always.' She addressed the table in a clipped stutter. 'It is true that we do argue sometimes but there have only been three arguments so far this summer not counting today. There was the golf club drop where we couldn't agree about how to redistribute the four thousand eight hundred pounds from the safe. There was the disagreement about how many people to include when we did the IT company drop, and—'

'Thanks,' Gedge interrupted, looking up from his phone. He seemed disturbed. 'That'll do for now, Ferg. If we've had a three-argument summer that's pretty standard.'

'No, last year it was six,' said Ferg. 'Firstly, there was the fight about the casino drop where Aidy hit Jay—'

Coke polished the press-studs on his skinny-fit shirt. 'Thanks for reminding me, Ferg. Can we give this a rest?'

'Anyway I've decided on how we're redistributing the Jaguar money, so no discussion necessary,' Gedge put his phone aside. I could see him making an effort to refocus before delivering his vote of confidence. 'I'm going to do it with Rendall,' he said. 'Teach him the ropes.'

As if my summer wasn't strange enough already, things got even weirder back home that afternoon. Chris was upstairs, packing.

'What's going on?' He was stuffing swim shorts and flip-flops into one of Dad's suitcases. 'Hey! That T-shirt's mine.' Chris hooked it out and threw it at me. It was my Payback tee from last summer, strictly private property. 'Going away?' I said, half-joking.

Chris grinned. 'Croatia.'

'You're kidding, right?'

'A bit of beach time, Buckaroo. And there may be a girl involved.' I watched my supposedly older-and-wiser brother throw a celebratory hip-swaying spin with jazz hands. 'Fives!' he said, holding out both palms. I left him hanging. 'C'mon. It's just for a few weeks.'

This was bad news. Dad was in Rotterdam until late August and the summer was going to be me and Chris together. 'You're meant to be keeping an eye on me,' I pointed out like a total spaceface. I didn't mention the exam he was meant to be retaking. He'd flunked a criminal law module at the end of his first year at UCL. Freshers' week, he told me – giving me the heads-up if I ever made it to uni – can become freshers' month. Freshers' *term* if you don't watch out.

'Yeah. About that.' Chris pushed his fringe from his eyes. 'Dad calls on Wednesdays right? Every Wednesday I'll be studying at Theo's. My phone will be off so we can concentrate.' Theo's father was a lawyer. The lie was logical at least. 'You take the call, spin a couple of stories. I'll be back before you know it.'

'You're serious?'

Chris sat me down on the bed. 'Listen buddy boy. There's this girl, Sofia. Did I mention Sofia?'

I nodded. 'The one with the butterfly tattoos.'

'That was Esther.'

'Oh. The one that looks like Ellen Page?'

'That's Laura.'

'Wasn't Laura "eyes like Megan Fox in aviators"?'

'No, that was Harriet. Anyway, we're talking about Sophie the Trophy, brah! The Croatian Sensation! Legs like – um – a mermaid with . . .' Chris faltered.

'With . . . legs?' I offered.

'Whatever. Her parents have this amazing clifftop villa. We got chatting after an exam before summer and one thing led to another.' I scowled. This always happened. Back when we were first conceived, Chris inherited the get-chatting-with-girls chromosome from my dad – the world's smoothest talker – and I was left with the making-a-tit-of-yourself-on-YouTube gene. You lose some, right?

'What about Malcolm?' Our cleaner. On a bad day, the only human being I got to talk to. He'd been hoovering around us for the last fortnight; mostly harmless but inclined to call the old man with Rendall-brothers updates if things got out of hand.

Chris made an airy gesture. 'Improvise. It's what actors do right? You'll be fine. I'll call a few times to check all's good.' He threw a beach towel over his clothes, rummaged through his bedside drawer and tossed a couple of pairs of sunglasses in. 'Phone charger, passport . . .'

A thought occurred. Chris had spent his way through his maintenance loan, generous allowance and overdraft. 'How are you paying for this, exactly?'

He plucked a card from the pocket of his jeans. 'The wonder of plastic, my friend.'

'That's Dad's spare business card.'

'Give the boy a prize!' Chris grinned, hugging the card close to his chest and swaying dreamily. 'Ah, Harriet . . .' he breathed.

'Sofia.'

41

Chris slammed his case shut. 'Yeah. That's what I said.' As he left, he had the audacity to pinch my cheek and jiggle my face. 'Be good, Buckaroo. I'll WhatsApp the holiday snaps.'

8
The Ruiz Drop

I swear, that night was a game changer.

I met Gedge at Arch 17 and we drove out along the dual carriageway, pulling off before the flyover and parking on an old industrial site – a poured concrete space the only remnants of some flattened factory. Columns lifted the carriageway clear of a weed-choked wasteland. Some joker had sprayed *Payback for president!* across them in red. Marx shot off in pursuit of something and Gedge grinned at him. Underneath the flyover it smelt of piss and oil.

'Nice,' I said as we lugged a pair of boxes through the litter-strewn shadows. The smashed carcass of a chipboard wardrobe, a fly-tipped sofa with its guts out, two oil drums on their sides – it was grim. 'What are we doing here?'

Gedge pointed. 'There's a homeless shelter just beyond the boundary there. This is a good place for the drop to go down.' He got me to help him drag an abandoned trestle table out into open space, a knackered pock-marked thing splashed with paint. We dusted it down.

'So – what are we up to?'

Gedge talked as we unpacked the boxes. Turned out they contained close to a hundred little shot glasses and we lined them up. 'You've watched a Payback drop before, right?' I nodded a little too eagerly. 'A drop,' he continued, 'is our way of redistributing wealth. We need to get the Ruiz money off our hands quickly in case the cops catch us with it.'

'Is there a good chance of that?'

Gedge shrugged. 'Well, there was that DCI at the hotel,' he said. 'Plus it gets harder the longer we go on. That's why we move each year.'

This was news to me. 'Where were you *last* summer?'

'East London. But then we found Ferg online and she's from 'round here. It's easier with her closer.'

I thought about Payback's young computer whizz with her clipped recital of lists and her flash-drive obsession. 'What's the deal with her parents?'

'They think she's at university. A month-long summer school for talented coders. The university think she has glandular fever . . .' Gedge gave a grin. 'C'mon. We need to get a move on.'

'Are we filming this one?' I said as we dug out the cash.

'No. There'll be lots of people. It wouldn't be right. Put five twenties under each glass,' he said, splitting the wad of notes and handing me half. 'It's best,' Gedge said, 'if the drop gives back what the criminal takes. Ruiz is a moneylender who loves a little property speculation. So this is for people whose lives have been destroyed by debt.'

'What, like homeless?'

Gedge produced the two bottles from the briefcase. He handed me one, then broke the seal on the other. We poured carefully; a nip of Ruiz's expensive whisky in each glass. Marx buzzed around our ankles and jumped for the tabletop looking for snacks. 'Right. Money for food and a shot of the good stuff. This is what it's all about!'

I'd never really been a charity sort of guy but setting up a cash-and-booze bonanza under a flyover, the last of the summer sunlight draining from the sky, felt *good*. We pulled our fox masks down and played bartender together.

Ian was our first arrival – a lean wiseguy in a waterproof coat.

There was Doug, who used to be a bouncer.

Chantelle, a woman in her twenties who'd fallen out with her mum and couldn't go back home.

Steve, a Glaswegian with a hacking laugh who closed his eyes, blissed-out by the smooth burn of his whisky.

It got busy and a queue formed. Some had battered rucksacks, filthy fingers and dirty hair. To start with I was shocked. I'd seen guys in sleeping bags before, drug-dazed and rolled up in doorways but I'd never seen them as real people, I guess. People with faces and voices and stories.

There was Mo, a teetotal Hindu who passed his booze to Gina but thanked us anyway.

I spoke to a girl called Astrid who had an old festival tent with her; she sat with Marx on her lap and watched the queue, pressing her face into the dog's neck and whispering to the little guy.

Andrei was covered in tattoos and had been a sheet-metal worker once.

Sasha was in her sixties, originally from Birmingham she told me, and had a dog called Bree.

A skinny guy with a white beard calling himself Elvis played a penny whistle.

An hour in, an ex-barman named Lyron started a fight with two other guys but Doug helped us pull them apart. Then we heard sirens on the flyover and people scattered, drifting quickly like shadows, heading back to the shelter or out into the city to find a doorway. Gedge and me ran for the van.

Back home that night, idling on the sofa and thinking about the people I'd met, I felt stupid and spoilt. I was the only person living in a house with space enough for ten. Beyond the windows was a lawn so big the gardener needed a ride-on mower. My phone went just before midnight. I picked up without checking, imagining Gedge or Kallie. I was wrong.

'Bellboy,' said a papery voice. 'I've not seen you around. Thought I'd check up on you.'

I stood up, itching with discomfort and suddenly wishing I'd never swapped the guy's whisky, never given him my number, never got involved. 'Mr Ruiz. Nice to hear from you.' The old man left me a pause and like an idiot I filled it. 'How can I help?'

'Would you believe my case turned up,' the old man said. 'And it got me thinking. I have a proposition for you Bellboy. One you might like. Come by tomorrow and we can discuss it.' He named an Italian restaurant I knew. Dad had taken us there for Chris's A-level results last summer. That suddenly felt a very long time ago.

'I don't know, sir. There are a few things—'

'You won't regret it Bellboy. I'd like to employ you. I understand you might be needing the money.'

I glowed with shame at the memory of Michelle sending

me packing. He'd been asking around. 'They open at eleven. I won't keep you long.'

I cursed myself even as I agreed.

Edison Ruiz had reserved a circular table near the door. He motioned me to sit, tossing a document wallet on to the immaculate linen. Sitting next to him, square-shouldered in a chalk-stripe suit, Gonzalez looked every inch the dude you don't mess with. He gave a chilly smile, interlacing his battered fingers.

'Bellboy,' Ruiz beamed. 'Thanks for coming.'

'Nice to see you Thomas,' Gonzalez added.

A waiter with a topknot poured us sparkling water. Ruiz opened the folder of documents, examining them privately before beginning. 'I'm curious about how my case came to reappear in the hotel,' he said. He left a pause so long I nearly started crying. Eventually he licked his lips and said, 'I'd like you to do a little investigating for me.'

Fear made me laugh. I'd just given away four grand of the guy's money. 'I'm not sure I'm the person for that particular job!' I managed. *They couldn't possibly know I was involved, could they?*

Gonzalez joined me in a broad grin and said, 'We think you are. You're resourceful, trustworthy, brave. You were committed to helping us earlier and we appreciate the efforts you made.'

'You weren't to blame for what happened,' Ruiz added.

They were serious. I put my hands in my lap so they couldn't see them tremble. 'DCI Sinclair is investigating,' I pointed out. 'I'm sure she's doing a great job.'

Ruiz made a face. 'I'm not a man who has ever put his trust

in the police. I'm sure Ms Sinclair is a capable woman but the scope of the investigation is, I'm afraid, beyond her.'

'Then – why me?'

Ruiz smiled. 'Good question.' He withdrew a stack of papers, fanned them on the table, chose one and skimmed it my way. I leant over to see it. A printout from a tabloid with the headline, DAWN OF VIGILANTE JUSTICE? PAYBACK RAID OFFICES OF TECH COMPANY. I knew the grab well. 'Are you familiar with this gang?' Ruiz asked.

'Everyone knows Payback.'

'Their membership is secret,' said Gonzalez, leaning forward. I caught a whiff of expensive-smelling scent. 'But they seem to be your age and recent reports have them here in this city. We have reason to think they were responsible for the theft of the briefcase. And perhaps also its return.'

I found myself holding my breath. *Why did Gedge make me return the case?* The guy had made a big mistake with that call. I wished I'd filled it with bricks and thrown it in the ship canal.

Ruiz adjusted his cuffs. 'Payback like a good villain. But I am just an honest man, using honest means to make a living in a business I have known for many years. I trade property, like thousands of others, and I help people with their debt. There's no crime here.' He sighed. 'It's sad that the nature of my work has been misunderstood. I'd like you to look into Payback so I can go about clearing my name.'

Suspicion crystallized as I watched them both sip their water. Gonzalez picked at a pastry with a cake fork. 'I wouldn't know where to start,' I croaked.

Ruiz exchanged a knowing smile with his right-hand man. 'We think we might be able to help there.'

'Really?'

More papers from the file. 'Property is my passion,' Ruiz said, pushing a list across to me. 'After the robbery we obtained and analysed every partially used city-centre lot – vacant spaces for commercial or industrial use. If Payback are still here, these are the kind of places they'll be hiding. Now you're a local boy.'

'I'm only here between terms,' I said, scanning the list. 'I'm at boarding school. I don't know the area that well any more . . .' A stranger in my own city, that was me.

Ruiz reached into his pocket, removed a folded wad of twenties and placed them between us. 'Two hundred,' he said. 'Think of a portion of that money as compensation for the stress incurred last time we worked together. The rest? Spend it how you like. Work your way down the list. Report back and the money's yours.'

I swallowed hard. This was a complication I could do without. On the other hand I could always turn up nothing and apologize at the end. And I could even give the cash away, right? I'd just met a roll call of people who needed it plenty more than me. I looked at the two men. There was something cold and frightening lurking under the surface of the conversation. Ruiz raised his eyebrows. 'I'll do what I can,' I said.

9
Being Peter Turtle

'New target. Blackhouse Langley LLP,' Gedge announced at our next meeting. 'Ferg?'

Becky activated the screen and brought up the website. We watched the blue-green projection as she scrolled through. Gedge pointed. 'A London law firm specializing in crime, fraud and licensing. Except they're the ones who find themselves making mysteriously large profits defending gang members and ensuring they escape punishment. Funny that.'

Their website looked like a rolling news bulletin; scrolling stories, headlines, business updates. 'We make sense of a changing world', the About Us section declared. There was a huge team of staff – stiff suits, bright ties, big grins – and a list of offices. Ferg clicked through a few. We got the idea.

'We'll need an under-the-radar, small-stakes grab,' Gedge pointed out.

'And something's sprung to mind I take it,' Coke said.

'Yeah. Ferg, let's have a look at the CCTV footage.'

Becky had hacked the office's interior cameras and we spent a few minutes looking at high-resolution shots of plush reception rooms, corridors, workrooms and offices. It didn't differ much from a hotel in a movie – marble, polished brass, immaculate furnishings, huge artworks.

'What are we looking for?' Kallie asked.

Ferg rewound and we watched again, studying a still of a conference room; oval table in dark wood, elegant chairs, wall-mounted screen for video links.

'The floor vase?' Coke asked, squinting at the image. There was a big dark egg-shaped thing in a glass display cabinet on the far side of the screen.

'It was made in 1932. A rare earthenware vase,' explained Becky, staccato. 'It's green-glazed with a peacock feather design. On its base it has an impressed logo and it's numbered by the makers. That means it's authentic.'

I've never been afraid of stating the obvious. 'It's massive.'

Gedge held a hand above the table, measuring. 'Four feet tall, a couple wide. Of all the artwork there – we looked at the paintings and sculpture too, looks like these guys are gifted all sorts of valuables – the vase is the easiest to remove and sell on.'

'How much?' Kallie asked.

'Twenty-five maybe.'

'Twenty-five. That's going to be a complicated drop,' Coke pointed out. 'Say Yate pays twenty-two. We keep our five per cent, and we've got a hundred batches of maybe two hundred?'

'Whoa,' I said. I was still getting my head around the maths of redistribution. 'I don't understand.'

Kallie laughed. 'Yate's our receiver. Our fence. He pays us for stolen goods in cash, maybe twenty-two thousand. We keep our five per cent to cover costs.'

Gedge finished. 'And we'll end up with a hundred batches

of two hundred quid to give away.'

'Personally,' Kallie put in, 'I'd make up *two* hundred batches of a hundred. That way we help more people.'

Coke sat up straight. 'We need to be looking abroad. Sharing money between first-world citizens is too cosy. I can name you five African nations where—'

Gedge held a hand up. 'Let's concentrate on the details of the grab first.' Coke bristled a bit then bust open an apple juice and chewed the straw furiously.

'The place is camera-heavy and uses fingerprint tech on the exterior door locks. We're going to need an inside man. Rendall, this one's for you.' Gedge skimmed a set of papers across to me. Mitsubishi Electronics, the top page read. 'Air con maintenance company,' he explained. 'You're their apprenticeship guy. Your name's . . .' Gedge paused. His lip quivered. 'Peter Turtle.'

Kallie was wetting herself. Coke too. Ludicrous.

'C'mon guys,' I tried hopelessly. 'No one's called Peter Turtle.'

Super-serious Ferg gave me a blank look, blinked and explained. 'That's not true. Someone *is* called Peter Turtle. He worked for Mitsubishi Electronics but then he moved to Glasgow. The law offices still have his details on their system.'

'It's a nice name,' Kallie said, right before dissolving back into laughter.

I sighed, wondering why I couldn't be an air con maintenance dude called Vin Diesel.

Mum used to come to all my performances.

Then, two years ago she got ill and couldn't any more. Dad tried once but I guess there's not much to enjoy in *Little Shop of Horrors* if you're a buttoned-up biochemist with a missing funny bone. The show was half-full that night and I remember checking the audience and seeing Dad through a gap in the stage curtains as the lights went down. By chance, there was an empty seat next to him where Mum should've been. I completely fell apart. Half an hour into Act One the director found me having a breakdown in the quad and led me back inside. She wiped my face, cleaned me up and lectured me into submission. I can't remember a thing about my turn as the lunatic dentist but Dad said nice things afterwards.

Six weeks later Mum died. I stopped enjoying acting. I gave it up. The drama teachers kept asking me to do lighting, stage management, anything to take my mind off it but I wouldn't even watch another show. I kept seeing empty seats. Everywhere I went, empty seats.

That made the Blackhouse Langley grab my first proper role in ages. My first, I realized, since the funeral. Riding the train, I remembered my attempt at a speech for the service – I had a little story rehearsed about how Mum had always supported me. But I'd seen an empty seat before I began and it'd set me off. Chris had walked me away from the microphone and Dad had taken over. Going over those memories on the train south, I don't mind admitting I went to pieces. In the end, a nice old lady knocked on the door of the tiny toilet to check I was all right. She ended up sharing her weird sweets with me until I felt better. I was a trembling mess as I rode the underground from Euston. Weirdly, though, no matter how cut up you are, there's only so many tears you can cry per sitting. Once I got to Notting Hill Gate and rode the escalators up into the sunlight I was feeling better.

And it turns out acting's like riding a bike – once learnt,

never forgotten. As I announced myself at the law office's reception I felt suddenly at ease. Almost happy. I swear I *became* Peter Turtle.

The corner of the receptionist's mouth twitched a fraction as I told her my name and gave the story about the faulty heating pipes in the upstairs offices. She typed my details with super-fast red talons, located my file and called the number on my card for confirmation of the job. 'There's nothing on the daily log about maintenance,' she explained, tucking the phone under her chin as it rang.

'Our offices have moved while we upgrade our servers,' I told her breezily. 'Maybe there's been an error.' Gedge had sorted the business cards, Kallie had lifted a badged-up boiler suit and tools, and Coke was on the other end of the phone, so I wasn't worried. It went like a dream.

'That's fine,' she said, concluding the call. I signed in. 'Have a good day, Mr Turtle. Please ensure you sign out upon completion.'

I gave a cheeky wink. The kind of thing, I figured, that Peter Turtle would do.

There was no one in the conference room. The vase was beautiful; a smooth, serene thing with this delicate crackle glaze over a stormy swirl of blue feathers. Along the street-facing windows of the room, recessed seats had been built over vented housing for air-con units. Black metal grilles protected crawl spaces alongside the pipes. It was here I would be hiding until the offices closed. Assuming these guys and gals knocked off at about eight, I'd be in there for maybe three hours. I was planning on sleeping for most of it.

I scattered some kit around me, fake-worked and made

sure I was recorded coming and going beneath the cameras. I rammed the bubble wrap into a crawl space. (Yeah. Bubble wrap. That, four pillows and a trampoline were all the equipment we'd need, Gedge had assured me.) Outside the conference room, phones rang and team members padded up and down corridors. Once or twice I was disturbed – a squat bloke in a three-piece suit apologized; later, a younger woman with impossible heels dropped into a chair and examined her eyeshadow in a compact before clocking me and shuttling off again.

Lawyers, it turns out, smell really nice.

Towards seven the receptionist cleared off and I loitered, making a meal of packing my tools away. I tucked my dust sheet, spanners and boiler parts under a pipe beneath the window seats.

Slipping into position, I pulled the grille up into place, used a screwdriver the size of a frickin' toothpick to secure it at its corners and lay on my side. I had room enough to move a little but it was like lying in a coffin. At least I had the pillows.

I must have been dozing lightly when I got the call because the vibration in my back pocket woke me. It was awkward reaching for my phone. I checked the time. It was just before eleven and the office beyond my grille was dark.

'Hey hey!' boomed Chris at the other end of the line. 'How's tricks?'

I winced and whispered, 'Now's not a good time. I'm in a bit of a situation . . .'

Scrambled interference, then Chris emerging through the static. 'So anyway, I just have to tell you about this place we're at. Remember that bar in Greece we went to with Mum and Dad – the one with the balloons? It's just like that! There's music – wait – you can listen . . .' There was the noise of talking, the clatter of glasses then, as Chris held the phone closer, an oompah band with an energetic drummer and an accordion player. 'Great, right? I swear it's the best place. Super-athletic starry-eyed ladies! Cheap drinks! Hey, Buckaroo. You've gone quiet. Where are you, in bed?'

'I'm hiding.'

'What? Sounded like you said you were *hiding*.'

'That's right. I'm hiding. In a crawl space near some pipes.'

'Where?'

'Notting Hill.'

A pause. In the background, a big cheer as a song finished. 'Right, well – good luck with that. Hey, say hello to Sofia! I thought it might be nice for you two to chat, y'know? She's excited to meet you!'

Great. 'Now's not a good time to be honest . . .'

'Thomas?' said a girl with a lovely accent. 'Chrissy has told me all about you! So cute!'

'That's nice,' I sighed, shifting position. 'So – how are things?'

'Oh it's so lovely here!' Sofia's happy slur suggested she'd been enjoying the hospitality. 'There's balloons and candles and this great band. There's a dance floor and a machine that makes bubbles. Life is good! So – what are you doing with your evening?'

'Oh, you know,' I said. 'I'm hiding in a crawl space in a lawyer's office in London.'

There was a pause. 'Oh. OK then. Well you have a nice time. I'm handing you back to your brother now.'

I hung up. While I'd been asleep, there'd been a text message too. I squinted at the alert, expecting an update from Gedge or Coke. Instead, a text from an unknown number. I rubbed my eyes and opened it, wincing at the ache in my back and legs.

In a way, it was the text that started to unravel everything.

I didn't know it at the time of course.

Heard about YOU, it said. *We NEED to meet.*

10
Slow-motion Social Media Disaster

To start with I figured it was a wrong number and texted back saying so. I thought that'd be it. But a second later I got a reply. *We need to meet TOM*, it said.

I typed *who is this* but the texts passed each other and one landed just as I hit send: *C-park half-pipe 6pm tomorrow*. The skateboarding place in the park near my house.

My texter didn't identify themselves but there were bigger things to stress about. I forgot the messages, switched on my phone torch and battled with the tiny screws until I could shoulder the grille clear and roll out into the office. I pulled my fox mask on, stretched and shook my hands free from pins and needles then hauled my kit out. Glass cutter, hammer, bubble wrap, packing tape, pillows.

My body buzzed with adrenaline and my face got sticky with my own hot breath. I weighed the hammer in my hand briefly then went to work. My first hit glanced off the glass. The stuff was pretty damn thick and I had to strike flat-on with all my strength to get it to shatter. Fortunately, when it did, the whole pane disintegrated in a downpour of silver, the shards small and neat. Drifts of glass beads collected every-where like tiny dice. I dropped my left arm into the vase the way we'd practised, pressing my palm flat against the interior, and from a stooped position used my right arm to lift it and carry it clear of the wrecked cabinet. The carpet crunched underfoot.

I went to work with the pillows, two inside the vase, three outside, securing them with bubble wrap and tape. It took twenty minutes. 11.30 p.m., five minutes to spare. I sweated and cursed as I finished the roll of tape and checked the vase, unrecognizable now, squat and fat in its padding.

Glass cutter next. The office windows, Ferg had said, were fitted with exterior alarms that responded to damage to the frame. A simple solution; cut the entire pane free and push it out and down into the street. I ran the diamond nib of the pencil-grip cutter hard and fast along the edges of the pane but I needed a few goes to get through the glass. My hands quickly got slippery and I kept dropping the damn thing, inventing a whole new family of swear words as I worked. By the time I was ready we were running six minutes behind schedule. I did my torch-flash message to the guys below, counted thirty seconds and shouldered out the pane.

The glass spun slowly then fell, end over end. I stumbled back from the gaping hole as cool fresh air rushed in. I waited for the crash but it didn't come which meant we'd got the positioning right at least. I risked raising my mask to wipe my face clear of sweat then got to work on my swaddled package. It was like lifting a baby elephant. I hugged the bundle against my belly and waddled to the window.

This time I could check the scene below before throwing the vase clear.

Blackhouse Langley were two floors above Linden Gardens, a leafy street off the Bayswater Road. And in the middle of it was the trampoline. Ferg had ordered us one of those ones you see in the gardens of big suburban houses – ten feet in diameter, raised on legs made from steel tubing and surrounded with a high mesh net. All I had to do was tumble the vase down accurately then follow Coke's roof map to a building with scaffolding where I would escape. Apparently.

It looked pretty damn ridiculous down there. I snorted with laughter at Gedge and Kallie, masked like brother and sister foxes either side of the trampoline, ready to adjust its position. Coke was in the van, filming from a sufficient distance to catch the graceful arc of the falling vase. Ferg was what she liked to call 'working from home', meaning hunched over a laptop in her bedroom, checking we hadn't ballsed up the alarm systems.

I hauled the vase up on to the windowsill. The pubs had called time and I could hear crowds of drinkers and see the late-night tourists, queues of taxis, the stuttering lights of cop cars and Deliveroo dudes hefting boxes on bikes between the shoals. I had to be quick. We should've been done by 11.35 p.m.

I was lining up the vase when it happened. A group of mates were weaving their merry way down our street. *Our damn street.* There must have been eight of them, all in their twenties, young professionals heading home. They still had suits on – extended after-work drinks maybe – and the girls were laughing, linking arms, leaning in to each other. I looked down at Gedge, who was giving me a frantic wave. We needed this done quick. I checked the trampoline again. One mistake and I'd lose us twenty-two grand and days of planning.

It was hard to concentrate because the gang had seen Kallie

60

and Gedge and were pointing and laughing. *A trampoline in the street*. Phones came out. Then one of the girls put two and two together and looked up. Next thing, I was being filmed. How quickly would this end up online? I ducked away from the window, bringing the vase down into the room with me. Maybe they'd get bored. I squatted in the office breathing hard.

I might have been imagining it but I could've sworn the noise in the street was building.

I did a furtive check. Definitely busier. Twenty or so people down there, I guessed. Camera flashes stuttered. I could see Coke; he'd left the van and was making his way towards the crowd, camcorder held aloft. I ducked back in a tropical fever of panic. Someone was shouting. More camera flashes. When I looked again I could see a bunch of passers-by on the Bayswater Road diverting down Linden Gardens to check out the melee.

What now? Gedge and Kallie were down there in the crowd trying to hold the trampoline steady. Coke was filming. Thirty people maybe. More coming.

Someone saw me in my mask. Phones were pointed my way.

'Fox!' a voice shouted. 'Robin Hood!'

I ducked back, heart galloping. It was official. We were in the middle of a slow-motion social media disaster.

11
Direct Hit

A few drunken souls sent up a chant.

'*Robin Hood, Robin Hood, ridin' through the glen!*' they chorused. More joined in. '*Robin Hood, Robin Hood, with his merry men!*'

There was no way we were hiding now. Maybe it was being Peter Turtle that did it; playing a proper role again for the first time in ages, but I figured we could turn a setback into an opportunity. How about we played to the crowd a bit? I waited until the next '*with his merry men*' and leapt up into view. 'Feared by the baaad!' I bawled in my best baritone, arms aloft, 'Loved by the gooood!'

Up went a gutsy cheer of recognition: '*Paaa-ay-back, Paaa-ay-back...*' The chant grew. '*Payback! Payback! Payback!*'

The noise was drawing more people. I was getting bellowing cheers and flashing cameras, just for singing. I couldn't help grinning under my mask. There was a proper crowd down there now and they were all cheering for me. Audience-wise, it was *Aladdin* times ten – the biggest I'd ever attracted. Coke was being buffeted even as he tried to film and had resorted to holding the camcorder above his head to scan the ruck of people. Gedge was high-fiving some guy, Kallie was getting a bear hug.

'*Payback! Payback!*' chanted the crowd.

I held my hands above my head as if proclaiming some sort of victory and there was an answering roar. Gedge began a speech. I'd never seen him talk to crowds before. He threw his arms out and bawled a chest-thumping polemic. 'This year, we've witnessed two billion pounds of tax cuts. *Two billion*. Respite for those who deserve it? Help for the poor? Extra teachers or doctors? No, no and no! Cuts that benefit the rich. This government *transfers wealth upwards*!' Cheers of agreement and encouragement. 'One billion cut from the welfare bill . . .' Gedge boomed, 'and handed to higher earners!' Angry faces roared. Cameras bobbed above the crowd. 'You a single parent with a kid? Earning a modest wage? You're worse off now!' There were calls of agreement, cheers and shouts. 'Well, we're here to change that. If the government aren't going to do the right thing – *we are!*' He was thumping a fist into his palm. The crowd was growing, the street a shifting mass of bodies. '*We're here to tax the rich!*' The place exploded at this. There must have been over a hundred down there, young people with live-streaming media feeds pulling in more. I'd never felt so alive. It was thrilling, dangerous. Only a matter of time before the cops arrived to break this beautiful thing up. The crowd was swelling, shifting, roaring and cheering. Fists pumped the air.

I saw Coke's camcorder point up at me, and I lifted the wrapped vase up on to the windowsill. There was an explosion of camera flashes, screens turned my way and a throaty cheer erupted from the onlookers. 'Pay-back! Pay-back!' I bawled.

The chant rose again and I led it. *I was actually in-real-life famous.*

Holding the pillow-encased vase steady with one hand, I did a little dance, a capering idiot-thing that ended when I bashed my head against the window frame and someone shouted, 'Get on with it!'

It hurt like hell but the chants went up again – '*Payback! Payback!*' – and I steadied myself, looking down beyond the crowd, beyond the sea of upraised phones, focusing on Gedge and Kallie's masks and the trampoline. I tipped the vase over the edge. It spun gently as it fell, a giant beach ball. And plunged into its nest. Direct hit.

I had roughly a nanosecond to enjoy my success before the bounce. Not part of the plan.

The damn thing took off again, springing up and away from its captors. Two upturned fox faces gaped as the swaddled package arced into the canopy of a nearby tree, trailing a shower of torn leaves. It snagged briefly on a branch before tumbling downwards. My heart gave a painful slo-mo boom, a single thud of blood as I anticipated a crash-landing.

But upraised arms captured the vase and wouldn't you know the beautiful thing pretty much crowdsurfed its way gently to the ground. The street exploded in celebration. I jumped and waved acknowledging the adulation. Coke made his way through the throng towards the van. I applauded the crowd like I'd seen footballers do at the end of matches and got answering cheers. Gedge was getting hugged, Kallie was posing for photos.

We'd left it too late. A cop van was pulling up at the top of the street.

Listen. It's worth mentioning at this point that I never

meant to start a riot. That wasn't my plan. None of what happened was my fault. The revellers had been drinking. It was just a case of miscommunication, yeah?

I pointed up at the cop van and shouted down to Gedge. I was terrified of getting caught, that's all. I'd kind of forgotten the crowd were even there. The next morning when the papers covered the story the phrase *incitement to public violence* was used a lot, like I'd been actually asking the crowd to intervene. I wasn't.

But that's what happened. As the cops came down the street the crowd responded to my urgent pointing and fanned out, moving up to prevent the law reaching us. One cop got through and made a break towards Gedge, running hard, baton raised. His helmet fell off as he ran. The next bit happened fast; I was nothing more than a slack-jawed spectator standing in awe at the window. As Gedge clocked the approaching officer his body softened into the coiled stance of a boxer. He brought both fists up tight against his chest, danced to the left as the copper slashed his baton, and flattened the guy with a single meaty right hook. That was it – one immense punch sent the officer shuddering to the ground. It was amazing to watch. The crowd roared again, shifted and split. A group of boozy guys had begun vigorously enjoying the trampoline, each leap accompanied by drunken whoops. Others had advanced towards the remaining cops. There were only five officers so I guess it might have looked as if they were hugely outnumbered, threatened even, but it was a peaceful protest, I swear. I could hear the remaining police demanding to be let past but there was a wall of revellers still cheering and shouting and they held strong. The law couldn't reach us and were forced back,

65

calling for backup.

Gedge and Kallie had rolled the swaddled vase down the street. Still the crowds pushed the feds back but there was no way Coke could bring the van directly beneath us as we'd planned. Gedge knew this too and waved up at me, indicating the alternative meeting place beneath the scaffolding of the building along the street and the two of them headed south, cradling our swag between them. A section of the crowd followed, cocooning them as they went, obscuring their escape from the helpless cops.

The whole thing was beautifully done.

12
Free Climbing

A week is a long time in social media but the events of that night were pretty much consistently shared, discussed, parodied, attacked and championed for the next seven days. On the drive back to Manchester that night we were all on a high, wired on adrenaline and the rush of success. I guess that goes some way to explaining how I forgot all about the text message until the morning after. I'd hammered my monthly data and run my batteries into the ground checking social during the drive home, then I'd collapsed into bed and left my phone on charge.

It wasn't until the reminder came through that I remembered it at all. *TOM C-park half-pipe 6pm*, it said.

Checking in with Gedge seemed to me the best idea. After a late breakfast I hopped a tram into town and walked across to Arch 17 to see what he made of it.

I s'pose I should've texted. Maxi waved me through, but only Ferg and Kallie were there when I showed up; Ferg eating biscuits and tapping away on a laptop, Kallie checking social and packing a bag. 'He's gone out,' she said as I skipped up the stairs. 'He's seeing Yate – making a plan for moving on the vase. Then working with Coke on the drop. Looks like you've got the day off.'

'Oh.'

'Cheer up. A day off's good, right?'

I shrugged. 'If you know what to do with it.'

Kallie grinned, zipped her bag shut. 'I know what I'm doing with mine. Climbing.'

I laughed. 'What, scaling buildings for the hell of it?'

'Indoor climbing,' Kallie said. 'You've never tried a climbing wall? You've never lived!' She shouldered her bag, tied her hair back with quick fingers and headed downstairs. 'Later.'

Out of nowhere I found myself saying, 'Wait. Hang on. I could come along. I mean – just to see. It'd be interesting.'

She shrugged. 'Sure.' As encouragement went it was hardly whole-hearted, but my brother Chris was the guy who got that. I could live with a shrug. I did a little skip of celebration. She rolled her eyes.

We walked sun-baked pavements across town, Kallie striding ahead and me scampering behind. It turned out the climbing place was a converted mill in the Northern Quarter. Inside, beyond a check-in desk where I shelled out a tenner of Dad's emergency cash for admittance, was a cavernous echoing space. The interior walls were white wood-clad structures punctuated with colourful quotation marks, the commas and apostrophes of weird hand- and footholds. Thick crash mats carpeted the floors.

'Back in a sec,' Kallie said and vanished into the changing rooms.

I watched one guy, whippet-thin, suspended beneath a high overhang, clinging to the sheer wall with chalky hands, scoping out his next move. The lunatic looked half a mile up.

My palms prickled just watching him. Nearby a couple of women chatted on the crash mats, hands on hips as they examined a tricky ascent. A gang of kids decked out in harnesses and hard hats were having a guided climb with a cheerful instructor dressed like a CBeebies presenter.

Kallie returned in black leggings and those weird rubber-soled trainers. She was dousing her hands from a bag of chalk at her hip.

'For grip,' she explained. 'Try some.' I attempted to dust my palms. 'Feeling nervous?' she said as she watched the stuff turn to glue in my hot hands.

'Somewhat,' I managed. 'Where are your ropes?'

She laughed. 'No ropes. Free climbing.'

'No way.'

'Not as hard as it looks, I promise. Now,' she tapped a finger against her chin. 'Where to start . . .'

'That one?' I suggested, pointing to a sheer section with a nasty overhang.

She sucked air through her teeth and narrowed her gaze. 'Tricky. OK then.'

She seemed to float through the early sections, her arms hard and strong, fingers vice-like but slowed as the holds became less frequent, eventually stopping to assess her progress, her whole weight supported on a single toe-hold. It was madness. I was dissolving on the crash mats below, my T-shirt sticking to me.

'Careful!' I bleated.

'I'm fine.' She didn't take her eyes off the wall, absorbed in studying pattern and distribution. 'Check out Catherine Destivelle,' she added. 'Next time you're online. My hero.'

'I'll have a look. A climber?'

'Amazing free climber.'

I stepped back to watch Kallie manoeuvre herself crossways, looking for a way up. I remembered the noise on the hotel roof the night we first met. I checked we were alone and kept my voice low. 'You really climbed the outside of the Midland?'

'Uh huh. With karabiners, though. Ropes and clips,' she added. 'The final section was hard. Did I ever mention how scared you looked in that roof garden?' She laughed at the memory. 'I was out beyond a screen of potted trees. You were bricking it!'

I got indignant at this. 'C'mon. You could've been a serial killer or something.'

Kallie looked down at me. 'Such a drama queen, Rendall.'

'Just got a vivid imagination,' I said. 'It's a curse.'

'You coming up?' Kallie beckoned then called across to the desk. 'Benjamin! Get my friend here some size nines will you?'

A staff member waved and trotted over. 'Thanks,' I said, reluctantly kicking off my sneaks while Kallie descended. I fumbled with the climbing shoes, my foolish fingers jumpy.

Kallie watched, shaking her head and tutting. 'Ready?'

I had no idea how heavy I was until that moment. Don't get me wrong, I've done press-ups. I've done three or four at once before, though that's going back a few years. Turns out nowadays I weigh a ton. And I had to raise my entire body weight using just my fingers. I puffed and sweated, struggling upwards, gritting my teeth as I made it a metre off the mats. Kallie, dangling artfully from an elegant arm, advised me. 'There. Further. Switch hands. Stretch, Rendall.'

I grunted and roared, my fingers slipping.

Kallie's language was baffling. 'Pinch it,' she'd say as I battled the wall. 'Undercut. Like this. A crimp here. C'mon. Bridge with your feet or you're going nowhere.'

'I think I'm going to fall. Kall, I'm losing my grip. Help.'

'It's like watching a water buffalo,' she laughed, pointedly not helping. 'In boxing gloves.'

'I'm serious.' I felt my grip fail. My arms burnt. I tried adjusting my feet.

Kallie reached down for me and did a throaty impression of a leading actor in a naff blockbuster. 'Kid. Take my hand. Everything is gonna be all right. Just . . . *take my hand.*'

We both started laughing at that. I reached up an arm, my face pressed against the wall. She withdrew hers, pretended we couldn't reach each other saying, 'Kid . . . stretch. *You can do this!*'

Then I fell. Turned out the drop was a matter of centimetres. I lay on my back on the crash mat doing a long falling Hollywood 'Nooooo . . .' Kallie hung from the wall above, fingers splayed, and returned my dying call adding dramatic slo-mo, trying not to laugh.

Then we went for cake.

In the cafe at the climbing place I told the Chris-leaving-for-Croatia story and Kallie nearly choked on her flapjack laughing.

'Your brother's funny! Not like Inesh. He's so suspicious. I only get to come up here because I lie about staying with cousins. Every week we get our story straight and Gita has to cover for me. It's a killer.'

We refilled our hot chocolates and talked for an hour. Kallie told me about her life in London, her mum, a lecturer with a neuroscience obsession, her school, college plans, university aspirations.

'Climbing's involved surely,' I said with a grin. 'You're awesome at it.'

'Thanks. At first, I only went along to keep a friend company, used to watch him climb. Then I caught the bug. I love it. But it's not my future.' Kallie paused, sipped her drink seriously. 'You want to hear the dutiful Kalima Shah written-in-the-stars family version?'

'Sure.'

'Mum reckons I'll be choosing Chemistry, Biology and Maths at A level, spending two years at my desk, getting straight As and studying Medicine.'

'Right. Not climbing, then.'

'Not if she's got anything to do with it,' she said, examining her plate and pushing crumbs about with her fingertips. 'She keeps telling me "education is freedom". Every week I get the lecture. "Get your degree first." I've heard it a million times.' Kallie sighed then brightened. 'Forgot to say – I checked you out online. That production of *The Sound of Music* is something else!' She dissolved into giggles while I tried not to recall my most humiliating performance ever; an am-dram nightmare at a local theatre the half-term before Mum got ill. 'Your *dancing*, Rendall. Shameless!'

'Yeah listen—'

'And the second act! Honestly. I've not seen *The Sound of Music* with audience participation before.' She wiped her eyes, tried to control herself and collapsed laughing again.

'Total accident. I thought it was a hen party,' I explained. 'I swear I had no idea they were real nuns.'

I had a good time that morning. There'd be precious few of those in the weeks before that summer ended. Kallie and I parted in the centre of town. I rode the tram home in high spirits. It wasn't until my stop that I realized I'd forgotten to mention the text message.

5.30 p.m. I was grabbing a jacket ready to keep my date with my mysterious texter when there was a knock on the door. I wandered over, lost in thought.

When I opened the door I swear it took everything I'd got not to collapse into confessional sobbing ('It was me! I admit it! I was the guy at the window, arrest me now for GOD'S SAKE...') because standing there was the policewoman from the Midland Hotel.

She was wearing a raincoat and holding up a badge. She had a big warm smile on her face. 'Lovely garden,' she said, indicating the expanse of front lawn. 'DCI Sinclair, remember? May I come in Thomas?'

13
Sinclair

I sat her at the central island in the kitchen, stunned. She refused coffee, flipped a notebook, checked her watch and said cheerfully, 'Nice place you've got. I won't keep you long.' My legs had liquefied. *Was Malcolm the cleaner due? He couldn't be witness to this.* Sinclair gave me a reassuring smile. *Had I taken my mask off? And she'd ID'd me from the footage?* 'I just need to talk to you again about what happened at the Midland Hotel.'

'OK,' I squeaked, thinking *Weird place to start. Cut to the chase, ma'am – Linden Gardens, fox mask, Robin Hood chanting, stolen vase.*

'The robbery you were witness to.'

I nodded. 'I told you what happened.'

'That's why I'm here.' I think I might have actually laughed with relief. Sinclair said, all curious, 'You were expecting something else?'

'No!' I barked, way too loud. 'No. I was just surprised. I was . . . I don't work there any more.'

'Yes I was interested in that part. Can you talk me through why you left your position at the hotel, Thomas?'

There was no way I was mentioning the trolley embarrass-

74

ment. 'It was for the best. My manager thought so too. I guess I was shaken up,' I said, hoping the half-truth was enough. Sinclair watched me, the silence widening. She could make conversations feel like unexploded bombs. 'I wasn't sure I wanted to be around the place. It reminded me of that night. I wasn't comfortable . . .'

'Right. I understand.' Sinclair thought for a moment. 'Was your decision in any way connected with this?' The DCI placed a photo on the table and pushed it across to me.

It was Gedge.

He looked five years younger. He had a black eye and was scowling at the camera from beneath a ridiculous fringe. I could see a loose-fitting grey shirt in shot but my eye was mostly taken by the white wall Gedge was standing against. On it, a series of lines indicated his height. I'm not the brightest but even I knew what that meant. 'I find that decisions are always connected to other decisions,' Sinclair continued, flashing me a breezy smile. 'Events to events, people to people; all by happy coincidence. You'd be surprised how often police investigations end up finding these networks. Like webs,' she added, spreading her upheld hands.

I made a show of studying the picture with furrowed brow, wondering what the hell she was on about. 'No, sorry. I don't think I know the guy.'

'Are you sure? Check again, Thomas.'

I didn't like the sound of that. *Was this a mistake?* 'Sorry,' I persisted. 'I don't know him.'

DCI Sinclair leant forward to retrieve the picture. 'It's important we locate this man,' she said. 'He has a history of violence. A criminal record for breaking and entering, perverting the course of justice, aggravated burglary. He might look slightly different now. Imagine him older, broader and stronger.' I made a show of conjuring this image as Sinclair continued. 'He's extremely dangerous. I'm concerned about your safety Thomas, that's all. But if you don't recognize him . . .'

The unfinished sentence hung. I stuck with my stupid story. 'Sorry.'

Sinclair smiled and shifted tack. 'Do have you another job now?' The kitchen clock said 5.45 p.m.

'No. Not at the moment.'

'Interesting. An officer came by on Friday and you weren't in. Now. Like I said before –' she bit the end of her pen – 'events connected to events. People to people. You *can* confirm you weren't doing employment of any kind last Friday?'

'No. I was with friends.'

'Who?' Sinclair's grip tightened on her pen. This was like some sort of nightmare. If I made up names she might check. If I told the truth she might recognize Gedge. *People connected to people. Lose–lose.*

'Kalima Shah,' I said, thinking of the climbing. Sinclair made me spell it and I did, my heart tightening with each letter.

'And how are you connected to Kalima?'

'We're just friends.'

'Is there anything you might have forgotten to include in your statement but have since remembered?' Sinclair said. 'Anything about your masked attacker?'

I shook my head.

'Were you aware of the fact that Mr Ruiz's case subsequently reappeared?'

I swallowed. My throat had gone tight. 'No.' The clock said 5.50 p.m. I was going miss my blind date in the park. 'Why would someone bring it back?'

Sinclair tapped the pen against her lips and said brightly, 'Exactly.' There was a pause so awkward I considered moving abroad and living a long and happy life selling sugared almonds from a tray on a Spanish beach. Sinclair broke it in the end. 'Thomas, can I ask you whether you climb?' I must have looked taken aback. 'Strange question I know, but . . .'

'Events connected to events?'

She pointed at me. 'Exactly! Climbing. Indoor climbing walls, extreme sports clubs, that sort of thing.' I shook my head. 'Right. Interesting. Any other hobbies?'

'Not any more.'

That was all it took. 'Any more?' said Sinclair.

'I used to act.'

'Exciting!' Sinclair said. I felt myself blush. Her pen was moving again now. She made me wait while she scribbled and said to herself, 'People to people, decisions to decisions. Amazing. It always works.' Eventually she clicked her pen shut with her thumb and got up. 'Thank you for your time, Thomas. You've been really helpful. If you do see the man in the photograph or remember anything else about the Midland robbery, please get in touch.'

I showed her to the door, exhausted. She turned before she left. 'Do you mind if I arrange a further interview? In case I find more connections I want to discuss.' She paused before adding, 'I have your number.'

I shrugged. 'Fine. But I've told you everything.'

Sinclair smiled and tucked her notes into her jacket pocket. 'I'm sure you have.'

Once she'd gone, I got busy on a full-scale nervous break-down. I'd missed my meeting in the park. The mysterious texter didn't get in touch again that night which was just as well. I spent most of it in the bath doing my stupid Zen breathing.

14

Bailey Heywood

I t was already August and things were about to get seriously busy. When I arrived at the arches the next day, Maxi Johnson was outside reading the *Mirror* in the sunshine, his dungarees open to reveal a Payback T-shirt. 'Safe,' he nodded. This time, he raised a weathered palm for a high five.

Through the workshop and up the stairs, Arch 17 was all frantic excitement. Marx bounced up at my legs, Kallie waved, even Coke looked as if he was prepared to tolerate my presence. I saw our leader through new eyes that day, recalling that head-and-shoulders shot of his younger self and Sinclair's summary of his criminal record.

But there was no time to dwell. Everything was focused on Gedge's announcement. *'Payback's most ambitious grab ever,'* he called it.

'Bailey Heywood,' Gedge began, 'is the UK's most famous and expensive wedding planner.'

We watched a gallery of pictures: tables draped in linen, floral centrepieces, rows of seats on lime-green lawns. *Bailey Heywood, Luxe Event Design House*, the website read. *Invitations and bridal showers, custom textile patterns, layered design elements*. Blah blah blah.

'This weekend,' Gedge continued, 'there's a show called "Understated Elegance: The Ultimate Wedding" at Halfpike Abbey, Wiltshire.' (Wiltshire, it turns out, is the big green bit outside Bristol.) We checked out a fresh gallery: a couple sitting astride two white horses, guys in kilts adjusting each other's cufflinks, a cloud of white doves exploding into flight. Kallie started laughing until Ferg scrolled to the ticket prices. Two hundred quid. 'And that's just the launch event,' Gedge explained. 'Book Bailey Heywood to sort your wedding, and prices start from sixty k.'

Coke said, 'Disgusting. Think what we could achieve if we had the budget for just a single society wedding.'

'Disgraceful right? And that's not all. Check this.'

Ferg clicked a link and read the text. '"At Understated Elegance, you'll get the chance to try a range of our specially commissioned jewellery, available for hire. Our team of expert appraisers will offer advice on how to incorporate these stunning pieces into your special day."'

'Ferg scroll down,' breathed Kallie.

Becky spoke, quick and nervous. 'We can get access to six different items of diamond jewellery but you have to make special appointments. There will be five sapphire necklaces, three brooches and four bangles . . .'

Gedge put a hand on her shoulder. 'Yeah. But security is too high on most of that. Ferg, give us the details on the pearls.'

'Pearls are produced in the soft tissue of molluscs and are made of nacre.'

Gedge waited, shrugged. 'And they're not big-time like diamonds, so less security. Plus, Yate will move them on for us quickly.'

'There are seven different pearl necklaces on display during the event.' Ferg projected the list. 'This one is the most expensive.' We all stared at the 'White South Sea Cultured Pearl Necklace'. It was spectacular. The text called it 'Leila's Veil' in honour it said, 'of Bizet's famous opera, *The Pearl Fishers*.'

'Estimated value, thirty thousand pounds,' said Gedge. 'Not big-time like the diamonds, so easier to swipe. Next: the site plan.'

We studied an interactive map showing a marquee built inside a walled garden. Inside was an open-plan area, 'the Ballroom'. Smaller rooms clustered around it, badged up with stupid names. 'Catalan Glamour', one read; 'Mysteries of India'; 'Undiscovered Orient'. Through the gates of the walled garden was a smaller space, 'Titania's Grove', and something called an orangery. One wing of the hall was to be used for dining. Costumes and jewellery were in the house too.

Gedge pointed to it. 'Leila's Veil will be there. Now, here's the plan.'

That Friday, Coke pulled up in the van at the end of my street and we queued our way out towards the motorway. Three hours later, somewhere on the edge of Bath, we parked in an empty lane that ran along the high wall of a country estate's deer park. The nearest village was a mile back.

'Ready?' Coke asked, switching off the engine.

I'd checked my bag repeatedly as we drove. Uniform and badges, shiny shoes, glasses, earpiece. ('They're ancient,' Gedge had said as he'd handed me my earbud. 'The reception's crap. Plus I can speak to each of you – but you can't speak to each other.')

I repacked my bag. 'Yeah I'm good. You?'

Coke unzipped a black holdall and checked his maps and schedule. He had a list of where everyone needed to be at what time, usually Gedge's role. 'He's been arrested more times than you've failed auditions,' Coke explained. *That figured* I thought, remembering Sinclair and the photograph. 'Lots of security at events like this are ex-law enforcement so he gets recognized. He'll run the grab remotely with Ferg.'

'We'd better check the sound,' I said, tension tightening my stomach. 'Ferg? Gedge?'

'Here.' Gedge's voice came through a howl of digital noise. He hadn't been kidding about the state of the tech. 'Becky's having a few issues trying to pick up your phones. We can see Kallie but not you guys. Move around.' We were at the edge of a field of wheat tumbling under a warm breeze, turning gold in the evening sunlight. Swallows dipped over its surface. I made my way along the lane, the wall of the deer park to my left.

'We see you,' said Gedge. 'We're in business. Time check. You got 6.26?'

Coke went over the wall first, landing knee-deep in last season's leaves and cursing the state of his deck shoes. We crossed the park towards the house. Soon we were skirting a lake in the twilight and heading up a hill to the ditches that marked the edge of the gardens. They were called 'ha-has', Coke told me, these weird trenches designed to keep deer out. His parents' house had one apparently. We crouched in the ha-ha unpacking our bags. I changed into my waiter's outfit.

I was a lad called Charlie Masham.

Ferg had found her way into the staff books of Wiltshire Quality Catering and chosen a kid called Guy Winter. I'd rung up and done my sick-kid voice – Guy had flu – and recommended a friend, Charlie Masham. Next I'd called Guy and pretended to be the manager telling him he wasn't needed for Friday. Poor fella sounded gutted. The following day Coke had nicked a uniform in my size and we were good to go. I pulled on the polished shoes and put my fake glasses on.

Then Coke and I pulled ourselves up the chest-height stone wall and over the fence.

I stood for a moment, taken aback. The house was an immense pale-grey manor of columns and carvings, steps and terraces. A hundred windows across three floors reflected the blaze of the setting sun. A trio of fountains glittered arcs of spray while white marble statues watched from recesses. Coke headed out across the gardens brushing down his skinny-fit chinos. I made for the kitchens.

The marquee was massive; white canvas rising to three peaks. Guy ropes pulled its skin taut and in places huge flaps had been lifted upwards and strung tight to form doorways. I nodded to a burly security dude at the entrance and waited while he checked his list.

'Charlie Masham,' I said. 'Catering staff. I'm covering for Guy.' The man ran a finger down a list then waved me through.

Inside a catwalk had been constructed and blokes who looked like roadies were testing lighting rigs, checking sound levels and messing with rows of chairs. Guests were coming in from the gardens, taking their free champagne and gasping at the sculptured paper chandeliers suspended above them. I went around the edge of the ballroom and out the other side, heading for the kitchens.

'Charlie Masham?' said a woman in a black dress at the desk. She leant over her list, clicking her tongue. I checked her badge. Jennifer. 'I've no Charlie Masham here.'

I'd already given my speech about replacing Guy. 'He recommended me, Jennifer,' I explained. 'We've worked together before at the Devonshire.' God knows if the Devonshire existed. It sounded like it might be a posh pub but if she called me on it I was done for. My heart cannoned but I managed a smile.

'You look too young for silver service.'

'I've done silver,' I said, trying to look put out.

'Phillip? Have we requested extra staff tonight?'

A bald bloke in chef's whites emerged from the kitchens wiping his hands on a dishcloth. 'Nope.' He gave me a long steady stare.

I held my smile and started the Guy story again. Before I'd finished he lost patience. 'Put him on hors d'oeuvres,' he shouted over his shoulder. 'If he ballses it up, call Guy. Don't care if he's at death's door.'

'Yes, chef!' I barked in agreement like I'd seen on telly.

Jennifer delivered the world's emptiest smile. 'Start time 6.45,' she said. 'Here's your badge.'

Carrying my first tray of food, I climbed the stairs out into the evening light.

Game on.

15
Being Charlie Masham

The next forty minutes were excruciating.

Chef was a slave-driving perfectionist. I got roasted big-time as I fumbled platters of pastries or disturbed the lie of his micro-salads. My trays tilted and wobbled. I found a hundred different ways to collide with or trip over the guests, and each time I did I got an earful of digital glitch.

'Easy, Rendall,' Gedge whispered. 'Get yourself together.'

By twenty past seven I managed to slip away. I weaved through the crowds on the croquet lawn and through the French doors into the main house. The east wing entrance hall was thronged with guests. I grabbed a tray and began rescuing empty glasses.

The costumes and jewellery were in the library at the top of a curved sweep of staircase. It was standing room only up there. By the window was a security guard, radio clipped to her lapel, hands behind her back and her hair in a tight bun.

There was a row of mannequins across the far wall of the room where the jewellery experts were engaging the crowd with tutorials. At the far end was a doorway covered by a velvet curtain. Occasionally a guest would be accompanied inside. The pearl expert was a tall lady with yellow nail varnish and earrings in the shape of half-moons. Around her the crowd was three deep, like the bar at the Midland on a busy weekend, and she was pointing out the elegance of Leila's Veil. The necklace looked beautiful.

Swapping the pearls now would be impossible but the first of the catwalk shows was due at 7.45 p.m. and according to Ferg, that'd be when everyone took their seats in the marquee. I was so deep in stressy contemplation that I didn't hear Jennifer. 'Charlie!' she hissed. As she spoke, I realized it was the third or fourth time she'd done so – and I hadn't responded to the name. Schoolboy error. She was at the top of the stairs, icy-eyed. 'Charlie!'

I plastered a smile across my face but it was too little too late. 'I'm calling Guy. I'm afraid you're not what we're looking for. Finish the job you're on, sign out and leave your uniform.'

I was making a bad habit of getting sacked.

'Gedge,' I said into my cupped hand. 'We've got a problem.'

I'd managed less than an hour in my role as silver-service waiter. From now on, Gedge made clear, I'd need to collect glasses, keep my head down and hide if I saw Jennifer.

I was meeting Kallie in the orangery at 7.35 p.m., a place accessed via the marquee and Titania's Grove. The grove turned out to be a walled area with a fountain. A low tree had been draped in hanging fabric. A woman with a chalk-white complexion plucked a harp. Young couples holding hands spoke in whispers, assessing the crazy crap around them and deciding a love like theirs was well worth the considerable outlay.

I pushed through the crowds and followed a path between trees. Here were three pools, each the size of a tennis court, bobbing with floating candles. Beyond them the orangery; a glasshouse with glittering windows and a pair of doors open on to a grove of trees complete with actual, real-life oranges. Plants crowded the walkways.

Inside the air was heavy with scented candles. The place was empty. No sign of Kallie.

Then she burst from the undergrowth holding a silk handkerchief below her eyes, humming a tune and accompanying it with a silly dance. 'Welcome to the palace of satsumas my prince.' She twirled up and down the aisles. 'Long have I waited for this moment. Tonight our two hearts become one.' She did this thing with her eyes where they went all dark and wide and laughed, discarding the silk. 'Dance with me!' she cooed.

I'll be honest; I wasn't the type girls asked to dance, even if they were mocking me. Before that moment the only person who'd ever danced even near me was a stage-school brat who joined me for a number in *The Sound of Music* and made a swift exit when I accidently elbowed her in the face. Kallie, on the other hand, was so cool that when I tried to speak nothing emerged except a husky stalker-on-the-phone thing.

She raised an eyebrow. 'Rendall, are you ill?'

I shook my head and had another couple of goes at getting my voice to work. 'Fine,' I managed.

'Good,' Kallie laughed. 'Keep it together. We need to go.'

'You're going to be OK with this?'

She grinned. 'The window's only six metres up. And have you seen the stonework? Way easier than the Midland.'

'At 7.50 p.m., I'll come up the stairs and into the library,' I said. 'I can keep them all occupied for two minutes.'

'That's all I need. Save me a slice of cake will you?'

The wedding cakes were displayed in a side room off the marquee. Mostly they were variations of the naff three-tier snowscape, frilly and ridiculous, and mostly they were too big to carry so my choice was easy. Once I'd bagged a neat small one I transferred it to a silver platter I found at the ballroom entrance, added a knife, a stack of napkins and a couple of bottles of fizz and headed for the house.

'Compliments of Wiltshire Quality Catering!' I boomed at the top of the stairs to the library, placing the cake and booze on a side table. 'Come and help yourself!' I was bang on time. Heywood's staff crossed the room and gathered around while I butchered the cake. The place was empty of guests and the mannequins with their jewels were unattended. I busied myself serving and pouring and (I remember congratulating myself on this) found a dimmer switch and lowered the lights a little to help Kallie out.

I only saw her once in the two thrilling minutes that followed. I was hacking a series of extra slices while I talked and I realized the sash window was now open, raised fifteen centimetres. I hadn't seen it happen. The pearls woman was telling us about some cousin's wedding.

'Anyone ever attended a Bailey Heywood event?' I asked. While we chatted, I saw Kallie make the swap. It was poetry. She was a lithe, dark figure over there in the shadows and her fingers worked quickly. She pocketed one necklace, attached the fake then flattened her body out and squeezed through the window.

I offered top-ups on the booze, the guard went back to her position and our little party ended. Everything looked exactly the same as it had five minutes earlier.

I swear if I hadn't stupidly brightened the lights again, it would have been another half an hour before pearls-woman noticed the swap.

As it was though, I did. And she did.

16
Nice Work, Slumdog

Not long after I raised the lights the conversation started.

'It's bizarre,' the expert was saying. She'd waved over the security guard and was rolling our fake pearl necklace between her fingers. 'Look. This isn't the piece I've been working with this evening. These are poor imitations.' The guard leant in to look. I wondered how far away Kallie was. I imagined ice-bright searchlights panning the deer park and a hooting alarm. Instead the two of them continued talking. I got closer. The security guard was giving a hushed account into her radio. She looked up. 'Of course we'll also need to contact your company's insurers.'

I heard the expert's reply. 'No need. These demonstration pieces are all imitations anyway.' She indicated our replacement pearls. 'These are an imitation of an imitation.' I turned, shocked, and managed to make it to a dressing table without collapsing. 'Pre-booked appointments only for the real pieces,' the expert continued, nodding towards the velvet curtained doorway. 'We take them next door where your colleague is based. It's all very discreet.'

My bladder went into freefall. *Kallie had lifted fakes.* I collected glasses and napkins while my mind hammered blindly. I must have let out a groan because in my ear Gedge whispered, 'Rendall? What's up?'

'So there *has* been a swap . . .' mused the guard.

'Yes. Someone has taken the ceramic copies. We coat them in a special varnish. It's only when you handle pearls you can really tell.'

The guard was examining the window now.

'Rendall?' hissed Gedge. 'Speak to me!'

'Everyone out please,' a security dude said calmly, entering from the top of the stairs. 'I want this place sealed until the police are with us.' He approached the pearl expert. A number of his colleagues followed him in and fanned out. 'Ma'am we can handle this quickly and discreetly but this is a potential crime scene now,' he said to her. 'Talk me through what happened here.'

Outside, I felt the sweat crawl on my scalp even in the evening cool. Assuming the law went with a city-centre team, a cop car coming from Bath would take less than half an hour. 'Gedge. Listen.' I lowered my voice. 'Kallie's got fake pearls. Copy that? Fakes. We've got twenty-five minutes until the cops come.'

'*What?*' Gedge gave a filthy curse. Even through a burst of static I heard him hissing instructions to Becky. 'Ferg will track the cops. Once she finds the car I'll let you know how long you've got. Listen, Rendall. Is Leila's Veil on site or are we pulling out?'

'No it's here. Beyond a curtain in a room upstairs.'

Gedge made a growl of frustration. 'Kallie's too far away. It'll be half an hour before she's back in position. The grab is down to you and Coke.'

I paced the lawn. 'They've sealed off the area. There's no way I'm getting back in there.'

There was such a long silence I thought the earpieces had finally packed in. Then Gedge spoke. 'Look around you, Rendall. From where you're standing, is there a single damn thing within the reach of the average working citizen? Do you see anyone who's struggling to make rent or heading to the food bank later? D'you remember why we're doing this?'

I stared at the first-floor window of the library. 'Yes.'

'Good. Find a way in.'

I dug out Coke's site map and checked it, muttering the most creative swear words I could conjure. What had been thrilling now felt like madness. The east wing was Fort frickin' Knox and it was time to bail.

Then something on the map caught my eye.

The first aid room was in the house – I'd dismissed it as impossible to reach. But a St John's Ambulance crew were using a nearby outbuilding as a break area. Green uniforms, first aid kits, defibrillators. That'd work, right? I paced for a minute, trying to put it together. Bailey Heywood's team had space set aside in the house for emergency treatment. Even the arsiest security guard would let a kid with a first aid kit through.

I started running. In Titania's Grove, the harpist was having a fag. I found the gap in the hedge indicated on the map and followed the light spilling from the open doors of an outbuilding where a guy in shorts sat white-kneed on a camping stool, nursing a brew.

'Mister!' I said, playing the Welsh-kid-having-a-bad-day card. My accent wasn't great but it'd have to do. 'Mister, come quick! There's been a fall and she's injured!'

The fella spilt his tea as he jumped to his feet, pulling out a pair of earbuds. 'Where, sonny?'

'Back of the marquee,' I stammered, veering towards Indian. 'A mother-in-law – the old lady with the purple hat!'

Bless him, the guy set off at a sprint. As I was going through his bags looking for a disguise Gedge said, 'Nice work, Slumdog. Coke's on the croquet lawn. Go.'

I arrived back a different kid. I'd bundled my waiter's uniform into a hedge and now I had a green short-sleeved medical smock with a youth leader badge and a first aid kit. I dragged my hair into a good-samaritan side-parting and plunged into the shadows that skirted the lawn.

'Rendall, is that you?'

I joined Coke, squatting low against some bushes. He was breathing hard and picking bits of foliage from his shirt with distaste. 'Had to short-cut through the shrubbery.'

'Right,' I said, opening my first aid kit. 'Gedge told you what's up?'

Coke nodded and mopped his brow with his handkerchief. He noticed my uniform. 'What's all this?'

I rattled through the supplies, my fingers jumpy. Chunky plastic tub of painkillers, bandages, asthma inhaler. 'I need you to be ill,' I said.

We hobbled across the grass to the French doors where a guard yawned.

'He's having breathing difficulties,' I said as Coke wheezed into the inhaler. 'I need to get him to the first aid room.' Coke fell to his knees spluttering and I had to drag him upwards. The guard looked alarmed. 'My colleagues are inside, they've got more training than me,' I said.

'The library is off-limits.'

'I don't care about the library,' I raised my voice over Coke, who was hamming up a cough. 'We need access to the ground floor where I can get this guy some medical assistance. Please.'

He let us in, thank God, and we struggled across to the far door. I hauled Coke through, closing it behind us. Inside the air smelt stale. Dust motes danced in the glow of a table lamp. Off to the right was a flight of stairs heading upwards.

'You'll never make it as an actor,' I told Coke.

'Where are we going exactly?' He was tucking his shirt in and straightening his cuffs.

'Past the library there's a room behind a curtain. The pearls are there.' I gave him my best motivational grin. 'And we're gonna find a way to them.'

17
Leila's Veil

Upstairs I pressed my ear to a door and, hearing nothing, tried the handle. A quick check confirmed an empty bedroom. We slipped inside.

The place was ancient – old-fashioned bedspread, antique headboard, dark wardrobe. We padded across to the window. We were above the croquet lawn and crowds were spilling out from the marquee now the first of the catwalk shows were done. We didn't have long before the cops would be rolling up the tree-lined drive.

'Gedge. We're in.'

Electronic interference and a muffled curse. 'Rendall. Ferg reckons you've got about five minutes. Copy? The law's with us in five.'

'Five minutes to find a way into the room,' I told Coke. 'Wait here a sec while I investigate.'

I slipped out into the corridor and crept forward just as a man was emerging from a door further along; a black guy with a chin-beard and chunky glasses pulling on the jacket of a blue suit. 'Young man. This area is restricted.'

I babbled an apology, improvising. 'I've lost the medical team!' For some weird reason, I'd gone Geordie. I couldn't even do Geordie. 'I was meant to bring an inhaler for a guest having an asthma attack and now I don't know where to go!'

'You're in the wrong wing,' he said. 'Take the stairs down, turn left at the bottom . . .' I saw the man's eyes widen at something over my shoulder.

Then Coke hit him in the face with a copper bedpan and he went down.

The sudden violence took me back. Aidy Coke had totally lost it. The clang of contact echoed for a moment as we both stared at the blood oozing from the fallen man's temple. He blinked once, semi-conscious.

'Bloody hell,' I spluttered. 'What are you doing?'

'And you say *I* can't act,' Coke said, steadying himself. 'Was that meant to be Geordie?'

The heels of his shoes raked wobbly lines in the carpet as we dragged the guy down the corridor. We passed a couple of doors and took a sharp left where a vase stood in an alcove. He groaned as we lowered him.

'We must be nearby,' I whispered, trying to keep it together. Coke was silent and pale. I knew one of the doors along here would be the right one. If we tried a few we'd surely find ourselves at the rear of the library behind the curtains – right on top of the pearls. Ahead, there were two doors that looked like they might be possibilities.

'Help me pull him,' I said. 'Then go.' I wanted Coke away before he did any more damage. 'You disappear and find a spot below the window. I'll throw the pearls down.'

At door one, we deposited the bloke and knocked. No response. Another six metres along I crouched over the guy, first aid kit out, and Coke knocked again. Door two opened.

I knew we'd got the right place; even the glimpse I got as I looked up from the unconscious man revealed a book-lined interior with a curtain beyond.

'This area is . . .' began a blond-haired man with fat fingers and a signet ring. Then he saw the reclining figure. 'Good Lord, is that Gavin?'

I was dabbing the wounded man's forehead, playing worried. 'I found him on the stairs. He may have slipped.'

The man turned and spoke into the room. 'Russell! Ged! We've got an injury here.' Coke took that as his cue to slip away, thank God. Soon I was pushed aside as the two security guards squatted over poor Gavin; one guy checking his pulse, the other running cupped hands down both legs to check for broken bones.

'Move him inside,' suggested Russell.

I stuck with Gavin, faffing with my disinfectant wipes. 'I'll get him some air,' I said crossing to the window and lifting the sash. Turning back, I took a moment to assess where I was. A small room separated from the library; chandelier with candle-shaped bulbs; fireplace; a rug in the centre and a modern-looking metal display cabinet. I took another second to run my eye across the cabinet. It had a glass top which was raised open. The inside was lined with purple silk. A selection of brooches and rings were displayed there, as well as the most beautiful pearl necklace I'd ever seen. Leila's Veil. The real one; the thirty-thousand-pound one.

'Do you know this man?' I said returning to Gavin, who groaned again, raising a shaking hand to his temple and wincing. He wasn't quite conscious but I didn't have long.

'Yes,' confirmed the blond bloke with the rings. 'He's a member of the house staff . . .' His attention was drawn by a sound from the main part of the library. 'Excuse me, gentlemen.' He slipped through the curtain into the room beyond.

Suddenly Gavin coughed himself into consciousness.

'Easy there mate,' said Ged.

Then the two guards both leant in. Russell was checking Gavin's pupils. This was it. God knows how I remained so calm. I stood, took Leila's Veil, balled it up in a sweaty palm, crossed to the window and threw it out into the darkness not daring to check if Coke was beneath me. Then I closed the window and busied myself with my first aid kit, barely thinking straight, terrified to look up.

Gavin was raising himself to a sitting position now, one guard either side of him. I swept up the last of my bottles and bandages. My uniform was sticking to me. I held my breath and calmly slipped from the room, following the corridor to the corner, every slow footstep an act of will.

Only when I turned out of sight did I begin to sprint.

I swear that St John's Ambulance uniform was like a licence to run. No questions were asked as I bolted back through the entrance hall and out on to the lawn. I squeezed my way between the shifting mass of guests, looking for Coke and trying to figure out where the pearls had fallen.

He appeared at the edge of the lawns, waving from the shadows. I knew he'd got them. We scampered through the gardens and out to the ha-ha, where we picked up the bag with my clothes in. Together, we sprinted across the deer park. It was so dark away from the lights of the house that we lost our bearings, nearly plunged into a fishing lake and ended up wandering along a line of woodland. Ironically it was the cops who put us back on track. Away to our left, a line of squad cars proceeded in single file along the drive. We spent an uncomfortable period face down in the grass until they'd gone then made a hasty recalculation and plunged into the woods.

It took us twice as long as we'd hoped but we found the outer wall. Half a mile along the road, we tracked down the van and gave a victory roar. We drove back towards the motorway, exhausted and elated, Leila's Veil in the glove compartment.

Two days later Payback met to go over the Heywood grab. We gathered around the table at Arch 17 to pick apart our mistakes.

I knew right from the start that Aidy Coke didn't like me much but as we discussed the grab I kept quiet about that sudden flash of violence I'd seen back in the house. I never mentioned it and neither did Coke. I felt guilty keeping secrets but I needn't have.

Soon enough I'd been finding out others were keeping them too.

18
Magnus Yate

Magnus Yate had a pavement cabin on Quay Street called Timekeepers. He fixed clocks and watches. We huddled under the eaves, Gedge watching Yate squinting through an eyeglass at the interior of a gold carriage clock, me checking a tabloid piece with the headline PAYBACK BEHIND STATELY HOME HEIST? Gedge rapped the sill of the service area and rather than turn, Yate held a gloved hand aloft and continued picking at a cog with a pair of tweezers. When he was finished he gave a grunt and opened his side door.

'Come into the back,' he said, eyeing me.

'Rendall's to be trusted,' Gedge said, squeezing into the hut. Behind Yate's working area was a room so small I could open my arms and lean on both walls at once. Yate and Gedge sat down. I got to watch from standing.

'What have you brought me?' Yate's accent was East London; he was a real geezer with an unsmoked roll-up behind his ear and fingerless gloves.

Gedge set a bag between them. 'South Sea cultured pearls,' he said. 'Aside from black ones, these are the best you can get. Single stones can be worth up to three grand each.'

Gedge tipped out the contents.

He'd removed the pearls from their chain, I noticed; they skittered free and the two men had to corral them together with cupped hands. They spun like milky marbles. I held my breath wondering how the hell we'd managed to lift them without getting caught. Yate rolled a pearl between finger and thumb and squinted an eyeglass into place. The little room was close and warm. I could smell the tobacco on Yate's breath, the sweat gathered in the damp wool under his armpits.

He coughed. 'Didn't see this one on your channel. Recent job? These are decent, Patrick.' He checked another, and another. Gedge tried to stretch his legs but the room wouldn't allow it. Yate removed his little magnifier and wiped his eyes. 'Well,' he said. 'A complete piece would've made life easier. Where's the chain?'

'We had an accident,' Gedge said. That was the first I'd heard of it. Maybe the piece had been damaged making its exit from the window of the reading room. 'Sold as seen,' Gedge added, an attempt at levity.

Yate didn't bother with a smile. 'I think we can do a deal. But before we discuss particulars, Patrick, there's something else we need to straighten out. Isn't there?'

Hovering behind Gedge, I couldn't see his face but I saw his shoulders stiffen. He tucked his feet beneath his chair. Suddenly his cap and skater shoes made him look like a kid facing a school interrogation. 'Listen,' he said. 'It's been a difficult period. Things haven't been as easy this summer. Let's set aside, just for a minute, the difficulties of the last month. Other than that I've been dependable, haven't I?'

Yate said, 'The golf club?'

'OK aside from that.' Yate opened his mouth but Gedge held a hand up. 'I know. I know – the casino chips issue too. I admit that wasn't great.'

Yate side-eyed him big time. 'Patrick, I have to watch you on TV and read about you in every paper I pick up. And then, in real life, I have to listen to your excuses. I'm bored. Now I'm happy to take the pearls in part-payment for everything. I can give you a reduced price and we say goodbye the best of friends, debts cleared.'

'Don't do this. We need the cash.' Gedge fanned his hands on the table before him, a gesture I'd seen before.

Yate wasn't having it. 'You're giving ninety-five per cent of your stash away. Keep some back. I'm not your bank, boy.'

Gedge fumed. 'Listen. Do you know how many people live in poverty in the UK alone? Thirty per cent of kids are classed as poor. That's four million people, pal. And they come from working families. Payback gives them money – that's the whole point. If we cut back on donations, we may as well quit.'

'I'm not your bloody bank.'

'Listen. Changes to benefits have just put another quarter of a million people into poverty. Now, d'you know the size of the catering bill for the House of Lords?'

Yate sighed. 'I'm sure you'll be enlightening me.'

'One point three million quid. Seventeen thousand bottles of champagne during a term of government. The state is rotten. All I want to do is fix it. Help people.' Gedge finished prodding the table and wiped his eyes. 'We've got two big grabs lined up and I swear to you – I *swear* Yate – we'll be straight in a week. One week. Seven days.'

'Or I break your legs,' said Yate.

I heard the breath catch in Gedge's throat. 'Yeah,' he said slowly.

'Glittering career as the new Robin Hood suddenly over. I break your legs. Say it, Patrick.'

'You break my legs.'

'Thank you Patrick.' Yate gathered up the pearls and tipped them carefully into their bag. 'Now, regarding the matter in hand, I'd be happy to pay fifteen for these.'

Gedge's voice was tired. 'C'mon. They're worth twenty-five, easy.'

'When I deal with high-risk customers, my costs go up.'

'Twenty.'

'Seventeen. Final offer.'

Gedge sighed. 'Deal.'

We walked back along Byrom Street. The clouds had cleared. Outside the museum, a mariachi band were doing a weirdly cheerful version of 'Bridge Over Troubled Water'. We stopped on the corner of Liverpool Street.

'Yate's hard work isn't he?'

Gedge took his cap off and ran the brim between his fingers. 'I've had that coming to me for a while.' He chewed his lip and replaced his cap. 'But seventeen k for those pearls? *Seventeen*?' He stared at the sky. His voice was uneven. It nearly broke as he said, 'We need more money.'

That evening, rattling around the house, I was plagued by thoughts I couldn't kill. Remembering it now, I reckon it was the phrase *we need more money* that bothered me. I'd always imagined Payback just lined up another job if the cash ran out. Or stopped until the following summer. Gedge though, had sounded life-and-death desperate.

I knew the guy was hiding things from us. Even aside from the criminal record there seemed to be secrets. Those papers in Ruiz's case for example, the ones he'd folded away and kept. And then making me pointlessly return the case to the hotel – as if he were almost sending a message. Now this fierce panic about money. I couldn't clear my head of it.

Yate had used Gedge's first name – Patrick. I decided to do some digging. Every time I'd sat in the kitchen with my tablet before now it had been on a strictly fanboy basis – me checking Payback uploads while Malcolm mopped the floor around the island – but that evening was different. I checked the dark garden, pulled the curtains across the windows and began work. *Patrick Gedge*, I typed. There were LinkedIn profiles, Wikipedia pages about dead musicians, an Australian politician and a boring roll-call of images – all grey-haired blokes in suits. Nothing useful. *Patrick Gedge Ireland* got me too many hits to handle, though I spent half an hour digging through the results. After a break and a couple of bags of crisps I had a brainwave and tried *Paddy Gedge*. Immediately things improved. There were references in the *Evening News* to delinquent gangs operating in Salford. A 'Paddy Gedge, 15' got a single mention in a longer article about a chain of betting shops targeted by young gangs. I dug some more. Twenty minutes later I'd got an opinion piece about troubled street kids which mentioned a BBC documentary. I dug it up on YouTube and watched. It was about an inner-city estate, centring on the north-west's immigrant Irish community. No sign of Gedge but plenty of other lads loitering on apocalyptic-looking housing estates. I looked around my plush kitchen and felt a stab of guilt as I made myself a hot chocolate. The film finished with a group interview – four lads against a red-brick wall under the sign 'Swinton ABC'. A quick search confirmed ABC stood for Amateur Boxing Club. I took a punt on *Paddy Gedge, Swinton Amateur Boxing Club*.

As soon as I saw the results I remembered that punch Gedge had thrown, flooring the copper in Linden Gardens. I was looking at photos and profile pieces for years' worth of Under 16s fighters. It wasn't long before I was staring at a black and white shot of Patrick Gedge, baby-faced and bare-chested, fists raised to camera. Alongside the picture was a paragraph of text. *Cork-born Paddy, a smart, technical fighter of a strong, muscular 154 pounds, hopes to compete profession-ally after Swinton ABC. 'I owe it to my mum to work as hard as I can,' says the young middleweight. 'We'd lost everything before we came over here. I'd like to make her proud of me.'*

I thought of the stuff amassing around us recently – Sinclair calling Gedge 'extremely dangerous', Yate's anger, Gedge's 'we need more money', the papers in the case . . . I knew one thing at least: Payback's talisman was more mysteri-ous than he made out.

As it happened I didn't have a chance to investigate further. I was wolfing down a cheese sandwich and sketching out a plan to search some of the properties on Ruiz's list – I badly needed to make a good impression if I was gonna finally shake him off – when I got a text.

It was my weird contact again. I'd missed our last meeting because Sinclair had shown up at the house. I read the new one. *Where were you? We NEED TO MEET TOM.*

I considered. *Something came up* I typed. *What's so important?*

Soon enough I got a reply. A new meeting: Cathedral

Gardens, centre of Manchester, tomorrow morning at ten. *Tomorrow*? I remember thinking as I climbed the stairs. *This guy must be desperate.*

Turns out I wasn't wrong.

19
This Close

In the high summer sunshine Cathedral Gardens was a motley mix of skaters, nerds, gamers and geeks. There was no way I was going to spot an individual amongst this lot. Thankfully I didn't need to. Someone recognized me and strode out from the middle of a group, crossing the grass in my direction. I watched him approach. He took my arm and spun me away.

'What *is* this?' I asked.

The guy had maybe a year on me, all vampire-goth, pale skin, his chin dark with a day's stubble, skinny frame under a long black coat. 'We need to talk, Thomas. You didn't show.'

'Show where?'

'The park,' said the lad. He rubbed his forehead unhappily. 'I asked you to come.' He put his hands in the pockets of his coat. I realized I knew his mannerisms from the videos. This guy used to be in Payback.

'You're Jay.'

'That's right,' he said. 'James. Becky's cousin.'

It fell into place finally. James Ferguson, cousin to Payback's IT super-geek Becky Ferguson. 'I'm your replacement,' I said.

Jay checked the street. 'That's right. I've been trying to get in touch. There are things you need to know, Thomas. Important things. Follow me.'

We crossed Corporation Street and stopped to talk near a statue of a man in a high-collared coat. *Robert Owen*, the inscription said. Leaning against its iron legs, Jay Ferguson rolled a cigarette.

'You left Payback. What happened?' I asked. I was thinking of Ferg listing last summer's disagreements. The casino grab, she'd mentioned, *when Aidy hit Jay*.

Jay rubbed his face and licked his roll-up shut. He looked a real stresshead. 'It was a bad time, Thomas. I thought Gedge would pack it in. The channel went quiet for a while. But then, this summer, there he was again and Becky couldn't help getting involved.'

I felt my defences rise at the mention of Gedge and Ferg. 'Becky's fine,' I said brightly, going for reassurance.

'Rubbish,' Jay said. 'She needs help. All that hacking – she's way out of her depth; you'd know that if you had half a brain. Her mum and dad paid for specialist support and they think she's at the university's summer school. Ha. *Summer school*. Her parents might believe she's taken care of but I know better.' I was flummoxed. Ferg – super-intense collector of colourful dongles and maker of lists – seemed fine to me. Maybe I hadn't been looking properly. 'Then there's the finances,' Jay said in a sudden change of tack. 'Check Gedge's black box. It's under his bed.'

'Black box?' I mocked.

'Yeah. Check the box if you want the shock of your life: Payback's bank balance. You guys are in big trouble.'

I shifted position at this. I'd been trying not to think about the broken earpieces we couldn't afford to replace, Yate's threat to go breaking legs, all the money we'd given away. I squinted into the sun. 'Go on.'

'Yate's at breaking point. He'll shop you guys to the cops if he has to swallow one more excuse, I swear. That's without rent arrears for various dormant HQs across the country.' I didn't know what rent arrears were but I was bright enough to get the gist. 'And then there's the Amelia Sinclair issue.'

My palms prickled at this. 'Sinclair?' I tried, looking all carefree.

Jay gave a crooked smile. 'Don't play dumb Thomas. She's really close.'

'To what?'

'To putting you guys into some young offender institution and Gedge into prison.' He held thumb and forefinger a couple of millimetres apart. 'This close to closing the net. I thought she'd got him last summer. He wriggled free. You guys won't see September, I swear. I'm getting Becky out. I'm here today to tell you to do the same. Bail before it goes down in flames.'

'Ridiculous.'

Jay got to his feet, held his hands up. 'Hey. I tried. I've done my bit. The rest is up to you Thomas.' I swore at him. Jay narrowed his eyes. 'You think you're clever and funny but you're an idiot. This won't end well. When it all goes wrong, remember I warned you.' He turned and left.

I tried to conjure some clever one-liner to send him on his way but I drew a blank and opted instead for, 'Screw you!' which at least had the benefit of simplicity.

After he'd gone I mulled it over. If Jay was right, things were looking bleak. But he couldn't be. Jay's perception was all warped because he wanted to protect his cousin, right? And yet when I tried to cheer myself thinking this way, it didn't work. The snags in the story bothered me and the talk of DCI Sinclair made my stomach shrink and my legs go watery. *What if Jay was right about everything?* I shook my head, trying to clear the thought.

No. There hadn't been a single item of proof.

That made me feel better. If Jay had really wanted to persuade me he'd have arrived with bank balances. Police reports. Recorded conversations, intercepted emails. Instead the guy shows up with fairy-tale talk of a black box under a bed. I could go straight to Gedge. Ask right out. Sort it.

I stretched my legs, thanked Robert Owen for the temporary hospitality and pulled on my jacket. Gedge had asked me to track down some costumes for a drop and I managed to forget Jay for an hour or so as I trawled charity shops and fancy dress rentals. By mid-afternoon I'd found what I wanted – five great get-ups the gang were going to love – bagged them, and hauled them home on the tram. By the time I was walking the last few sunny streets to the house, I was even whistling a cheery tune.

That all stopped when I saw a cop car across from the house.

Vauxhall Astra, window down, driver's head cocked to one side like she was watching me in the wing mirror. Sinclair raised a hand in greeting.

'Thomas,' she said, turning. 'Have you a minute?'

I dropped the bags in the drive and carved out a hollow smile as I crossed towards her.

'Offside rear door please,' said Sinclair. I had no idea what that meant. I tried doors, beginning with hers, stupidly, and Sinclair had to smile patiently and say, 'No, Thomas,' until by a process of elimination I got the right one.

I settled myself in the back and she turned to talk. She had a tablet with her. 'I have a few questions I'd like to follow up. Not in connection with the robbery at the Midland Hotel, Thomas. My team and I are looking into related incidents.' She paused and smiled. 'Earlier this month, two cars were stolen from a shopping mall in North London. Soon after the robbery, footage was posted online, apparently filmed during the theft.'

I let out a long breath going for shocked. 'Wow, really?'

'I've also got further footage from an incident in central London last week,' Sinclair continued cheerfully, swiping the tablet to bring up a video. Coke's footage from the Blackhouse Langley grab; jumpy handheld shots over the crowd. Some spaceface in a fox mask dancing in a window.

I laced my fingers to stop them jumping and said, 'That's Payback. They're famous. Everyone knows Payback.' I tried a grin. She was watching me. 'Why are you showing me this?'

Sinclair smiled. 'Buzzcuts for Biscuits,' she said matter-of-factly.

My head went down at that. The DCI laughed.

Guess I'd better tell you about my YouTube channel.

20
Nuclear Sunrise, Baby

Three years ago, I was a self-obsessed risk-taking show-off. Hard to believe, I know. It was a puberty thing. Anyway, Year 9, the week before a nationwide fundraising TV marathon and school had gone crazy about raising money. I had this killer idea. I'd get my head shaved and my payment for this embarrassment would be a single Bourbon biscuit. Hilarious, right? People would make donations to see it live and pay double if I was brave enough to post the footage online. 'Buzzcuts for Biscuits' was born. I forget how much I raised but I beat the rest of the year group put together. Everyone at school visited my cobbled-together channel. The big-time beckoned.

About a week later some Year 7 lad bet me a Jammie Dodger that I wouldn't leap a line of kids on his BMX. I was no cyclist but a kid in my year offered to be my cameraman and made a ramp on a lathe during DT detention. Loads of lads volunteered to lie on their backs at the bottom of the hill, getting braver (or more psychotic) the further away they positioned themselves. I pedalled flat-out down the incline and took off. The back wheel of the bike struck the last boy right in the Cinderellas. I took a comedy tumble and the unfortunate lad roared in agony. He cried so hard he was sick. Later his mum went ballistic and the head teacher made me write a letter of apology. But we'd filmed the whole thing so we uploaded it and Buzzcuts for Biscuits went small-time stellar. I had six subscribers and seven hundred views.

Soon other people started hearing about it and over the next two years I got offered biscuits for all sorts of stuff. I did a thing with shaving foam. A few things with shaving foam. I agreed to be the victim of a mock kidnap during school sports day, acting the hell out of it. In the snowy winter of Year 10 I created a sledging challenge – Sledgicidal – and asked people to nominate the craziest places to ride the snow. I ended up skimming my ass into the side of a bus at some traffic lights. Someone got hold of an edible bra and pants (I know, who knew? Turns out they're made from little sweets strung along lines of elastic . . .) and I got fully made-up and mimed to a tune called 'Babes Never Die' in exchange for a Jaffa Cake. I did pretty much anything. I knew it was going well when a prefect from the year above said to me, 'You're the Buzzcuts kid, aren't you? God, you're such a *tart*.'

In the run-up to my Year 11 exams I'd not had much time for Buzzcuts. The last upload had been my April Fool's post; an uninspired video of me burning my class notes and dancing around the flames dressed as a witch in a wig. One comment said, 'Buzzcuts has lost it.' It took me weeks to copy up my missing notes. A single custard cream had been my only compensation. The site had been dormant since.

'Events connected to events,' DCI Sinclair said. 'People to people. Like fate.' Then she hit play on her tablet. I had to watch one of my Buzzcuts uploads in the back of a cop car, which was bad enough. Worse, Sinclair had picked one of the

Mr Boom-Boom ones. I used to think Mr Boom-Boom, my fireworks alter-ego, was hilarious and last autumn me and a couple of guys from school had gone all out on him. I got biscuits in return for setting fireworks off in all sorts of places. Sinclair had chosen the video we shot at the park. We'd rigged the roundabouts, slides and climbing frames with rockets.

So I had to sit and watch myself capering like a pre-schooler, hopping from foot to foot Rumpelstiltskin-style. We'd found some imported Chinese fireworks, their names rendered ridiculous in translation, but after each rocket went off I'd shout them anyway. *Whoosh* went the rocket. 'Haunted Fish!' I yell. *Boom*. 'Festival Balls!' *Fizz*. 'Freddie Mercury!' The film ended with me executing some atrocious body-popping and declaring 'Nuclear Sunrise, baby!'

It's no exaggeration to say I have never been so relieved to see anyone hit pause on anything ever in the history of time, ever. The frame froze with me leering at the camera through my mask. I had a pumpkin mask from Hallowe'en and over the course of three capers it'd sort of become part of the Mr Boom-Boom aesthetic.

Plastic masks. Suddenly I could see where this was going.

My phone buzzed against my thigh but I couldn't check it. Sinclair pushed on. 'Now, have a look at this,' she said enthusiastically. The night of the Jaguars: three foxes standing side by side, arms folded. 'Payback,' said the text scrolling along the foot of the screen. 'The Redistribution Solution.' Sinclair checked my face as she indicated the screen. 'We think this character here is Patrick Gedge. I showed you his photo, remember?' I watched the foxes creeping through the Westwater Mall, the blood thumping in my ears. 'These two here,' Sinclair observed, pausing the movie, have the same height and build as previous Payback members but this one . . . ' she indicated me; I stared neutrally at my lower back, the flash of white above my black jeans – 'only appeared recently. We don't know him.' To me the figures looked unmistakable. But only to me, I told myself. *Sinclair can't be sure or she wouldn't be asking.*

She placed the tablet on the passenger seat. 'What interests me Thomas,' she said, 'are the connections between these films.'

I recovered pretty quickly and gave a pitch-perfect gasp of astonishment. 'You're not saying *I'm* involved are you? That's Payback. I admit I've done some stupid things before but that's *actual* Payback you're talking about.'

'See it from my point of view. Two physically identical suspects, and when we do some digging, lo and behold a tendency to lark about in masks.' My stomach was tight as a wire knot. 'Now, what if Payback had got themselves mixed up with a certain Mr Ruiz, who was staying at the Midland Hotel while you worked there? And what if they had stolen something of his?'

I bit my lip and looked at my hands. I couldn't hold her gaze. 'You've lost me,' I said.

'Thomas you seem a nice lad. I've got a son your age and he's got the same energy and bravado. I understand.' I almost collapsed into weeping confession but looked out of the car window and managed to hold it together. She passed me her card and said gently, 'Whatever you're getting caught up in – stop. Come to the station or call me on this number. I've been unravelling connections and I've nearly got this gang. But I think you're the one to help finish this.'

'Me? Why me?'

'Oh, you know. People connected to people. You're the sticky guy. The person in the middle that holds everything together. And you don't even know it.'

'I'm not involved!'

'We can still get you out without charge.' She raised her eyebrows. 'Understood?' I nodded, poker-faced. 'Call me.' I nodded again. 'Good. Off you go and enjoy your day.'

I felt sick. I watched Sinclair drive away then fumbled with the house keys, legged it upstairs and dry-heaved in the toilet for a couple of minutes, a chill sweat pouring from me. When I'd regained control I splashed my face and checked my phone for the text that had arrived during the interview. It was Gedge, summoning me. I swiped my tablet awake and found my search history for the night I'd typed *Paddy Gedge* into Google. I brought up the boxing profile and read it again. *'I owe it to my mum to work as hard as I can,' says the young middleweight. 'We'd lost everything before we came over here. I'd like to make her proud of me.'*

I paced the kitchen trying to think through the panic.

We'd lost everything. I typed, *Bankruptcy, Patrick Gedge, Cork.* A few pages down I got a PDF of a piece from the *Evening Echo.* BANKRUPTCY HELL FOR CORK FAMILIES ran the headline. *Bernadette Gedge spoke of the torment of foreclosure at the hands of an American capital firm who has recently become a big player in the Irish property market. 'They know nothing of the suffering of local people,' said Mrs Gedge, 38, mother to one son . . .*

I was starting to understand Payback's leader. Self-educated, thrill-seeking, passionate but also super-secretive, driven by the suffering of his mother and, if Sinclair had her way, soon to be tracked down, cornered and slammed behind bars.

Things weren't looking good for Paddy Gedge. And if they weren't good for him, that meant they weren't good for me.

21
Burnin' Bad Guys

I hauled the costumes across town towards Arch 17, pausing under a halo of pigeons to work my way through a pack of supermarket donuts, settling my stomach, fighting down fear. I'd planned out exactly what I was going tell the gang about Sinclair – it was time to come clean and call a halt to everything. Maxi emerged from beneath a Jeep, waved me through, and I climbed the stairs and dragged the door open.

I'm not easily taken aback. But this really threw me off my stride.

Gedge, hands on hips, was engaged in a close examination of a naked male clothes-store mannequin. He had a tumble of shopping bags around his feet. Marx was dozing on the cobbles next to him. The plastic torso was that of a muscled man, arms by its sides. The head had a movie-star face with a chiselled chinful of comic-book stubble and was topped with a synthetic wig of thick black hair threaded with grey. It was wearing nothing but a pair of sunglasses.

Gedge thrust a thumb at the dude in the birthday suit. 'What do you think?'

This was what he'd texted me for? I picked my words

carefully. 'Why are we looking at a life-sized replica of Channing Tatum . . . *in the buff*?'

Gedge gave me an irritated glance. 'Eejit. You brought the costumes?' I nodded, offered him a donut. He shared it with Marx, examining the mannequin again. Evidently he saw what I meant because he snatched the glasses off and tumbled the hair a bit.

'Ah!' I said. 'Jose Mourinho?'

Gedge sighed and began digging about in the bags at his feet, pulling out a pair of black jeans, a crumpled white shirt, shoes, a jacket. 'Let's get him dressed. That'll help.'

I shrugged. 'Whatever.'

Somehow the simple act of clothing the thing helped me concentrate; begin to push the Sinclair problem away. *She can't possibly know our identities for certain. All she has is unconnected video footage, not a scrap of proof, just like Jay. She'd been looking for a reaction.* We put the mannequin on its back and yanked a pair of black jeans up the legs. Marx loved this; he leapt and scampered, climbed on to Jose's chest, dismounted with a leap, nosed my bag of donuts. Turned out the jeans were two sizes too tight. We could pull the zip of his flies up but there was no way we were getting the button shut. Gedge covered the gap with a leather belt and I put some socks on him. Together we added the shoes then lifted the mannequin upright and tried to get a white shirt over his shoulders and down his stiff plastic arms. It felt good working together. I whistled a choice tune from my feel-good playlist, stroked Marx, felt my worries soothe.

Aidy Coke clattered down from the mezzanine to see what was going on. 'Who on earth is this?'

'Channing Tatum,' I said, trying to do the buttons on the guy's shirt. Dressed, he was actually looking more like James Bond.

Coke laughed. 'Who is it meant to be? Eddie Redmayne? Benedict Cumberbatch?'

Gedge swore. 'C'mon guys. It's obvious isn't it?'

'A young George Clooney?' Coke asked brightly. He glanced at Gedge to check. There was a disappointed silence. Coke sucked on his apple juice. 'George Osborne? Max George? Is it *anyone* called George?'

'Just *think* about it,' Gedge raised his voice over our sniggering. 'Think a second. It's for the Bailey Heywood drop. We'll dress him up then burn him as we hand out the cash. Now do you see?'

'Guy Fawkes?'

'No!' Gedge stamped his feet in frustration.

I was still laughing when Kallie appeared at the door and clocked the mannequin. 'Why have we got a statue of Steve Jobs?' she said.

We put a jacket on the dude, I managed to get a half-neat tie around its neck and Coke straightened the cuffs and smoothed the creases from its jeans. When we were finished we all stood back, imitating Gedge's silent consideration. Ferg came downstairs to join us and we all gathered in a semi-circle around it.

'Well?' said Gedge. There was still a snap of irritation in his voice. No one wanted to risk a guess. 'It's *the man*!' he spat eventually. 'You know. The *stickin' it to the man* . . . man.'

I made a vaguely positive noise. Marx joined in, barking and making three rapid laps of the room.

Kallie nodded vigorously. 'I see that now,' she said, the edge of her mouth twitching as she swallowed a smile. 'It's clearly the man.'

Becky said, 'Which man?'

'*The* man,' Coke said. 'The symbol of control and oppression from the civil rights movement in the sixties. I've got to give it to you Gedge, it does look like the man. Though also a lot like Benedict Cumberbatch.'

Even Gedge grinned at that one. He reached for a placard, holding it up for us. It was a metre-long painted wooden sign, black with red lettering stencilled neatly across it. *Payback* it said. Orange flames rose around the text: *Celebrating two years of burnin' bad guys.*

'Burning bad guys?' Coke asked.

'Yup. Rendall?' Gedge flapped a hand at my bags. I launched into my speech, handing them out.

'Gedge'll be Robin,' I began. 'The rest of us get to choose. Look – there's Friar Tuck,' I unfolded a monk's habit and wig complete with shaven tonsure, 'one of us gets to be Little John – check out these boots! One of us is Alan-a-Dale—'

'Who?' asked Kallie.

'The minstrel. Y'know – singer. And one of us is Maid Marian.'

The silence was borderline awkward as I finished unpacking. Eventually Kallie clapped her hands together, eyes bright. 'Love it!' she declared. 'Can I be the monk?'

Coke indicated the placard. 'But why the flames?'

'Ah!' I produced the plastic longbows I'd bought from a kids' toy shop. 'We're all going to be shooting these,' I said, handing them around and indicating our mannequin, 'at him.'

While the rest of my year group stressed their heads off about exam results, I spent that Friday night riding a flatbed truck through Birmingham city centre dressed as Maid Marian, firing burning arrows at a dummy and throwing money into a crowd of eager weekenders.

It should've been an absolute blast in theory but the Bailey Heywood debacle easily wins worst drop ever. It was the planning that let us down. We didn't anticipate the riot police for one.

Or the size of the fire.

This is how it was meant to work.

The man, hair neatly combed and shoes polished for the occasion, was gaffer-taped to a steel crowd-control barrier so he stood up. Gedge's sign was hung about his neck like a giant bib. We'd pulled his head off, stuffed his interior with flammables (paper, straw, cardboard), doused them in lighter fluid, popped the dude's head back on and readied our bows and flaming arrows.

Then we'd put him on the back of a bright red flatbed truck. The truck was Coke's idea – the kind of thing you'd see dressed up as a float in a parade, kids playing steel drums on the back, chugging through a street party in a city near you. At a hundred quid for the night it was, he assured us, a complete bargain.

The man would be lashed to his barrier towards the driver's cab end, facing backwards so the assembled crowds could see his sign. At a safe distance from the mannequin would come the cash from the sale of the pearls, just over sixteen grand assembled in a neat grid, three hundred and odd packs, each with fifty quid in fivers all ready for us to pick up and throw. And everything would be placed on a wet blanket of fire-retardant nylon.

Fire-retardant, we were to discover later, is not the same as fire-resistant.

You live and learn, right?

22
Hen Do from Hell

It started well. The night was warm and dry; thin trails of cloud blushed orange by city lights. Crowds spilt from bars and restaurants. A band was busking at the corner of New Street and Bennetts Hill, their singer pogoing enthusiastically. A guy sold helium balloons from a stall and the staff of a cocktail bar (all regulation black T-shirts and skinny jeans) handed out little plastic shot glasses of something with crushed ice and mint. We'd been hard at work on social and pulled a happy, enthusiastic crowd. We'd figured the feds would take an hour to notice the disturbance. A cheer went up when the truck arrived. Phones were raised and the event began, live-streamed to a thousand online platforms. Coke drove at a stately pace, Kallie alongside him in the cab, waving from the window in her monk's habit; Gedge and I were balanced on the back. I had a long purple dress and veil, Gedge was head-to-toe in Lincoln green with a fetching pair of knee-high leather boots and brandishing a loudhailer. *'Robin Hood, Robin Hood, riding through the glen . . .'* went the chant as we motored slowly down New Street. *'Feared by the baaad!'* I screamed, falsetto. *'Loved by the gooood!'* Watching the video back later that night – the bit before it all went south – I admit I made the drop look more like the hen do from hell than a serious political statement.

The redistribution principle was this: anyone in a Payback T-shirt qualified. That way, Gedge said, we'd get a crowd of students, radicals and liberals, 'Kids with their hearts in the right place,' he called them. Yeah it was open to abuse, he argued, but it was unlikely we'd get a crowd of oil barons and oligarchs in disguise right? Fifty quid would mean nothing to them and everything to the rest. ('Everything?' Coke had said, rolling his eyes. 'It'd be better sending it abroad. I can name you five African countries where . . .')

The crowd exploded when we began throwing out the bundles of money and cavorting with our longbows, shooting plastic arrows over their heads. Gedge was inciting anger again. 'Ordinary UK citizens,' he yelled, pointing into the crowd, 'like *you*, and *you*, and *you* – pay over forty per cent of your income in tax. *Forty!* What about the rich? What's the figure for the top earners?' Answering shouts and calls. '*Thirty-three per cent!*' Gedge howled to outraged cries. 'Make more, pay less. Well we're here to change that!'

As we crossed Temple Street and I listened to Gedge, my internet research came back to me and a thought struck. Gedge came from Cork. Not part of the UK, right? Yet he always referred to domestic politics. I wondered why an Irish guy who'd only spent a few years over here was so fixated with our problems. But since Temple Street was my cue, I forgot all about it and busied myself dipping arrows in lighter fluid instead. 'We're here to change that!' Gedge continued, parading back and forth with the packs of notes. 'Here, have some of their money!' The crowd boiled and roared as the cash sailed into their midst. 'Payback are here to tax the rich!'

Gedge was shouting. 'We're burnin' the bad guys!'

I concentrated on lighting my arrows as the notes flew above me. They burnt quickly when lit – the arrows, that is – their plastic tips fizzing and melting. I fired a few at our mannequin, hitting him in the chest and drawing a roar of approval. The man burst into flames quickly, the first indication we'd over-doused him with accelerant. In a matter of moments he was a rippling gauze of heat, entirely swallowed. I was suddenly very glad of the water canisters we'd lined up at the back of the truck. His sign went up in seconds too, his hair disintegrated. The plastic stank and belched nasty smoke. And the heat was a white wall pressing against our backs as we turned our attention to the cash. Sweat ran in wet streams down my face beneath my Maid Marian veil as I worked.

The crowd was alive with Payback T-shirts. I threw money out to teenagers, to homeless guys with rucksacks and dirty faces. I hurled a bundle out into a sea of waving arms, I placed a packet in the brittle hands of an elderly lady dwarfed by her XL Payback hoodie, I passed it out to exhausted-looking shift workers, skateboarders, labourers, a big, bearded guy getting buffeted on his mobility scooter. I skimmed a bundle over the heads of those crowding the truck towards more distant figures; a guy with a headful of red dreads, a group of women in supermarket checkout uniforms waving their T-shirts like flags, a taxi driver thrusting his chest out and pointing at our logo.

Then, at our backs, I heard our effigy groan and crack, begin to tip. The man was seriously unsteady, looming behind me like a flaming skeleton. The tape lashing him to the crash barrier had burnt through and his legs were starting to buckle.

I threw another cash bundle out into the waving arms of a group of students, gave a howl and leapt around a bit for the smartphone screens. My longbow succumbed to the heat, softening and sagging. There was a roar of laughter as I flung the remains of my useless weapon out into the darkness. I was reaching for another bundle of cash when the man – evidently tired of me sticking it to him – collapsed forwards. I yelped and leapt away, landing on my arse and rolling. Gedge gave a roar of panic and dropped his loudhailer. The man had fallen on the money.

Our pile of cash went up in flames.

Gedge made a crazy attempt to lift the melting mannequin using an outstretched foot but the heat was too intense. 'Water!' he yelled.

We scrabbled for the containers. My sweaty hands trembled as I tried to unscrew the purple cap. Once I'd got it open I realized I couldn't lift the damn thing; we'd over-filled it and raising the slippery, hot plastic was like trying to manoeuvre a rock. Gedge had more success – I could see him hauling it up to shoulder height and begin pouring a glittering arc of water over the man and money. The neck was too small. We'd borrowed containers that poured water in demure little streams like teapots. Clouds of thick smoke rolled outwards in filthy drifts. Gedge tossed his empty canister aside and yanked mine upwards, pouring again. I tried crawling towards the cash on my hands and knees, soaked in water and coated in dust and ash, but I couldn't get close to the disintegrating notes. My dress was on fire. I backed off, opened a third canister and tipped it on its side so a wave of water flooded the truck and poured out over its edges on to the street. Gedge crashed to his knees, his canister rolling out of his grip.

I was aware of a voice on another loudhailer yelling instructions and through the smoke I saw the flashing lights of cop cars. There was a line of police in black helmets with riot shields. The drop was over.

'Hang on!' I heard Coke scream and the truck changed direction, the engine giving a high-pitched roar and the gears crunching as he swung a left and we parted the crowds and hurtled up a side street. There was nothing to cling to and I slithered towards the rear of the truck until Gedge grabbed me with a meaty fist.

'Stay low!' he yelled, grabbing the chassis of the vehicle with one hand and lying face down in the water. I did the same. We accelerated. Increased speed meant increased drag, currents of night air fanning the flames. Burning bank notes fluttered and twisted over our heads. The fire roared around my ears and I smelt my hair burn. Coke made a screeching loop around the same roundabout three times, chose an exit and floored it. Our steel barrier came free and tumbled end over end on to the central reservation. The flaming remains of the man were scattered across a dual carriageway as we roared out of town. Blackened banknotes eddied off into the night in glowing streams.

I clung to the truck and clung to Gedge, terrified and weirdly elated as the fire died around me.

I had to scrub myself pink in the shower that night and throw away my clothes.

23
Three Points of Contact

The next day I felt empty and listless. I kicked around the house getting short-tempered, tried to watch TV, got tetchy at my playlists and found myself sitting on the end of my bed staring at a bedside picture of Mum and me. I must've been seven, dressed as the captain of the *Titanic* for a presentation assembly. I'd only had five lines in the performance but, frightened of screwing it up and certain this was my big break, I'd memorized the entire script. I looked skinny and ridiculous in the picture, dwarfed by my officer's jacket, the cuffs turned over to reveal a pair of immaculate white gloves. Behind me, Mum had her hands linked across my chest and was kissing the top of my gold-trimmed naval cap. Nearly ten years ago, I thought suddenly. Back when things seemed certain.

I couldn't think about it or I'd lose the plot. I decided to go climbing.

It was better being busy, heading across town to the place Kallie had shown me. I remembered that free morning together with a sort of hazy pleasure and rode the tram enjoying a dumbass daydream in which I got ridiculously good ridiculously quickly and impressed Kallie leaping from outcrop to outcrop while she watched. Less water buffalo, more gazelle.

I was no gazelle that morning but marginally less crap second time around. Ben slung me a pair of climbing shoes and offered to show me some moves. We worked on something called flagging – a weight–balance trick that used the wall to help with support – and rockovers. 'Arms straight!' Ben kept telling me. 'Three points of contact!' he'd remind me as I tried hanging from my hands. And when I was too scared to try a foothold, 'Trust the rubber!' he'd say, indicating the soft-soled shoes. I wasn't brilliant but by the end of the hour I was sweaty, exhausted, and a damn sight happier.

It's amazing how quickly that good-time feeling can disappear. Heading home, I'd cut through a backstreet of lock-ups and crossed a couple of zombie car parks when I saw someone waiting for me. Tall, dark-haired, hooked nose, black raincoat, Italian loafers.

'Thomas.' Mr Gonzalez raised a hand, leaning against a shiny German car.

A jolt of stressy electricity thumped beneath my ribs. Despite my best intentions, I hadn't done a thing about the properties they'd wanted checking. 'Hello,' I said. I managed to find a smile from somewhere. 'Just been scoping out a few of the candidates on your list.'

Gonzalez looked as if he'd been waiting for me; expecting my cover story. Like he'd been following me around. *He knew.* The guy's smile was paper-thin. 'We were wondering if you could drop by the restaurant and give us an update.'

The small of my back went hot. 'Sure. How are you fixed tomorrow?'

'This afternoon.' Gonzalez opened the door of the car.

Classical music drifted from the cool interior. 'Two o'clock, Thomas. Don't be late.'

He spun the wheel and moved out into traffic. I checked my phone, it was midday. If I got a cab, I thought, my heart charging, I could zoom from place to place and get a few of them covered, scribble some notes and pretend that . . . I shut my eyes. This was never going to work. Ruiz was going to tear me apart.

I could skip the country, I thought. *Find Chris in Croatia.*

Somehow I managed to breathe. No, calling a cab was all I had. We could drive a loop around the edge of the quays through Pomona and Cornbrook. I could take notes from the back seat. From there I'd just have to blag it.

I was fifteen minutes late to the restaurant, knackered and jumpy but with three pages of scribbled notes and Ruiz's dog-eared list of sites in my sweating palms as I pulled the door open and headed for the same table as before.

Ruiz was pouring himself a coffee from a silver pot and talking on the phone. I half-expected fury but his eyes were hooded and his face emotionless as he watched me slip in and take a seat.

'Right,' he said into the phone. 'Interesting. And not unexpected.' He pinched the bridge of his nose with bony fingers. 'Thanks Robert. He's here now. We'll discuss that.' He put the phone on the table.

I made a show of sorting through my notes. 'Here's what I've got so far,' I began.

He held up a hand. 'Let's not spend time on evasion.' I was well over fifty per cent sure what evasion meant but my face must have indicated otherwise. 'You haven't been fulfilling your side of the bargain, Bellboy.'

'I have! Look I've got some notes for you.' My hands trembled as I pushed them over.

He didn't waste his time checking. 'You may have gathered these at the last minute but Mr Gonzalez informs me you've been spending a lot of time elsewhere.'

The room was very hot. 'I don't know what you mean.'

Ruiz tipped his head. 'You do. London. Bath. You've hardly had a moment to complete the task I charged you with. And when you *have* been here in the city . . .' Ruiz sipped his coffee and smiled. 'You've been spending your time in two locations. A Victorian property in Chorlton . . .' I felt my throat constrict and my bladder loosen. I swear I've never been so frightened, '. . . your family home, Mr Gonzalez informs me – and a lock-up here.' He stabbed the map I'd pushed across to him. *Gonzalez followed me.* I'd never noticed a thing. 'So I can't see how you might have carried out the work we discussed. It's impossible for you to be in two places at once, yes?'

'It's been a busy time,' I croaked.

Ruiz raised his white eyebrows. 'Really? I was under the impression you'd lost your job, Bellboy. That's why I hired you.' He licked his lips. 'I'm interested in what you find so fascinating about these archways along the riverfront.'

If someone had offered to swap everything I owned in exchange for escape from that room right then, I'd have taken it. Sonos wireless speaker system, skateboard, games console, designer T-shirts, box-fresh high-tops: *Have them all. Just get me the hell out.* 'My brother's stuff's stored there,' I improvised. 'He's away and my dad packed up all his gear. I've got a key and I sometimes go and get old DVDs and clothes.' I

132

began warming up. 'There's some camping equipment too. Tent, sleeping bags, a barbecue. I've been thinking of taking a holiday with some mates so I've been going through the stuff with them.'

'Like you said,' Ruiz was deadpan. 'A busy time.'

'I'm sorry sir. Maybe it'd be better if you found someone more suitable. I don't know these places too well.'

'Maybe so,' Ruiz took a long sip of his coffee and replaced the cup gently on its saucer. 'Maybe so.' He indicated the door.

I've never made a swifter exit in my life.

Outside I checked for Gonzalez. The street was busy and I didn't know how or where to look – my eyes made random leaps from face to face, terrified of spotting him. I made a break for Deansgate, half-running, half-walking, checking the pavement behind me. I'd never wished for something so hard as I did during that journey – that I hadn't given Ruiz my number, taken his case back, agreed to help him. If someone had offered me back the carefree life of the Tom Rendall who rode laundry trolleys along hotel corridors, I'd have bitten their hand off. In a coffee shop I chose a table in the shadows at the back and knocked back a hot chocolate, my stomach gnawing at itself. I kept checking the windows, strung out and exhausted, waiting for the fear to subside.

There was a dog-eared copy of the *Metro* abandoned at the next table. I flicked through it, starting with the sport and working towards the front desperate for something to take my mind off the chaos around me.

Ten minutes later my heart lurched hard.

On the inside front page was a picture of me.

I stared at it, imagining Sinclair in an office somewhere tacking the article to a corkboard bristling with me-related evidence. The net was closing in, Jay had said. *Get out while you can.* Gedge had been cropped out of the photo so it was just Maid Marian silhouetted against the raging blaze. Like Sinclair had said, *physically identical . . . a tendency to lark about in masks.* The DCI would be bringing us to justice. Ruiz was coming to finish us off. Yate was about to start breaking legs, there was the question of the secret black box . . .

I had to tell Gedge about everything, I reasoned, sweat springing up on my forehead. I couldn't carry on like this.

I scanned the piece to see what the writer had got. *Direct action pressure group renowned for theatrical thefts . . . civil resistance . . . wealth redistribution . . .* There didn't seem to be anything compromising, thank God. I felt myself relax microscopically. *Ill-judged mischief-making that could have resulted in serious injury . . .* it all seemed pretty standard. Except for the line, *quite what the group have against 007 remains a mystery . . .*

I saw the headline last and sighed. Gedge would be gutted. PAYBACK BURN EFFIGY OF JAMES BOND, it said.

24
The Black Box

'**E**ver heard of someone called Stacey Healy?' Gedge asked me as I climbed the stairs, Marx yapping excitedly at my heels. I was still twitchy and terrified. 'Her name came up in the comments on the channel. She's asking us for help.'

I couldn't concentrate. 'What?'

'A plea. From a woman called Stacey Healy in the video comments. She wants us to help her. Rendall, you OK?'

I wasn't. If I had been, maybe I'd have asked all the right questions. Ferg skim-read our video comments but it was a long, often hopeless task. It was nice to see stuff like 'You guys are the best!' or 'Robin Hood got nuthin' on Payback', or 'Keep stickin' it TO THE MAN!!!', and it was good to check-out the suggestions for new grabs, often meticulously researched. But most of it was narrow-minded trash from red-top-reading spacefaces who'd blame cancer on immigration if they could. I'd stopped checking.

This particular one had grabbed Gedge though, and when he indicated it I could see why:

I love your videos, please help. I've lost everything. I'm alone and I have no money left and I've lost everything especially valuable and important things, can you help?

'What do you think?'

I wiped my eyes. Arch 17 was a state. Gedge had the melted remains of his mannequin and scraps of burnt clothing gathered in the corner surrounded by a drift of partially incinerated fivers. Our costumes, torn, inside-out, occupied the tabletop. Coke was sitting straight-backed at the table using a little nail-clipper to get his blackened hands clean and Ferg was tapping keys in the corner. Kallie, Gedge said, was back in London placating her bully of a brother.

'Maybe,' I managed. 'Listen, we need to talk. There's a few things I have to explain.'

Gedge shrugged. 'Sure. After this though.' He read the closing section of the comment. '"The company is Nelson Repossessions and they've taken all my things. Please help if you can, Stacey." Now, Ferg's been doing some digging,' Gedge said.

Becky activated the projector and we watched the picture sharpen on the far wall. *Nelson Repossessions*, it said. And underneath, *Our team of experienced Enforcement Officers are trained and ready to recoup a range of assets. We'll offer an efficient, professional recovery service you can trust.*

The big guy was relentless. 'OK,' I sighed. 'So – what's repossession?'

Coke looked at me like I was pond life. 'The recalling of goods when owners can't keep up payment.'

'Usually it's cars, houses, big-money items,' Gedge added. He seemed tense and irritated. The *Metro*, I noticed, was folded on his chair. Maybe he'd seen the James Bond balls-up. 'These guys will collect everything you have to cover debts,' he said. 'Everything.'

Marx padded between us under the table. Coke began

talking. I got the sense he was resuming an argument he'd been asked to drop. 'I don't see this as a Payback concern. I sympathize. But she can't afford to pay us. She needs Citizens Advice or something...'

I watched Gedge straighten his cap, lean forward against the tabletop and spread his fingers. 'Recent statistics show UK working households are nearly four hundred pounds a year worse off this year than last. That can be the difference between staying afloat and drowning. This woman is a victim of the system and she's asking for our help.'

Coke sniffed. 'How much did we lose last night? Two grand? There's no way we'll be reaching our targets if we use the time we have left to—'

'I don't care about targets right now,' Gedge said flatly. It seemed to take the air out of the room. Coke had no reply.

In the end Ferg asked, 'What does she want us to do?'

Gedge shrugged. 'Let's meet her see. Becky, stay here and find everything you can on Nelson. Particularly where the stuff goes once it's repo-ed. They must have a warehouse or something. Rendall, you're coming to pay Stacey a visit. I need you doing your best face-that-everyone-trusts, OK?'

'Sure thing,' I sighed. 'Just us?'

Gedge eyed Coke. 'Aidy, you should come too.' Coke couldn't keep the surprise from his eyes. 'I know you don't see this as important. Come with. Let's see if Mrs Healy can change your mind. First though, why don't we take Marx for a walk, eh? Just us two.'

Marx nearly exploded at the sound of the word walk, leaping eagerly at Gedge's thigh, skittering in circles and racing down the stairs.

Coke stood reluctantly. They headed out.

I sighed as the door slid shut downstairs. I couldn't find the right time to talk to Gedge. There was always something more important happening.

'Ferg,' I started. If Jay was right, this was a girl out of her depth. 'How's things?' I tried, staying all chirpy, determined to get to the truth.

'I'm trying to access Nelson's staff rota.'

'Good job,' I said with a smile. There was a moment of mammoth awkwardness. 'How's life? I mean, how do you feel?'

Ferg considered this a moment then turned to face me. 'A series of nerve endings send electrical impulses to my brain,' she said. 'The same as everyone else.'

I laughed. 'Yeah. Never mind. Just making small talk.' I gave a dismissive wave. 'Not important.'

'OK.' Ferg resumed typing.

I headed downstairs and slipped behind the screen that Gedge used to separate his bedroom from the chaotic storage area and considered the tangle of sleeping bag, sheets and books arranged there. Piled on the floor alongside the bed were a battered copy of *Quotations from Mao Tse Tung*, a dusty classic the size of a breeze block called *The Conditions of the Working Class in England* and other books with titles like *Live Working or Die Fighting*, *The Rise of Disaster Capitalism* and *Treasure Islands: Tax Havens and the Men Who Stole the World*. *Serious bedtime reading*, I thought, shifting them aside. I felt stupid kneeling on the cobbled floor, peering under the bed. Like betrayal – as if looking for the stupid box was backing Jay over Gedge. But since my expertly analytical probing of Ferg had revealed nothing, poking around under the boss's bed seemed the next best course of action.

It smelt of dog. There was Marx's popped football, a lot of dust, a balled-up pair of jogging bottoms and a single sneaker. Jay was a fantasist with a grudge, that was all. I pulled back and was about to stand up again when I saw something tucked away in the shadows. I lowered myself on to my stomach and shuffled forwards, stretching a hand out into the darkness. I could feel it was clothing. A coat maybe. I gave it a yank, pulled it clear. A grime-choked hoodie with a white-on-black image across its front – a hand manipulating puppet strings and beneath, the words 'New World Order'. Marx had been using it for a bed; it was coated in hairs. I was bending to cram it back when I saw the hoodie had been screening something. I checked the door to Arch 17, listened to Ferg's nimble fingers click as she hacked us into Nelson Repo, then dropped to my stomach again. I inched forward through the dog hair and spiderwebs. It took a few goes to pry it towards me but pretty soon I'd pulled it clear.

It was an old Converse box. Jay's use of 'black box' had made me think of aeroplane flight recorders, not trainers. I took a long breath, the box on my knees. My jeans were filthy. I'd have to brush myself clean after I'd taken a quick peek.

I slipped the lid off.

Inside were papers, photos, letters. Lots of letters, in envelopes. Some had been neatly torn open and the letters left within, some looked as if they'd been read and replaced. A lot were postmarked from Cork so I guessed were from Gedge's family. There were court summonses, solicitors' communications, notifications from the police. I felt rotten

139

even looking at it. Then I found a sheaf of papers I recognized. They were still folded across the middle, just as I'd seen Gedge do when he took them from Ruiz's briefcase. I remembered the look on his face as his eyes had roamed the pages – the burn of excitement in them. I opened them up.

Lists of bank accounts, companies, contact details. At the top was an outfit called Ruiz-Chaves Holdings LLC and underneath, alphabetically arranged, its subsidiaries and sister companies. Edison Ruiz part-owned a list of operations spanning two pages. There were investment banks, casinos, bookmakers, debt-acquisition companies, payday loan providers. For a second, scanning nervously, I couldn't see why Gedge might have found it that interesting.

Until.

Bailey Heywood Events Management, the list said. I went cold. Blackhouse Langley LLP. And under that, Nelson Repossessions, Westwater Retail. I recognized other names from past grabs, going back beyond this summer into last year: Lucille Deutsch Investments, JSR Casinos.

I folded the paper back amongst the letters, trying to think. Mindlessly, I rifled the rest of the box. There was worse to come. Under the papers was a mobile phone, a cheap one-use burner with its own SIM card by the looks, and a tiny box. I'd seen boxes like it before, the type of thing you might buy a ring in. I lifted the lid.

'Jesus,' I said to myself.

There were five pearls in there. *Leila's Veil.* The meeting with Yate came flooding back. The two of them over the laminate tabletop in that tiny office, trapping pearls, Yate saying, 'a complete piece would've made life easier,' and Gedge telling him how it had been damaged. It hadn't

140

been damaged. He'd snapped the chain, pulled the pearls free then kept some back for himself. I scrapped for breath, wretched.

Then I heard footsteps on the cobbles outside.

25
Gorse Hill High-rise

I crammed the lid on the box – I couldn't be sure the pearls hadn't rolled free as I did so – and rammed it deep beneath the bed, then stuffed the hoodie after the box, pushing them both as far under as I could. Next, I straightened Gedge's books, my hands slewing the piles into each other, my heart a hot ball. I was on my feet as the door was pulled open and slipping out between the screens, brushing dirt from my top, sweating and frantic.

Coke appeared first. 'Rendall,' he said. 'Are you all right?'

'Just fallen down the frickin' stairs,' I grumbled. 'Nearly broke my neck.'

Coke barked a laugh. 'Such a drama queen.'

Gedge, following Coke through, fired me a, 'What happened?'

I stammered my crappy cover story a second time. 'Nearly broke my neck,' I repeated as a finishing flourish.

Gedge watched me wince at my non-existent bruises as I brushed myself down. 'Eejit,' he said. He passed me and headed up the stairs. 'Ferg!' he shouted. 'Gimme some good news!'

I followed Coke up, aching with shame. Things were falling apart.

Stacey Healy's Gorse Hill tower block was surrounded by a sunken car park. The wind corkscrewed crisp packets and newspapers. Weeds thrived in cracked concrete.

I hadn't been in a tower block before. Stacey's flat was on the seventh floor but the lift had been vandalized so we slogged up the stairs. The walkways smelt of cigarettes and engine oil. On the seventh floor we walked past boarded-up flats. One had a pile of disgorged junk outside its door – a toaster, ironing board, mop and bucket, a pair of yellowing pillows.

Stacey Healy was a sallow-faced woman with deep wrinkles and chewed fingernails. She showed us into an empty room – a nicotine-stained box with a single window, threadbare carpet, one chair, a low table and a bowed sofa. We sat, Gedge in the middle, Coke and me tipping against him as it sagged. Stacey brought tea from a kitchen that looked as if it had been stripped of equipment and we sipped from chipped mugs. Mine had *Strictly Come Dancing* on it. Coke put his cup on the table and wiped his palms on his cashmere cardigan.

Stacey smoked, braiding her bleached blond hair as she spoke. 'Thanks so much for coming,' she said. We waited while she wheezed and coughed. Her accent was gentle, Irish. 'I didn't know who else to turn to.'

Gedge waved a dismissive hand. 'You're grand, Mrs Healy. Don't worry. How can we help?'

'Aww. What part are you from?' She smiled, hearing his voice. 'Cork?' Gedge nodded. Stacey blew against the surface of her tea with fag smoke and her eyes went distant. 'Love Cork.'

'How can we help you Mrs Healy?' Gedge took a custard cream from a plastic plate.

'Call me Stacey.' She smiled sadly. 'Gary – my ex – he got himself into problems. He's inside now. Three years, they said. I couldn't pay the rent, not with my wages. They started repossessing a month ago.' Stacey indicated her front room. 'I'm running low as you can see.'

I'm not usually lost for words but Stacey's flat rendered me speechless. Without a fridge, she was eating from tins piled in plastic bags on the floor. There were folded stacks of clothes next to their discarded hangers. The carpet's pale patches marked the absence of TV, storage cabinet, chairs. Coke, sitting stiffly and holding his breath, couldn't have been less comfortable but Gedge was remarkably at ease.

He sat forward, chewing another biscuit and nodding. 'It's hard. Stacey, you mentioned in your comment a picture of the items you're concerned about.'

We watched as Stacey nudged the burning tip from her cigarette and pinched the paper nimbly, saving the rest for later. 'Give me a second.' She left us alone.

'What are we doing here?' Coke hissed, turning to us once she'd gone. 'This isn't us. She needs a charity, Gedge.'

I wondered what had gone on during the walking of the dog. Whatever had been discussed, Coke's position hadn't changed. Gedge's fists were balled up tight and he struck his knees as he whispered, 'We *are* a charity. Have some compassion! Look around you!'

'I am. I just don't see why we're here.'

'Is this a good thing we're doing? *Is this good?* Huh?' Gedge hissed.

'It's a private concern. There's no public money at stake...'

I figured I should mediate. 'What if we hear her out OK? Let's just calm down.'

Stacey Healy was at the door, a photograph in her hands. Gedge coughed apologetically.

'Most of what's gone was my mother's.' Stacey sat down, relit her fag. 'I treasured those things. This is her jewellery box and wedding ring.' She slid the photo over to us. We all leant in. An engraved box, silver, and next to it a ring on a fine gold chain. Items from another time – a time of plenty. 'I just need them back. Mum would turn in her grave if she thought I'd...' Stacey stopped and bit her fingernails. Tears trembled beneath her lashes. 'I didn't know who to turn to,' she continued. 'I've seen you all on telly. My niece loves you and shows me your videos all the time. I don't know if it's too late. They auction all the stuff they take.'

This was news to me. 'Sell it on? So you might never see it again?'

Stacey started to cry quietly. Gedge gave me a *nice work, spaceface* look then said to Stacey, 'They hold items for a period first though. When were they taken?'

'Last week.' She gave us the date – six days ago, it was – and Gedge scribbled it on the back of the photo. 'Can you help?' Stacey asked.

Gedge smiled. 'We'll see what we can do.' I could sense Coke's disapproval in the stiff way he rose from the sofa. We said our goodbyes.

I considered swiping a biscuit for the walk back but thought better of it.

*

145

Ferg had filled Kallie in – back on the train from Euston for another 'stay at her cousin's' – by the time we made it across town. We all gathered around the Arch 17 table. Becky stood in the projector light, hands bunched awkwardly in the pockets of her jeans, and told us what she'd found. 'Nelson Repossessions own property in this park.' A screen-grab showed a warehouse in the centre of a fenced business park surrounded by compounds of parked cars and a wooded area. 'This bit here is Nelson House.' She navigated the website and showed us the glass-fronted curve of an office building flanked with neat trees and paved walkways. 'When goods are first repossessed they are stored in the lock-ups. Then they are cleaned and prepared and moved to Nelson House for public auction.'

'How long are they stored for?' Gedge asked.

'Less than a week. The duty rotas show assets moving all the time. I tracked the recently repossessed cars. They stayed for six days between repossession and re-sale.'

'That's bad. Can we work out where Stacey's stuff is?'

Ferg nodded solemnly. 'Repossessed goods have storage codes and different types of goods are stored in different places. There's vehicles, furniture, electricals, personal items ...' Becky tugged at her fringe. 'They're stored separately and auctioned separately. That's everything I know about it.'

Gedge rose, reaching for his hoodie. 'Right. Let's go and check out this business park. If Stacey's stuff was repo-ed six days ago, we're on the verge of losing it for good. Kallie, we'll need binoculars. Ferg, bring the laptop and we'll see if we can access the site plans. Coke, can you start work on a legitimate way in? If we're quick we can—'

Three staccato thumps sounded on the outside door below.

We froze. Gedge held up a finger and the five of us stood in a silent circle, waiting. Strangers didn't come to the door of Maxi's place out of hours. And Arch 17 wasn't a registered address so no post, no bills, no cold callers. Coke picked up the dog and cradled him. Marx wagged his tail, panting contentedly, tongue out.

A brisk voice from below. 'Greater Manchester Police. Open up please. I need to talk.'

Kallie held her breath, cheeks inflated. Gedge's eyes were narrow and his jawline tight. I recognized that voice. It was DCI Sinclair.

I physically winced at the next three thumps. Sinclair called again. 'Hello? Police. I need a word please. Could you open the door.' The lock was rattled and the door clattered on its runners. Then there was silence.

We waited, wound tight. Eventually Gedge's shoulders moved and he leant forward across the table releasing a long breath. We all followed suit.

Coke stroked Marx and leant over the mezzanine, looking down at the door. 'She's left us a note,' he said.

26
Half a Dozen Margheritas

We argued in the van. A lot.

'This is it!' Coke spat. 'We're finished. Who led the law to us?'

Gedge drove with his arms rigid, eyes flicking to his wing mirrors as if he feared pursuit. 'It might not be the end. Just let me think a minute.'

'We were OK until Rendall showed up,' Coke pointed out. 'Two whole summers, no problems.'

'Christ!' I spluttered. Part of me was furious. Another part, much bigger I admit, was embarrassed in case he was right. I'd never given the DCI the smallest hint of our whereabouts but if Gonzalez could follow me to Arch 17, Sinclair and her team could too. I felt sick.

'That's rubbish,' Kallie said. 'Maybe the drops have got too big. We were lucky to get out of Birmingham in one piece. Leave Rendall alone.'

Gedge pulled up at a set of lights and ran a hand across his mouth. 'It doesn't matter why she's on to us. Could've been the Midland Hotel, could've been the Jags. Forget *why*. We need a plan.'

'I'm pulling out. That's my plan right there,' said Coke.

Kallie gave a gasp. 'Whoa! Aidy. Don't overreact.'

'I'm *NOT*!' Coke exploded. He began beating the dash with a wildness that made me remember his violence at the Bailey Heywood grab. Gedge looked alarmed and pulled over. 'Let me out!' Coke yelled. We shuffled along the bench seat, opened the van door and let him steam up and down the pavement. 'We need to split. We need to vanish! Oh God,' he said quietly as if realizing it for the first time, 'I'm meant to be going to university.'

Gedge pulled Sinclair's note from his inside pocket. He'd been the only one to read it so far. 'Kallie, get him inside.'

'This is the biggest argument we've ever had,' Ferg pointed out quietly. 'Even bigger than the fight at the Lucille Deutsch con.'

'Useful to know,' I said, deadpan. Ferg said thanks which made me feel bad. Kallie dragged Coke back into the van.

We all shuffled along and Gedge said, 'You guys need to see this. So let's all *calm down*.'

Coke nodded slowly, fists on his knees. We gathered round to read.

FAO Patrick Gedge and Payback. This is Greater Manchester Police. We have a proposition for you, Sinclair had scribbled. She wrote like she spoke – irritatingly cheerful. She'd used green ink. *It could benefit us both. The situation is urgent. Please contact me directly to discuss the matter. I've included a copy of my card.*

Gedge held the card up. 'Our friend Amelia Sinclair,' he said. 'Anyone had any further contact with her?' Everyone shook their heads. Except me. 'Rendall? You've got something to say?'

Payback – my family, pretty much – was falling apart. I

had to summon some positivity from somewhere but I didn't have the guts for the whole truth. 'Yeah,' I said, furrowing my brow. 'She was the one who interviewed me after the Midland Hotel grab remember?'

'Just the once?'

I paused, nodded. 'Just a few minutes in the lobby that night.'

Gedge bit his lip and spoke almost to himself. 'So how's she tracked us down? And what does she mean?'

'It's a trap,' Coke said. He removed his glasses and began polishing the lenses, lips pursed. 'She's tricking us. Whatever you do, don't call that number.'

'So – what *should* we do?' Kallie asked.

Coke replaced his glasses. 'We need to clear the arch of evidence. The laptops, pen drives, papers, costumes . . . oh God. We're finished.'

'Wait. One thing at a time,' Gedge said. He was calm enough to refold the letter and pocket the business card before saying, 'What if she means it? What if there is a proposition?'

'Nonsense. It's got trap written all over it,' Coke pointed out, his jaw tight.

'C'mon. What might she have to discuss? Anyone?'

I felt the heat rise around my collar in the silence that followed. Gedge tugged at his beard and stared at the street for a slow minute. 'Right' he said. 'We're here to help Stacey Healy. Her stuff went six days ago. It's due for auction *now*. So we finish this job first. Trap or not, Sinclair will give us a chance to think it over.'

Coke went rigid. '*What?* Give us a chance to think it over? Gedge have you *lost your mind*? She'll be pulling the place apart with a team of officers as we speak. It's madness! What does anyone else think? It can't be just me ...'

'Hey. This isn't a democracy,' Gedge's voice was cold and firm. Under the surface, I swear I saw fear. 'The note is addressed to *me*. She has a proposition for *me*. I need time to consider that. We finish the job in hand, I call her tomorrow.'

'I'm out.' Coke reached for the door.

I needed to contribute something that would get things back the way they were. 'If it's a trap,' I offered, 'why the note? She could've brought a whole gang of cops and bust the place open then and there.'

Coke paused, considering this.

Gedge gave a curt nod. 'What he said.'

The clouds broke and the sun climbed as we passed binoculars between us, scoping out the Nelson warehouses from the parking lot of a shut-down shipping company across the way.

Kallie focused on the electronic gates. 'There's a pair of guys in the gatehouse.'

'Nelson's database had the shift patterns on it,' said Ferg, twisting her fingers together. 'There are two guards on at any one time but they overlap shifts so the same guards don't leave at once.'

'Staggered patterns,' said Gedge.

We watched a van pull up. 'Here we go. Delivery,' said Kallie. She nudged Coke. 'Go on.'

'They're checking ID,' Coke reported emotionlessly, glasses propped on his forehead and binoculars up at his face. It was the first thing he'd said for half an hour. He'd been ice-cold since the bust up in the van. 'Chatting. Second guy calls reception. We're waiting, waiting ... checking delivery schedule. And ... they're in.'

'What's that, forty seconds?' Kallie asked. 'A minute?'

Gedge scribbled notes. 'Let's put Rendall in the cab of the truck.'

'Those windows look a nightmare,' Kallie said, handing the binoculars to me. Nelson's warehouse wobbled into view behind a mesh fence and Kallie guided my hand upwards as she explained. 'Look. Super-modern. No old sash windows or metal frames.' I scanned the buildings. Nelson House was the central block, gleaming from behind its shield of trees. Around it a grid of roads ran between big storage buildings with shuttered fronts, open bays with stacked goods and, towards the back, a number of fenced lots filled with parked cars. Beyond that, the strip of woodland we'd seen on the website.

'The place is massive,' I said. 'How do we find a wedding ring in all that?'

Gedge turned to Ferg. 'Becky, any sign of that site plan?'

'Nothing yet.'

'We're going to have to be invited in,' Gedge said. 'Drive right through those gates there.'

'This is ridiculous,' Coke said. 'I could be clearing the arch ...'

'*One thing at a time!*' Gedge had thrown his notebook down and that got everyone's attention. 'For God's sake. This is likely our last grab, right?' He adjusted his cap and took a breath, collecting his notebook and smoothing it in his huge hands. 'So let's stay calm. We can do both. We find a way in, we get Stacey's stuff, we clear the arch of anything incriminating, we lie low. Tomorrow I contact Sinclair and find out what she wants. Questions?'

Kallie swallowed. '*Last grab?*' she said, eyes shining

with sadness.

Gedge rubbed his forehead. 'Yeah. Listen,' he sighed. 'A few weeks ago I got an email from my mum. She's back home in Cork. The council's moving her. She needs help shifting her stuff. Then there's getting her settled, finding a job. I think I'm gonna have to move back.'

'What? For a week or two?' Kallie asked.

There was a pause. 'No, it'll take longer. She's not so well.'

I tried to pick through my thoughts. Sinclair's note. Jay's advice to get out. Gedge's letters from Cork tucked away in his black box. The list of companies. The presence of the five hidden pearls – that made *no* sense – unless the pearls were a way to help his mum, maybe? And what about this sudden obsession with Stacey Healy? Was he doing one last good turn then skipping the country and leaving us to clean up the mess? Or take the rap? Gedge watched a gang of gulls wheeling over the tarmac. 'It's been important. We've made a difference. And we've had fun right?'

'Yes. My favourite grab was the Bailey Heywood grab because the jewels were beautiful,' said Ferg. 'My second favourite was the Lucille Deutsch con because even though Jay didn't like it I did. My favourite drop was the soup kitchen drop during the first summer. My second—'

'C'mon, boss!' Kallie said. 'The Jaguars! The Casino steal! Good times!'

Even Coke managed a smile at that.

Gedge looked at each of us in turn and borrowed Kallie's phrase. 'Good times,' he said, before his expression hardened. 'Guys. Stacey needs us. So – last grab.' He indicated the compound beyond. 'How are we getting through those gates. Ideas?'

'Pizza,' I offered. Gedge had been ready to take notes. Instead, he bit the end of his pen. I pressed on. 'We go in with half a dozen margheritas, there's a mix up about who ordered them. That'll work, right?'

There was a considered silence.

'I'm not breaking and entering any more,' said Coke. 'No way.'

Kallie turned to Gedge. 'What d'you think?'

Gedge tapped his teeth with his pen. 'Pizzas,' he said, staring out across the compound. 'Right. I think we'll be needing a delivery van.'

27
Lying for a Living

Despite his foul mood, Coke did a great job lifting a pair of magnetized signs for Donnie's, a local pizza place which proudly declared its product '*howlin' hot!*' Kallie tracked down some company overalls and a huge Donnie the Pizza Dog suit, complete with comedy feet, dog head and a huge two-for-one placard.

The van was getting the magnetized signs. Gedge was getting the overalls. I was getting the dog. You can imagine my glee. The suit smelt bad and inside temperatures were borderline volcanic.

I sat next to Gedge in the van, my furry pockets bursting with pizza flyers, skin sticky with sweat and shame as we pulled up at the park gates just before 5 p.m. Gedge had hoped one of the guards might have disappeared for sandwiches and he was right. I lifted the dog head and flashed the remaining guy a grin from beneath it, chewing gum and going for cheerful-Brummie-in-fancy-dress.

'Evenin'!' I handed over the clipboard with the delivery notice. 'Six pepperoni, two margherita, one seafood, one Fiorentina. Doughballs and six bottles of Fanta,' I told him, leaning out of the cab.

I didn't get the response I expected. The security bloke squinted up at us, brow furrowed. He was looking beyond me. Gedge's face wore a frozen grin.

'Don't I know you?' the guard said to him. He folded his arms and leant out of the gatehouse window. 'I swear I put you away once. How long have you been out?'

Gedge leant over his steering wheel. 'Don't know who you mean, mate, but you don't mean me.' The dog head hid my face. Which was good because I reckon I hadn't managed to keep my expression neutral. I was remembering my internet research – Paddy Gedge the promising boxer and tearaway who'd lost everything in Ireland before coming over here to start a new life.

'Still lying for a living, are you?' the guard asked.

Gedge gave a laugh. 'This is ridiculous, mate. Like the dog said – Donnie's pizza delivery, that's all.'

'Gone straight have you? Likely tale. Go on – tell us your name.'

'Dean.'

The guard grinned. 'Nice try. I swear it's you. Hang on. *Gedge*, right? I still speak to my old mates on the force and the word is you're this close to going down again.' The guy made a tiny gap between his thumb and forefinger. My heart bucked under my ribs. A big articulated truck had pulled in behind us. We couldn't even reverse out.

'Listen,' I said through the gaping mouth of the grinning dog. 'This is Deano. I've known Deano for years. Who's this other guy you're on about?'

'Oh he's got you fooled too has he?' laughed the guard. The driver of the truck hit his horn and the guard leant forward and waved. 'In his youth, "Deano" here was responsible for

156

half the burglaries in Salford. I know because I was the investigating officer for—' The van behind us sounded its horn again. 'Hang on!' shouted the guard.

I held a hand up. 'Listen mate. We've got fifteen deliveries to do tonight and this is only number five.'

The truck-driver opened his door, bless his arse, and climbed down. He was a grizzled weightlifting type with tattooed biceps and a mega-beard. 'I'm half on the carriageway here,' he growled. 'There's a hell of a queue building up while you have your cosy chat.'

'Just a second!' The guard side-eyed us. 'You're up to something. I know it.'

'He thinks we're criminals,' I said to the truck driver, leaning out of my window. I grinned through the dog's mouth. 'Do I look like a criminal to you?'

The driver squared his massive shoulders. 'Just get a bloody move on!'

'Open up, will you?' I moaned at the guard, thrusting a furry thumb at the trucker. 'Wolverine's going ballistic out here.'

I've never been so relieved to see a pair of gates open in my life. We drove round the edge of the Nelson compound, scanning buildings and squinting at signs. Some of the lock-ups had their shutters open. I saw furniture, washing machines, TVs. Fenced bays held other goods: rows of stacked solar panels retrieved from the roofs of remortgaged houses, garden furniture and three compounds of cars in numbered bays, each behind a high wire-mesh fence. Gedge pulled over.

'OK. Have a good look around. Stay on your phone. Ferg is checking through the order of work and getting close to a decent site plan. Once we know where the stuff is, you swoop.

And Rendall – you won't have long.' I rolled on to my stomach and fell gracefully out of the van. Gedge passed me the pizzas. 'That guy on the gate arrested me once. I need to clear out. *Dammit*. Our last ever grab and it's down to you.' He grinned. 'No offence.'

I dropped the food at the reception of an office near a set of Nelson lock-ups. The woman behind the desk made a fuss but I held up my doggy paws and did my *hey ma'am, just doin' my job* act. 'Got the delivery address right here,' I finished, waving a clipboard. 'Maybe a colleague ordered them in. Enjoy!'

I left her giddily calling the staff down for a feast. Outside I noticed that some of the lock-ups were rented to other companies and had their own offices and letterboxes. I pulled my flyers out and moved from building to building, making my way towards Nelson House pushing stuff through letterboxes as I went. Each lock-up had a small security booth; either empty, or occupied by a solitary guard. A bear-sized bloke was watching TV with his feet on the desk of a warehouse area smoking lazily. Further along, a chatty security team patrolled the repo-ed cars swapping gossip. I waved my pizza flyers cheerfully at them.

The parking spaces outside Nelson House were full, lights blazed in the reception area and the automatic doors hissed open and shut in an endless cycle. There must have been a public auction on. Car after car was pulling up and their owners emerging. There seemed to be a lot of those blokes – they're everywhere these days – who tuck a crisp white shirt into a pair of jeans and wear polished brogues. There were cufflinks, sports jackets, business suits, heels. None of the attendees, I reckoned, looked like the kind of family who might have their stuff repo-ed by Nelson.

My phone pinged. I dragged my doggy gloves off and dug it out of my hairy pocket. A text from Gedge, giving me a screenshot of an overhead map. It took me a second to orientate myself. I was pretty sure he meant the high-roofed warehouse directly across the car park. Its main doors were open. Inside were rows of freshly valeted cars, stickered up for auction. I moved low against the wheel arches checking for CCTV and counted five wall-mounted cameras which I guessed fed into the screens in an office twenty vehicles along. I could see a woman holding a kettle as she chatted to a reclining figure. Both had security uniforms.

I scuttled the length of the hangar praying they were overweight desk-jockeys yawning before their mind-numbing monitor feed. At the bottom of a set of metal stairs was a colour-coded floor plan, just like Ferg had said. I scanned through *motor-vehicles*, *audio-visual/electricals*, *computers*, *domestic white goods*. Each had a designated colour code. *Antiques* (purple) was section seven on the second floor, *personal valuables* (orange) next door in eight. Stacey's stuff would be in one of those.

I took a last breath of fresh air, replaced the dog-head, and crept upwards.

28
Chelsea and Nadim

The second floor was like a cavernous open-plan superstore with pathways between stacked piles of goods. I passed a hill of fridges and washing machines then a quadrant of plasma TVs. There was a bizarre collection of gym equipment; there were paddleboards, canoes, dinghies, hiking and climbing supplies. There were also more CCTV cameras so I stayed low.

The antiques section was full of dressers, fancy old mirrors and wardrobes; not what I was after. The next bay along was personal valuables. Even from where I stood I could see the bay-number hung over an empty space. The whole area had been cleared but stupidly I checked it anyway – like there was going to be a wedding ring and jewellery box handily abandoned there. Six days, Ferg had said. Everything had been moved for auction. Payback's last ever lift was going to end in failure. I kicked the floor in frustration with a hairy foot.

Here's a heads-up: it's hard to discreetly throw a fit dressed as a dog. I was still stamping about when I heard steps on the stairs.

They must've seen me on their monitors. Along the far wall were a set of offices. I scampered across the huge space and slipped inside an airless room of filing cabinets. No cameras in here, I noted with relief. I took the dog head off, listening for footsteps. My damn phone went and I nearly dropped it trying to mute the ringtone. I swiped the call open and hissed, 'Not now. In a situation.'

'Buckaroo!' bellowed my brother. 'Picture the scene. I'm lying on my back looking at the stars on a beach at sundown. The sand, brah! The most beautiful thing I've ever felt!'

'Chris...' I whispered. 'This is a bad time.'

'So go on, humour me. Where are you right now? Still working at that hotel?'

'I can't talk.'

'The reception's crap! I was saying I'm on a beach lying here next to Sofia.' I struggled with the volume button, crouching behind a filing cabinet. 'So before I hand over ... hello? Still there? You've gone quiet. What's up?'

'I'm hiding in an office in a pizza-dog onesie.'

'Oh, right. OK then. Listen – want to speak to Sofia?'

'Not right now . . .' Too late. I heard the phone being passed across. 'Hi!' I whispered, going all super-polite. That's boarding school education for you. It's frickin' Pavlovian.

'Thomas!' chirped Sofia. 'How are you?'

'Yeah. Good.'

'We're enjoying the beach out here. The night is warm. We have wine. There's a fire. And a guy with a guitar playing "Stairway to Heaven". Life's good, you know?'

Outside there were footsteps. 'Excellent,' I said. 'Sounds great.'

'You're quiet. What are you doing on this lovely evening?'

'Nothing much. Just . . . nothing.'

There was a silence. 'Oh. OK then. Have a nice time. I'll

hand you back to your brother now.'

I killed the call, closed my eyes and tried to think. The footsteps were nearby and I needed some sort of cover story.

'Hey, Nadim,' I heard a woman's voice from outside. 'C'mere.' She was pretty close – just beyond the door of my hiding place.

''Sup, Chelsea?' said her partner, approaching.

Ten seconds later I had a plan. I started getting undressed. Pretty lucky because that's when Nadim came into the office. I'd managed to get down to my pants. 'Oh my God,' I said. 'I'm so sorry.' I can't explain why I thought a Russian accent might suit the occasion but that's what came out of my mouth. Sometimes the magic just happens.

'What's going on?' The woman, Chelsea, reached for her radio.

Nadim winced at the sight of me. 'Awww, kid. I don't want to see this.'

I babbled. 'I know, I know. I'm so sorry. Can you help? It was a – how you say? – stag do. Things got out of hand.' I tried to blush. Ever tried blushing to order? It's a damn sight harder than it sounds. 'There was vodka. I fell asleep in car.'

'This is a high-security compound,' said Chelsea. She had a super-tight perm and painted nails. She didn't seem impressed with the accent. 'What the hell are you playing at?'

I cringed guiltily. 'I'm sorry. They've dressed me in these ridiculous clothes and I've no idea where I am.'

'You're a bit young for a stag do aren't you?' Nadim pointed out.

'My uncle's,' I said, going for tortured and hungover. 'Oh, Father will kill me.'

'I should expect so,' said Chelsea, producing a notebook.

'I'll need your details.'

'No. I mean he'll really kill me.' I'm such an embarrassment I actually drew a finger across my throat for clarification as I gathered my stuff up and moved beyond them into the warehouse. 'Many apologies comrades. I won't do again I promise.' I made a show of awkwardly getting dressed, thinking *Bikes*. I'd seen them somewhere beyond the white goods.

'Your name.'

Nadim didn't look convinced any of this was necessary, bless him. I turned my attention his way. 'Please don't make me do this.' I paused and bit my lower lip.

Nadim gave me an apologetic shrug. 'Protocol. What's your name, son?'

I sighed. I hadn't planned anything beyond the stag-do story. I pulled on the pizza dog costume, trying to think of a Russian name. For some reason, I couldn't conjure up a single one. 'Jock,' I said.

Chelsea raised a single eyebrow and held my gaze. 'Surname?'

I panicked, grinning.

'Surname?' Nadim repeated.

'Block.'

He folded his arms slowly. 'Your name is Jock Block?'

'Correct.' I was blushing now that I didn't need to. 'Like the actor,' I added, 'but with different vowels.'

'Don't play games with us!' Nadim blazed.

Fair point. I made a break for it.

It was hard to run with that stupid dog's head and I tumbled over a rowing machine on my way. My shins stung as I scampered onward to where a line of bikes leant against each other. Deeper in I could see some super-sleek special ones but I only had time to mount the nearest. It had a basket on its handlebars.

I wobbled unsteadily. The damn thing was stuck in fifth gear and creaked as I set off. I picked up speed, weaving past washing machines, Nadim shouting somewhere behind. I skidded low, pedalled hard and headed for the stairs. Someone was climbing up them towards me. A third guard. I cursed and swerved right again – found myself doing circuits round the upper floor, going nowhere. Halfway around lap two, security realized what was going on, stopped running and changed direction. I slithered to a halt.

I swear that three-point turn was the most awkward manoeuvre in the history of high-speed transport-based warehouse escapes. Chelsea was on her radio as she ran, calling for backup. I hauled the bike around and started going again. The most laughable getaway ever eventually ended when I found the stairs and rode down them, brakes squealing, wheels thumping and slithering. I fell off at the bottom.

Picking myself up and righting the bike, I scanned the lower floor.

The roll-top door had been raised and another two uniforms were making their way inside, drawn towards the noise. I pedalled around the exterior wall using the cars for cover. The stairs behind me echoed with descending boots. Desperate for breath, I cowered behind a van, listening.

It took a few minutes for them to head for the stairs. I mounted the pedals and shuddered back into action, the open door an invitation at the far end of the building. Someone spotted me and shouted. My legs were burning.

I bulleted out into the parking lot, pursued.

29
Dog on a Bike

The red-brick face of Nelson House was spotlit in the early evening. More cars were pulling in. I veered left then swerved on to a drive punctuated with bone-jarring speed bumps. I hammered along, knackered and gasping, dog's head lolling.

This was ridiculous. No one fails to spot a dog on a bike, right?

I pulled into the woodland, ditched my transport and ran for the trees. When I was deep enough in I threw myself into the undergrowth and hid, panting. The bracken swayed and crunched. My costume was damp with sweat and stinking. I used a fallen tree for cover and watched Nadim pace the parking lot, his cap under his arm. When I was sure I'd got away with it I followed the cover of the trees, examining the back of Nelson House looking for a way in. If Stacey's stuff wasn't in the warehouse, it was in there. And given the number of people who'd already arrived, I reckoned the auction was about to get underway.

That's when I saw the kid with the notebook.

He was outside a horseshoe of single-storey outbuildings attached to the house, chewing his pen, thinking, writing, then thinking again. I watched as he read something aloud, grimaced, ran a line through it. He was about my age. Beyond him was an open door. My way in.

I didn't have a fox mask with me. But I figured since this was our last ever grab, I'd be fine without. He looked up as I approached, dog head under one arm. He was taken aback at first but smiled at my comic shrug.

'Long story,' I said.

The lad pocketed the notebook. 'What's going on?'

'Glad you ask,' I said. 'Listen. You've heard of Payback, right?'

Inside the building was a scruffy meeting room. Staff sat around a plastic table while a woman poured tea into polystyrene cups. Everyone looked at me and I waved, embarrassed, as my new friend, Marshall his name badge said, began a high-energy introduction.

'I know it looks ridiculous,' I said, helping him out, 'But it's true. I'm from Payback. I need a way inside. Can you help?'

'Where are the rest of you? There's five isn't there?' one asked.

A thin balding guy narrowed his eyes. 'Loads of people could say they were Payback though, couldn't they?' There was a murmur of agreement.

I had an idea. 'What about we watch a video?' I placed my phone on the table and we all gathered around. Marshall chose Blackhouse Langley ('It's the *best*!' he declared) and we watched me prancing in a window.

One fella made a face. 'Maybe? At a push?'

'Guys! It's *obviously* me!'

'Go on then,' a woman said with a smile. 'Let's see the dance.'

There was no getting out of it. I sighed, put the dog's head down and threw some shapes. I wasn't expecting applause but I'd hoped for a bit more than expressionless silence. 'Aw come on,' I pleaded. 'What else would I be doing breaking into Nelson Repo in disguise? I need access to the auction lots. I'm looking for a wedding ring and a jewellery box.'

'There's no love lost for Nelson in this room,' a woman said, indicating the state of the place. 'Bloody zero-hours contracts.'

I took my chance. 'Exactly!' I fired off an account of Stacey Healy's story. As I was going through the details one guy rose and left the room. I soldiered on. When he returned he had a uniform with him. I hissed a celebratory *yessss* as he handed me a spare shirt, a pair of black trousers and some old boots.

As I climbed out of the dog suit they all did a bawdy rendition of that slide-trombone song you hear when people strip, whooping and cackling.

When I was done one woman, indicating my abandoned costume, said, 'D'you want to take Donnie the Pizza Dog?' When I told her she could keep it she gave me a grin and said, '*Smokin'* hot!'

Outside Marshall waved at me to wait. 'Listen,' he said, jogging alongside as I strode towards the main buildings. 'I could help. I mean – give me a chance. I just want to be able to say I've been part of a Payback steal.'

'I don't want to get you into trouble.'

'We could pretend you're new at work. Or a visitor I'm showing round or something.'

I slowed. That sounded promising. 'Go on.'

*

'Lot 242!' the man behind the podium bawled into the microphone as we ducked through crowds towards the lots at the back of the hall. 'A Victorian dresser, mint condition. I'll take bids beginning at two hundred.' Hands around me shot up. 'I have two, thank you. Two twenty. Forty . . .' The prices rose, stalled at just under four hundred pounds, then rose again.

The area where the lots were displayed was roped off. There were two young Nelson staff standing side by side at the entrance.

Marshall gave them a wave. 'This is Kevin.'

'I'm an apprentice,' I said as I approached. My subconscious had chosen a Liverpudlian apprentice, it seemed. Luckily the accent was mint. 'Trying to learn about antiques. My boss said I had to look the lots over again and take notes. Marshall said you wouldn't mind. I'm not very good at identifying – um – Georgian . . .' I faltered, only half-sure Georgian was a thing. I rephrased. 'Furniture made during the reign of Queen Georgia . . . anyway. I just need to brush up a bit.'

'Know the feeling mate,' one of them said. 'I was terrible in school.'

I grinned along, nodding like a dashboard dog. 'I promise I'll be in and out. Gonna make a few notes . . .'

The dude unclipped the rope. 'Don't be long. Wait – hang on.'

I froze, listening to the blood thump in my ears. I was sure I'd been rumbled. 'Wha?' I said.

'He's a king.'

'Eh?'

'*King* George. Georgian.'

I cleared my throat and smiled. 'Yeah. I knew that.'

Marshall led and we snaked between piles of labelled furniture heading for the silver collected on a table towards the back. We passed neatly stacked chairs, an elegant dresser topped with porcelain vases and lamps. There were pictures, photographs in silver frames, plates and bowls.

'Lot 243!' I heard the announcer declare. 'The first of a number of bundled lots of silver items, mostly ladies' jewellery . . .'

The silverware. We didn't have long. I hooked my phone out and checked Gedge's picture. Marshall studied it closely, zooming in, then we examined carved oval boxes with velvet interiors, music boxes with ballerinas on top, cigar boxes with little locks, compacts and handheld mirrors, lockets and keepsakes.

I heard the smack of a hammer as another lot closed. 'Lot 244!' the voice declared. 'A collection of period silver music boxes.' A guy in overalls and a Yankees cap came in. We threw ourselves into thoughtful poses. Marshall flicked through his notebook as the dude regarded us suspiciously, lifted a tray of silver boxes and returned to the auction floor with it. We sagged a little as he went.

'We haven't got long,' Marshall whispered.

We resumed our desperate search. 'Lot 245! Assorted silver jewellery boxes and keepsakes.'

'Here!' Marshall said. 'This is it, right?' He had a tarnished box, small and neatly decorated. I fumbled for my phone and double-checked. *Yes.*

'We need a ring too!' I hissed. There were thirty or forty rings, each displayed in a glass-topped cabinet. Silver ones, platinum bands, gold ones – each simple, no stones or decoration. I lifted the lid on the case.

At my shoulder Marshall checked the photo. 'There's no way we're going to . . .' As he fretted I tipped the case on its end and funnelled the whole lot into a pile. 'Whoa.'

'I'm having them all,' I said, dumping a handful into the box and following it with a second. 'Better safe than sorry, right?' The guy with the overalls was on his way back. 'I need to go,' I stammered, pocketing the booty. 'Thanks, Marshall.'

He beamed, blushing. 'Changing the world,' he said, 'one steal at a time.'

We high-fived like a pair of fanboys. Then I legged it.

30
Handover

Gedge and me watched Stacey's flat window from the street across the road where a Caribbean takeaway was doing good business. We'd arranged to hand over at eleven but the windows were dark up there.

'Doesn't look exactly welcoming does it?' Gedge said, checking the time. 'Still, there's a few minutes.'

This was my moment, I figured, to tell Gedge everything. Ruiz following me to Arch 17, the Jay conversation, Sinclair closing in . . . and there was the small matter of the black box to clear up as well. I needed to know what the hell he intended to do with his bonus pearls. It wasn't going to be an easy conversation. I took a breath, determined to get it over with. 'Listen,' I said.

A low light came on in Stacey's window. Gedge smiled. 'Excellent. Let's do this.'

I cursed myself as we crossed the street. The lift was back in action and we rode it in silence, Gedge running his hands down his hoodie, securing the bulge beneath it, ready to pull the box and ring clear once we were safely inside. On Stacey's floor it was dark. A cop car came past in the street below and we held our breath. I briefly wished I was down there outside the takeaway, drinking and laughing with Kallie or a bunch of mates.

Gedge knocked on Stacey's door and it drifted open. It hadn't been shut properly, let alone locked. There was a light inside. Gedge looked at me and I felt, for the first time, unease become fear. I could see he felt it too. He pushed the door.

As we stepped inside a breeze ran through the flat and somewhere a window rattled in its frame. I could hear a taxi blaring its horn in the street below. We took a few short steps into her corridor. It was empty. Stacey's bags of shopping had gone.

When Gedge moved towards the living-room door it wasn't with the natural ease of a guy about to win the love and respect of a destitute victim of the system. He was wound tight, knees bent, head cocked; his boxer's stance. I followed suit. The door ahead was made of rippled glass. I could see a source of light beyond. Gedge pressed the handle down and pushed. We stepped in.

Whatever dwindling part of me was still expecting normality in Stacey Healy's flat – Stacey, fag in hand, rising from the sagging sofa and saying, 'You're back! Did you get it?' – disappeared at that moment.

The room was empty. I mean, it had been pretty empty before. Now there was nothing but a carpet. No sofa, no chairs, no sparse kitchen equipment, no chipped mugs or plastic plates. It was like it had never been lived in. Except the walls. The walls were papered in tacked-up pictures and printouts. In the centre of the floor was a small, still creature on its back in a black and sticky pool.

I heard Gedge stop breathing. At first I thought it was

engine oil, but it didn't smell like oil – it was sugary and metallic. The creature was Marx. Eventually I nudged the big man forward and he dropped to his knees next to the little animal. Its fur was matted and sticky, its head turned strangely, the glitter gone from its eyes. Gedge let out a long, shaky breath.

Then there were the walls. Photos of Gedge, predominantly, but also Kallie and Ferg – some screen-shots captured from CCTV, some taken with a long-lens camera, black and white, digitally enhanced, all shot during the Nelson grab. There were fewer of Coke and me, but plenty enough. Scattered amongst the images were printouts bearing our names – helpfully highlighted – our addresses, schools. There were copies of birth certificates, national insurance details. Gedge's criminal record was displayed over seven or eight sheets of typed police reports all tacked up in a line. My school reports were up there. A complete Payback exposé. I was going to jail.

It took every fibre of strength and courage I had to crouch close to the poor creature. 'Is he dead?' My tongue was thick and dry.

'Still warm,' Gedge said, his voice trembling as he placed a hand against the dog's little rib cage. When he drew back he had two wet circles of blood on the knees of his jeans. 'Oh Jesus . . .'

I rose from my crouch and stepped away from Marx. Blood had pooled on the carpet around my trainers. Now there was a neat red tideline along the white edges of my soles. And I was leaving sticky red footprints. 'Oh my God,' I gasped.

Gedge held up a hand and we both stood stock still, looking at the devastation we'd somehow mixed ourselves in. There was a mess of prints from both of us and the smudge of Gedge's knees. All around us was an incriminating gallery of photographs and personal information. It must have been Ruiz. Gonzalez hadn't just been following me; he'd tracked us all and his pictures had been blown up and mounted for public consumption like a museum display.

'We need to tear this stuff down,' Gedge said, wiping his eyes clear of tears. Understatement of the year, right? He pulled a handful of papers down from the wall, balled them up in his fists and hopelessly examined the size of the job ahead of him. 'These won't be the only copies. We're wasting our time.'

That was when we first heard the sirens.

They were distant but multiple. Not just a pair of cop cars, three or four. Seeing my shock, Gedge went for positive. 'They might not be for us,' he said. I could see in his eyes he didn't believe it but he sniffed, wiped his face again and pushed on. 'Late-night bar fights, burglaries, gang brawls – it's busy out there.'

Even as he was speaking I could hear them draw closer. I think I lost it for a few minutes. I said 'Oh my God' a lot.

Gedge had to shake me back to sanity. 'Take them off,' he said, indicating my sneakers. He pulled the jewellery box and ring from beneath his hoodie and tossed them aside.

'Careful with those,' I said numbly.

'Rendall – they're fakes. We got stung.'

I'd been so slow. Of course. I pulled my trainers off – getting dog blood on my hands as I did so – and bundled them under my arm. The sirens were louder again. The gluey slo-mo spell of the last few minutes was broken. I saw the open kitchen window properly for the first time. Someone had brought the dog here, cut it and left it to bleed out, then

174

escaped. Maybe it happened just as we were watching the flat from the street.

I could see blue lights as I made it out on to the walkway again, looking for the fire escape. I heard the squeal of brakes – cars pulling up. Doors slammed. I knew my bloodied hands had left smudges of red in the carpet and I knew that meant a thousand terrible things. But we had no more time. We couldn't go down, the street was alive with cops.

I followed Gedge along the walkway in my socks, running for my life.

31
The Sting

Two floors down we found the metal fire escape. Gedge was leaning over a concrete wall, examining the alleyway below as I reached him. The cops must have started cordoning off the street; I could see queues building up by the railway bridge.

The law would be climbing the stairs and finding that grotesque scene any minute, clocking our bloody footprints, examining the dead animal, the gallery of photos and documents.

'Here! Thank God.' Gedge was pointing over the edge of the wall. Some three metres beneath us was our escape; a flight of iron steps. There was a fenced balcony that served an old fire door. Gedge swung his legs out over the edge. The drop loomed. He rolled on to his front, gripping the wall, and lowered himself, his feet scrabbling.

I assessed the position of the mesh-metal gantry. Gedge extended his arms and tried to look down. If he missed it he'd drop like a brick in a lift shaft. I checked the other side of the roof. There was torchlight – someone was climbing the far stairs. 'Go!' I said.

The balcony was small and rusty. The drop yawned.

Gedge released.

He crashed into a graceless heap. I heard the old steel of the fire escape lurch and groan.

'I'm all right.' His voice came out breathless. I swung my legs over the wall, let my arms take my weight and cycled my feet uselessly against the brickwork. 'Wait until . . .' Gedge began. The last thing I saw before I lowered myself was a cop reaching our floor. I let go.

I'm pretty sure I landed on top of him. Our combined weight was bad news. The fire escape shifted and buckled. I saw it come away from its rivets, sections of brickwork exploding into powder. Little showers of rusty metal splintered the air. I rolled out against the railing.

There was an ominous creak and – I swear I experienced my first ever full-body cardiac panic at this – a gap opened between fire escape and wall. The rusted gantry was coming away from the building. The whole construction was going to crash into a twisted mess and we'd be skewered inside it in the alley below.

Gedge made it to his feet and pulled me up. I felt like I was roller-skating on the deck of a cross-channel ferry. The structure shifted beneath us with every step. We stuck close to the wall, trying to rebalance the teetering metalwork. Somewhere above us torch beams flickered as cops searched the high-rise.

It was a slow and terrifying journey but by the time we reached the lower floors it seemed more secure. Looking up we could see the top of the structure leaning drunkenly. No one could possibly follow.

Somewhere beyond the alley we found the dripping lower levels of a multi-storey car park and squeezed through a gap between cobblestones and concrete to drop inside. We'd begun snaking between the sleeping shapes of cars when I finally found the courage to say it.

'Why did you make me return Ruiz's case?'

Gedge ignored me at first, opting instead to mop his brow and issue a slow exhausted breath. 'What?'

'You were sending him a message, right? Threatening him somehow. Did you leave a note for him or something?'

'Rendall, I've no idea—'

'He's stung us because of something you did. It *must* be.'

Gedge was silent as we wound our way to the Carver Street pay barriers and from there to the Chester Road, where we hid in an abandoned shopfront. Cop cars came and went as we watched.

'I'm right, aren't I?' I didn't want it to be my fault, that's why I was pushing him. *I'd* been the guy who'd taken Ruiz's two hundred and done nothing. But that had all happened because Gedge wanted the case returned. I kept coming back to that. 'Just say I'm right,' I pressed. But there was nothing from Gedge as we trudged down Bridgewater Way. He was taciturn, hands in pockets and head down when the cop cars passed. 'This is all your fault!' I spat, terrified.

The big guy ignored me. We walked the rest of the way in silence.

The arches were alive with noise and movement when we got there.

I gripped Gedge's arm and we hovered behind a queue of parked cars. I cowered against the wheel arch of a BMW watching from a safe distance. My body began a stressed-out rejection of the last hour's events. I felt like I was dying.

178

Outside our underground parking lot were two police vans flanked by a pair of cars, their blues flashing silently. Inside the lights were on. We moved closer until we could see officers making their way along the interior arches, hammering at doors. Maxi's Auto-Service already had its door drawn open and lights on. A team of uniformed police were moving in and out of the space, carrying equipment.

Watching the cops, I spotted the one I'd expected. Sinclair was in a calf-length raincoat and trainers, talking on her mobile phone. One of her team emerged with Becky's laptop, dragging a tangle of leads.

'That's Sinclair, right?' Gedge observed, his first words in half an hour. 'I thought she'd give me longer. Coke always said we should get ourselves some decent lawyers.'

Nothing seemed real. 'So how do we get out of this one?'

Gedge shifted and sat with his back against a car, no longer watching the police. He'd seen enough. 'Stacey bloody Healy. A whole grab set up to incriminate us,' he said.

'Made Stacey Irish, too, so you'd sympathize with her.' I held my head in my hands. 'Dammit Gedge what have you got us mixed up in?'

I suppose I deserved what happened next, piling the pressure on the big guy like that, directing all the blame at him. I'd played my part, I knew. And that part was about to compromise me.

My mobile buzzed. As I reached for it I threw a glance in the direction of Arch 17 and Sinclair.

The cop had a phone to her ear.

32
Cooper Goes Boom

'Thomas. It's DCI Sinclair here. I think we need to talk.'

I guess my face said it all because Gedge's eyes went wide and his raised shoulders said *who is it*? I gave a dry cough and tried to speak. 'DCI Sinclair?' I gave Gedge my best meaningful gaze while my stomach lurched. 'How can I help?'

'Thomas, I'm near Victoria Station railway arches looking at a particular lock-up. I have a warrant to search the premises. Listen, can you get yourself here as quickly as possible? Do you need me to organize a car?'

'No, no. I'm nearby. I can come.' Gedge's jaw dropped, then his face darkened. I held a hand up to him. 'I'll be there.'

Gedge wasted no time once I'd hung up. 'The cops? Calling you? What the hell!'

'Wait,' I tried. 'It's not like that. Just—' Gedge swung at me and I ducked back, holding my palms out.

He dropped into a boxer's crouch and spat the words at me. 'It's not just me that's got us into this. You're twice as bad! Cops!'

'Calm down, Patrick. The DCI came to my house. She knew I'd worked at the hotel and she was hassling me . . .'

'So you blabbed, huh? Told her about Payback. Jesus!'

'No. It wasn't like that. I never said a word. She was after you but I denied everything.' Gedge was advancing again. 'I said I didn't know you. *I told her nothing.* She's been persistent that's all. Sit down will you? She'll see us.'

I pushed him back towards the parked cars, a hand on his shoulder. He was breathing heavily as he sat. He swore, slamming his huge fists against the pavement. When he looked up, tears stood in his eyes.

'Wait here,' I said. 'We can still sort this.' Gedge was all skittish and jumpy and I felt like some sort of weird horse whisperer. 'Let me handle this. Maybe she wants to deal, like she said in the note. You got your phone?' He nodded, chewing his lip. 'I'll call you. Sit tight.' Eventually, I got him calm. Then I broke from cover, crossing the street towards the arches.

Sinclair turned as I approached and wordlessly indicated Maxi's. We passed through his workshop and climbed the stairs to Arch 17.

The cops were tearing the place apart. There was a constable sitting on Gedge's bed, dusting his books for prints, his evening's work spread around him. The black box had been excavated. Each letter had been separately bagged and lay catalogued side by side on the mattress. Ruiz's list of companies was face-up in the middle of it. I couldn't see the pearls but I saw Marx's ball; a sad little half-deflated thing. I felt tears rise.

'We now know this is where Payback are currently based,' Sinclair explained, leading me upstairs where a team of three younger coppers were bagging up Becky's stuff, the laptops dissected on the central table in a tangle of tech; hard drives labelled and packed, trackpads, cooling fans, disassembled motherboards, bundles of wire. Her flash drives were sealed in individual plastic pockets.

Sinclair said, 'Gentlemen, a moment please.'

A guy with a moustache gestured at the tabletop and said, 'Ma'am there's a lot still to be done here . . .'

Sinclair held up a hand, fingers splayed. 'Five minutes gentlemen.' The cops clattered reluctantly downstairs and the DCI smoothed her choppy grey hair then turned to me. 'I've got a busy night ahead of me Thomas and I need to be quick. There's another incident I'll have to attend to shortly . . .' She shook her head. 'I won't keep you long.' It sounded a lot like she hadn't connected the Stacey Healy nightmare with us yet. She indicated the room with a curt nod. 'The team have been through the place. I have enough material here to close down Payback. But maybe there's something else going on here. Something much more important. I left a note to that effect recently.' She fixed me with a meaningful gaze.

'I don't know what you're—'

'Something even bigger.'

I sighed. There was no point lying any more. 'We stole a briefcase from Edison Ruiz in the Midland Hotel. Ever since, he's been trying to track us down.'

'Well well,' grinned the DCI. 'I must say, the two of you were pretty convincing the night I interviewed you. Pitch-perfect performance Tom. Frightened hotel porter in the wrong place at the wrong time.' She shook her head at the memory. 'I knew, though. I just *knew*. People connected to people.'

'Events to events . . . yeah, you said.'

Sinclair smiled. 'Cooper will be delighted,' she said and

not taking her eyes from me, raised her voice. 'Cooper. You were right!'

'Ruiz?' came the voice of another cop below.

'Yup. They'd targeted him.'

Cooper gave a satisfied chuckle. 'Boom,' he said.

Sinclair rubbed her hands together. 'Here's the thing. A week ago we received an anonymously delivered file of information that conveniently led us here. Detective Constable Cooper was of the opinion that Edison Ruiz was trying to manipulate our investigation. To accelerate it in a particular direction. Which meant he was hiding something.' Sinclair folded her arms. 'When property magnates and portfolio-recovery specialists like our friend Ruiz start getting helpful, I get suspicious. And Cooper – he gets *really* suspicious.'

I'm not the brightest. 'Portfolio recovery – what?'

'He buys debt,' Sinclair explained. 'Then makes huge amounts of money on it.' She stretched. 'I think what we have tonight is an opportunity. Ruiz has been in London today. This evening, according to his tickets, he boards a late train to Edinburgh from King's Cross. By tomorrow, he'll be in Scotland. After that, if our sources are correct, he'll be flying back to the States. His train passes through York in a couple of hours. We have just a slim chance to arrest him on a number of charges. But English forces have limited powers in Scotland. Basically, we need Ruiz before he crosses the border. You follow?' Yeah, I followed. 'Now, tell me how much money you took from Mr Ruiz.'

'Four thousand,' I said.

'I see.' Sinclair settled herself against the table, her chin on her chest, her lower lip thrust out. We stood together in silence.

I was being led by the nose somewhere I wasn't clever enough to see but to hell with it. 'Detective Sinclair?' The DCI looked up. 'Is there any way me and my friends can help?'

Sinclair gave a little delighted grin as if a tricky puzzle had fallen into place. 'Well now. There's an idea,' she said. 'Why don't we discuss that. I don't suppose you could get in touch with a young man called Patrick Gedge, could you? You may remember I showed you his photo once. Who knows, perhaps fate will be kind and he'll be nearby.'

Sinclair had us pinned. I called Gedge. He'd weathered the storm and calmed down, thank God. 'You need to hear this,' I said. He listened. When he'd hung up I tucked my phone back in my jeans. 'He'll be five minutes.'

'Ah! Excellent,' said Sinclair, clapping her hands. 'Now Thomas. What if Payback, sick of being hounded by Mr Ruiz, were to grow a conscience and decide to return his money?'

Hesitantly, I cleared my throat. 'Go on.'

DCI Sinclair gave a satisfied nod. 'Are you familiar with what we coppers call "marked bills"?'

33
A Bad Week to Quit Menthols

'**H**ang on a second,' Gedge said after Sinclair had finished making her proposal, 'why not do this yourself?'

We were outside the arches, facing each other and talking in low voices, the DCI with her hands thrust deep into the pockets of her raincoat, the wind tugging at her hair.

Sinclair looked back at Maxi's place as Cooper emerged with an armful of evidence bags. 'Gents, it's impossible to get approval for an operation like this in the next two hours. I know what my superintendent will tell me if I wake her up with this. Risk assessments, operational approval, costings. And time is one thing we haven't got, right?' Sinclair pulled a packet of cigarettes from her pocket and tapped one out. 'I picked a bad week to quit menthols,' she said, grinning at what was evidently meant to be a joke. 'Do you mind? I rarely do this. Only to celebrate those moments when connections come together.' She lit up and blew a stream of minty smoke skywards. A late tram clattered past. 'So,' Sinclair continued, hugging her raincoat against her with one arm, holding her cigarette in the other, 'I have to work with what I've got. Which, fortunately, is a crew of thieves and con artists with extensive experience of heisting bad guys. Lucky me, eh?'

'This is crazy,' Gedge said.

Sinclair arched an eyebrow. 'That's a matter of opinion. Work with me and I'll arrange that your criminal records are expunged.'

Patrick Gedge straightened at this. He ran a hand across his chin – mostly, I guessed, to keep his mouth from falling open. 'For real? You'll clear my history?'

'And those of your friends. Of course we'd need you to close down Payback. But if you work with us I'd be prepared to declare a truce. Ruiz is the bigger prize, gentlemen. The man needs stopping.'

'Stopping doing what?' Gedge asked.

Sinclair examined the tip of her cigarette and pursed her lips, reluctant.

'Buying debt?' I asked. It didn't seem that big a deal to me – just one more misdemeanour in a world crowded with them.

The DCI peered into the underground space and watched her officers work. 'My son's hoping to go to university,' she said. 'Probably something you're considering too. Do you know how much it will cost him?' I shrugged. I'd heard Chris complaining about loans, but I hadn't been paying that much attention. 'Close to fifty thousand pounds,' Sinclair said. 'He's going to begin his adult life fifty thousand in debt.'

I whistled softly. Fifty k. It dwarfed the sort of grabs we'd been doing over the summer.

'Why are you telling us this?' asked Gedge.

Sinclair smoked. 'The government lend the money to students. Then they sell the debt to companies specializing in portfolio recovery.'

'Ruiz?'

Sinclair nodded gravely and spoke through a cloud of exhaled smoke. 'He's pulled this trick before. Ruiz can then raise the interest rate, increase fees, skim huge profits. It could net him tens of millions even before the money is returned to government coffers. That's taxpayers' money going into private bank accounts, all off the back of eighteen-year-old kids trying to get an education.'

Gedge, eyes wide, said, 'Legally?'

'That's the worst thing. We can't touch him for it. Except we've got him on other charges. Buying off competitors, bribing government officials; all the details are on a laptop he has pretty much permanently chained to his wrist.'

'*The* laptop?' I said.

Sinclair pushed her fringe off her forehead and eyed us both. 'Exactly. You know what you're looking for. Acquire the laptop for me and,' Sinclair fanned open the curled fingers of each hand like a magician, 'Poof! Your records are expunged. No charges brought.'

Gedge deliberated for at least a full second. 'Deal.'

The DCI flashed an impish grin. 'Good. We'll start by giving you the four thousand pounds you owe him. Your reason to meet.'

'What's our story?' I asked.

'You regret what you've done. You've had enough of him pursuing you. You'd like to repay what you took. At Newcastle station, you make the handover and get us the laptop.' She took us through it. 'We'll have a team with a car waiting for you just outside the station. The train takes fifty-five minutes to get there from York.' She checked her watch. 'Do the deal fifteen minutes outside of Newcastle station – just before two a.m. Hand over the cash, seize the laptop. Walk calmly

187

through the ticket barriers, act natural, cross the concourse. My officers will pick you up and drive you back south.' Sinclair tightened her jaw. 'If anything goes wrong – I mean *anything* – and you can't disembark, get off at the next station, Alnmouth. We can even rescue you from Berwick. But on no account leave it beyond that, or you're climbing into wild moorland and before you know it, Scotland. You're over the border and you lose my protection.'

'Great,' I said.

Sinclair rubbed her palms together. 'You'll be needing to call your team, Mr Gedge. You're welcome to use your secret offices. Think of it as one last operation, eh? It'll be fun.'

Gedge shook his head at the DCI and grimaced. I knew what the big guy was thinking: it still didn't solve the Yate problem and it didn't bring Marx back to life. But it gave us some sort of way out. He made a call. 'Kallie,' I heard him say as he spun away from us.

Sinclair smiled. 'By the time Ruiz reaches Edinburgh, we'll have enough evidence to put him behind bars for a very long time. I'll have closed down Payback. And you'll come home squeaky clean, Thomas. Win–win–win.'

An hour later Coke and Kallie had arrived and Gedge had walked us through every conceivable laptop steal, most of it in language I didn't understand. We spent twenty minutes plotting something called a rip deal before the big Irish lad put his head in his hands and declared it dead. We discussed and ditched the possibility of a fiddle game (Coke tried explaining this one to me; apparently it was a classic involving a violin and a restaurant bill), and another half an hour was spent arguing the chances of us playing cat in the bag with the cash – I gathered this one was some sort of switch, though I couldn't grasp the details. On the floor below us Cooper and Sinclair spoke in low voices, checked their watches, and reminded us of the time.

'We're driving you to York in twenty minutes, folks!' Sinclair called up.

'OK, wait. Let's talk about what Ruiz is expecting,' Gedge said, rubbing his face and eyes.

'A switch, obviously,' Kallie said.

Coke chewed his thinking-straw. 'Except there's no time to set anything up. Any change-raising game takes too long. What else have we got?' He counted them off on the slim fingers of a single hand. 'Beijing tea? Doubtful. Pigeon drop? He knows us too well. Middle switch? Not without a decent laptop and a chance to hack the . . .' He stopped, defeated. 'Any news of Ferg yet?'

Gedge shook his head. 'Phone's switched off.' I reckoned I could explain that one – Jay had convinced his cousin to leave us. But now wasn't the time to mention Jay. Whatever we did, it would have to be without Ferg.

'Are we being too subtle?' I asked. They looked at me. 'If he's expecting something impressive couldn't we just . . . grab the laptop and run?'

Coke winced. Kallie grinned.

Gedge paused midway through an elaborate scratch of his beard, 'Wait.' He wagged a finger at me, his eyes brightening. 'Rendall's got something. We throw a straight-up accomplice distraction, maybe two or even three at once and we bust and run.'

Coke's lips tightened into a line. 'Precision timing needed if we're to skip at the right station. And what's to say Ruiz

189

doesn't follow?'

'He's got to be sixty,' Kallie laughed. 'I like our chances in that race.'

'C'mon.' Gedge drummed the table. 'What would we need? Couple of bottle bombs?'

Kallie said, 'A jack-in-the-box?'

Coke nodded. 'And a smoke alarm's always useful.'

'Rendall's right. Without Ferg we need to go old school.' Gedge said. He tugged at his beard and grinned. 'This is starting to feel like a plan.'

34
Jack-in-the-box

We checked and double-checked it on the drive to York. By 1 a.m. we were taking our seats in Carriage A, the one at the back of the train where they stored the bikes and super-size suitcases. Ruiz was tucked up at the front in first class, eleven carriages away. No need to crowd the guy, right? Timing was everything.

Our carriage was low-lit and silent with sleepers. We sat rehearsing our lines until the train pulled out and we left the city behind. I watched Gedge remove his money belt – a slim pouch he'd lashed across his waist beneath his hoodie – and tuck it in his lap so he could check the cash again. The train galloped through night-time farmland and fields and later, moorland. Outside was the velvet black of countryside darkness. Coke tracked our little blue dot speeding north on his phone.

Newcastle was forty minutes away when Gedge gave us the nod. 'Let's stretch our legs,' he said, taking Kallie's jack-in-the-box – a bottle-bomb concealed in a cheap briefcase – with him. Game on. I swung my backpack on. I'd be swiping the laptop and, I figured, probably carrying it by hand as I charged across the station. The bag was there as backup.

We made our way up the train, carriage by carriage. There were four first-class carriages at the front, H through to K; quiet spaces with tables, paper place mats, glasses and napkins. Turns out first-class passengers are different to standard. A night-owl with a generous gut browsed the *Telegraph* and sipped a tomato juice. Two identikit business blokes with eye-masks tried to out-snore each other. All around us people stretched and slept. We passed through, stepping over boutique shopping bags and stiletto heels. Ruiz's tickets, Sinclair had told us, were for K, the final first-class carriage. We'd decided upon two groups. Me and Gedge would continue, Kallie and Coke would hang back and enter on cue, giving us an element of surprise. They took up their positions. The doors to J hissed open and I followed Gedge through. We passed up the aisle looking left and right at each table just in case. A guy in a pair of chunky cans nodded to his music and an old-timer faffed with a crossword. We reached the end of J.

This was it. Carriage K.

The door hissed open. I flexed my fingers, calming myself, getting my lines ready. K was quiet. Halfway along, a south-bound train rushed past in a blur and we steadied ourselves against the lurch before resuming our walk, looking left, right. K wasn't quiet. *K was empty.* We reached the last table, the one with the seat numbers that matched those Sinclair had given us.

The napkins and glasses were undisturbed. No one had been sitting here.

Gedge turned, jaw tight and eyes blazing. We made our way back down carriage K. By the door, Gedge tucked Kallie's case up on to the overhead luggage rack. He gave me a nod, satisfied with its position, and we re-checked J. No Ruiz.

'Next one,' I whispered. 'He must've moved.'

We re-walked H. No sign of the old man, so we huddled by the toilets in standard class. Gedge checked his phone and swore. 'Newcastle in thirty minutes,' he said. 'Where is he?'

A bad feeling sat in my gut. 'Are we being played?'

Gedge made a call. 'Kallie, we can't see Ruiz. Take Coke and search A to F. Text when you spot him, don't approach. Stick to the plan, stick to your lines.' He adjusted his cap. 'C'mon. Let's do it properly this time.'

We retraced our steps. I could see stars and a slice of moon through the left-hand windows as we shot through Durham, rocking like a speeding cot. In D we passed Kallie and Coke coming the other way. We were careful not to acknowledge each other but their expressionless faces told us everything. No joy. *We've been tricked* went my mind as we walked the aisles back towards first class. *Ruiz isn't on the damn train and we're in some sort of unsprung trap; the kind you only see when it snaps shut.*

We reached K again and followed the length of its empty interior back to the tables at the front.

Where was Ruiz? Or was this the work of Sinclair? *Who's playing us?*

Gedge and I turned tail and tramped half the train back to the middle. The four of us convened and huddled shoulder-to-shoulder, steadying ourselves. We weren't ready for this. Coke had designed and rigged a sensitive smoke alarm to the toilets in first class and was all set to hit *boom* as we pulled into the station. Kallie's case was in position; Gedge and I had worked on a flow chart of conversational options; we'd rehearsed every conceivable aspect of the negotiations.

'Yeah. Everything except the mark going missing,' Coke hissed when I pointed this out.

Gedge was obsessed with the time. 'Newcastle in eight minutes,' he said. 'Ideas?'

'We wait this out,' Kallie whispered. 'There's two more stops after this, right?'

Coke was tracking our dot again. 'Alnmouth and Berwick. After that we're into the lowlands.' No one needed to spell out what that meant. Sinclair's protection would vanish and we'd become every Scottish copper's top priority.

'Plenty of time,' Kallie whispered. 'We've got to hold our nerve. Maybe we missed him.'

Gedge winced. It was the first time I'd seen him really shaken. Even at Stacey Healy's place he'd bossed the situation, held it together and steered us out of trouble. 'My record,' he said to himself.

Coke looked up. 'Pardon?'

All eyes on Gedge. 'My record. I need to clear my record. I need that laptop.'

'The grab's still on,' I said. 'We can do this, OK?'

Gedge looked out of the window and his eyes widened. I turned. We were slowing down. An announcement informed us we were now approaching Newcastle. Gedge looked at each of us in turn, his gaze intense and frightening. 'Ideas. C'mon.'

Coke straightened his hair and ran his palms down his shirt. 'You said K was empty? Let's go there and wait for him.'

'Take up our positions as normal,' Kallie nodded.

'Go through our lines again, plan for him showing up, bail at Berwick if there's no sign,' I added in a whisper.

Gedge considered this. The platform came into view and

the train slowed. There was a squeal of brakes and I watched the blur of waiting-room lights in the darkness, red metal benches, a pop-up coffee place shuttered for the night.

We drew to a halt. The four members of Payback stared at the open door of the carriage. Gedge had this weird look of longing – for a second I thought he was on the edge of making a dash for it.

I could see the ticket barriers. Somewhere beyond, Sinclair was sitting in a cop car waiting to whisk us away. All we had to do was walk.

The doors slipped shut and a whistle blew. We pulled out of the platform.

Gedge looked at the floor for a second then closed his eyes.

35
Crazy Wrong

We walked the train. Gedge locked himself in a toilet to count the cash again. Kallie pressed her nose against the windows and watched dark mountain silhouettes roam the distance. A yawning staff member passed us pushing a trolley of drinks and snacks.

Alnmouth came and went. Gedge had us spread out along the length of the train, each watching the ticket barriers and moonlit platforms. No sign. Alnmouth to Berwick was another forty minutes. We hung in first class K, checking the empty space one last time. I actually began feeling relief during that final leg of the journey. I wasn't going to have to see Ruiz again. No need to chant my lines and memorize my options. I could stop sweating and staring and biting my nails and instead find a train to take me home.

'Guess this is it,' Gedge said. He hauled himself up, heavy with regret. Together we watched the train slow and Berwick – the last station in the country – scroll into view. 'Let's go.'

It was then everything went crazy wrong.

Ruiz seemed different from the moment the carriage door hissed open; cold and unperturbed. He passed under Kallie's case and walked the length of the carriage to the table where we sat. Behind him, Gonzalez pulled a shade down across the glass of the sliding door, a blackout blind badged with the logo of the train company and the word 'private' printed beneath it. The emptiness of carriage K had been arranged for our benefit. I watched Gonzalez walk to join us. He had the laptop in a black zip-case in one hand, the other in the pocket of his coat. He took his left hand out of his pocket. I'd never seen a pistol with a silencer in real life but I'd seen them enough in movies.

While we'd been stupidly waiting two stops for the old man to board the train from the station platforms, he'd been somewhere nearby all along. Maybe he'd climbed aboard in Newcastle, maybe he'd hidden himself right from the start. It didn't matter how he'd done it, we were cornered at our last-chance station.

'No one goes anywhere,' said Ruiz as he sat. He used a tone so conversational it seemed as if we were back at the bar of the Midland Hotel. Gonzalez joined us, resting the gun on the table. 'The train's staff have been informed of the private meeting taking place here,' Ruiz went on, 'and won't disturb us. No one is leaving.'

The train slowed to a stop, air brakes hissed and passengers descended. Someone dragged a case on wheels past our window. Berwick was a pane of glass away, and as unreachable as a distant planet.

'We have your money.'

Thank God for Gedge, with his straight back, steady stare and level voice. I found myself straightening too, getting ready with my lines. Gedge slipped the money belt from around his waist, placed it on the table, unzipped it and

197

arranged the dough. Four rubber-banded packs of twenties, crisp and neat. Maybe we could get this done super-quick and still be out of here before Scotland.

'Mr Gedge,' Ruiz said, dropping his bombshell casually. 'It's very unlikely I'll be interested in your money. The bills will be marked, am I right?' No one said anything in the terrible pause that followed. 'I'll take that as a yes,' Ruiz said. 'Now. Let me tell you the story of what happened here this evening. I was travelling to Scotland to conduct some business. As we crossed the lowlands towards Edinburgh, I was set upon by a group of young criminals who have been systematically victimizing me over a long period. They offered to buy me off . . .' he nodded at the four neat piles of cash, '. . . but I suspected the money to be bogus and I challenged them.' While Ruiz spoke, his companion took the cash and placed it before his employer. Ruiz gave a small smile of acknowledgement before continuing. 'They became violent.'

I felt a slow sink of dread. A shrill whistle sounded. There was a jerk as the train pulled out. We were heading for another country. Somewhere south Sinclair would be driving home.

'They produced a firearm. There was a scuffle,' Ruiz said, 'and despite the efforts of Robert here, who always acts with my best interests in mind, that firearm went off. Sadly one of the gang was seriously wounded.'

I wiped my eyes with a shaking hand, wondering where Ruiz's story was going. Gedge was stiff and alert. Kallie closed her eyes, and tears spilt down her cheeks. The old man's accomplice raised his gun.

Coke was closest to them, sitting with his legs out across

198

the aisle. That's the only reason it wasn't me. I've thought a lot about that since. Gonzalez fired; the noise as neat and precise as a blowpipe.

The bullet went right through Aidy Coke. I can still see it now when I close my eyes; a little black dot like an insect emerging from the top of Coke's leg in a burst of blood.

He went down with a scream.

Then he cried out a couple of times until Gonzalez stood, crossed to him and kicked him into silence.

I couldn't see Coke – his body was curled up in the footwell beneath the seats – but I could hear his desperate, whimpering breathing.

Kallie was crying. Rather than comfort her, I opted for a series of unstoppable panting palpitations, my heart battering my ribs, my body shaking. Ruiz raised an eyebrow at me. Once the horror had run its course I managed to get a grip. Gedge cleared his throat and straightened his cap. He'd gone weird, his face cold, his eyes fixed like a statue.

Ruiz straightened his tie and resumed. 'I was held at gunpoint for some time. Then as the train pulled in at Kirknewton, my attackers attempted to finish me. Thankfully, Mr Gonzalez was on hand to defend me. If it weren't for him . . .' Ruiz shook his head. 'Suffice to say, I owe him my life. He was able to wrestle the gun from the gang and use it to seriously injure – possibly kill – a second unfortunate member. The four of them escaped, two nursing potentially fatal injuries that will prevent them getting far. I'm afraid they each wore masks for the duration of my ordeal so I can't give any accurate identification. But I feel confident that, given the setbacks they suffered, they will be unlikely to trouble me again.'

In the silence we listened to Coke breathe hard and fast through clenched teeth. I could see his bare ankles above his Italian loafers. The deep blue of the aisle carpet had gone wet-black and sticky. Gonzalez watched us, his face like stone. If we didn't do something one of us would be next.

Ruiz cleared his throat, unzipping the laptop and powering it up. 'Mr Gonzalez – if you'd be so kind as to run the numbers on these bills,' Ruiz said. 'If they're marked they can stay here. If not, I'll take them as some small compensation.'

Gedge sneered. 'Compensation,' he repeated, barely able to utter the word. 'And did compensation ever occur to you as you destroyed communities?'

Ruiz looked blank. 'Mr Gedge, I trade debt. I don't destroy anything.'

'Oh yeah? Tell that to residents of Cork's community housing. Tell that to my *mother*.'

Ruiz ran a papery hand across his chin, cold-eyed. 'If your family couldn't pay their debt that's their concern. I did good business.'

I'll be the first to admit I'm sometimes slow. But not on this occasion. *The newspaper article about the American company bankrupting Irish families.* That company was Ruiz-Chaves Holdings – it had to be. Edison Ruiz had ruined Patrick Gedge's family. Payback's two-year roster of smash-and-grab raids – Blackhouse Langley, Bailey Heywood, JSR Casinos, Westwater Retail, Lucille Deutsch Investments – made sense at last. Payback wasn't about redistributing wealth.

The old man smiled at the irony. 'Mr Gedge, I'd like to wager the rest of your crew thought your intentions were noble and political. Turns out they've been helping you exact personal revenge. That's all.'

Across from me Kallie was wiping the tears from her cheeks carefully and neatly with the backs of her hands. She gave one meaningful look beyond me. The case at the far end of the carriage up on the luggage rack; her jack-in-the-box.

I looked at my reflection in the black sheen of the window. I ran through every possibility that didn't include me trying to rescue the situation. Gedge didn't deserve my help. The summer's work was a sham. I'd been tricked into risking everything.

But then I remembered Astrid . . . and Lyron, Sasha, Nathan and all the other homeless people we'd helped; I remembered the crowds at the Robin Hood drop; the T-shirts, the calling voices, the smiling faces. We'd made a difference to *them* right? And that had to mean something.

I took a breath and started my act. My voice came out pretty clear and level. I said, 'What if this meeting was being filmed, Mr Ruiz?'

36
Paper Birds

Ruiz pursed his lips until they went pale. I could see his eyes flicking from seat to seat up to the luggage racks towards the front of the train.

'Your story wouldn't sound so convincing then, would it?' I said and remembering my classmate's handheld video camera, Buzzcuts for Biscuits and Mr Boom-Boom, made it all up as I went along. 'We've got a neat little TX350 – high-def, full-colour even in low light. The pictures are transmitted to mobile devices over a range of thirty metres. The angle we've chosen captures the whole carriage of course.'

The lines in Ruiz's skin deepened as he frowned. He took the gun from Gonzalez, weighed it in the palm of his hand then pointed it at my face. At my *actual face*. I froze, mesmerized. A nod from Ruiz and Gonzalez moved down the carriage. It didn't take him long to connect my imaginary camera with Kallie's case.

This is how it went down.

I watched, keeping my head still. Figuring I was about to die, a cold clarity came over me. Gonzalez reached for Kallie's jack-in-the-box. He appraised the case in his hands, checking for recessed lenses. I held my breath. The train swayed and rattled.

'Open it,' Ruiz said. Gonzalez placed the case on a nearby table. Kallie had been working on it all afternoon. Ruiz's grip on the gun was steady and strong.

Ever posted a palmful of sweets into a litre of Coke, shaken it like hell, and run? I have. Buzzcuts for Biscuits *lived* for that kind of jape back in the day. Bottle bombs, Kallie had told me earlier, worked in the same way – harmless but noisy. Gonzalez reached for the catches. Aidy Coke, I noticed, had gone quiet, a danger sign I hoped to hellfire Ruiz hadn't clocked. This was all going to be about twisting back and down when the bottles blew. Death or glory.

I heard the click of a catch then caught a throaty bang. A mist of spray burst across the ceiling. Gonzalez gave a shout. I flung myself against my seat as the gun went off. A window exploded over my shoulder and I jarred my head against the table. The air was a roar of glass – a mist of iced beads peppering my skin. My left ear was sticky with blood. The outdoors bellowed into carriage K, wild draughts whipping. I half-saw Gedge leaping from his seat and throwing himself at the old man then I was out on the aisle with Gonzalez over me. He kicked me hard in the head and I sprang up, knocking him over. Banknotes were everywhere in whirling clouds like crazy confetti. I stumbled over Coke's outstretched leg, slipping in his blood and heard him yowl with pain. An alarm was braying.

Kallie was beating the case against Gonzalez. I staggered back and found myself standing on the gun. I stooped, picked it up, wheeled around and pulled the trigger, aiming for the remains of the window. The rest of the glass exploded outwards and was dragged in a sideways cloud over the moor.

Noise and chaos. I could feel the train slowing as the alarm blared. I grabbed the laptop, slammed it closed and leapt on to the table, holding it against my chest.

The dark moor was very close through the broken window; shadows of heather and bracken and wet peaty pools of black water zooming by. How fast do trains go – a thousand miles an hour or something? This particular one seemed to be doing close to light speed. *I'll be having a word with the driver if I ever get through this*, I thought.

'What about Coke?' Kallie shouted as she saw me poised and trembling.

'Go!' Gedge shouted at me, grappling Ruiz. 'Go!'

The wind slammed into me as I edged forward. A river of fluttering cash poured out over my back, paper birds streaming out into the night. I noticed there was glass in the turn-ups of my jeans as I squatted at the shattered window.

I began a long and crazy scream then threw myself out into the darkness.

The ground rose up and hit me hard. Then it came back to do it again – big meaty thumps that jarred my bones. I wondered how the actual moor was able to do that. Then I realized it was me, bouncing. Each bounce brought a whip-crack claw of moorland heather.

I must have stopped eventually. When I came to I was lying on my front. My head spun. I'd lost a tooth, my mouth was full of blood and my left arm seemed weird – I couldn't move it to push myself upwards. When I looked, my shoulder was poking out of my jacket at an unfamiliar angle like it wasn't my shoulder at all.

The train had roared onwards into the night and I was

alone in a black nothingness. The agony made me weep. I managed to roll on to my back and found myself lying on Ruiz's laptop. It was in one piece. I sat up and checked myself over, shouting with pain, and stuffed the laptop into my bag. Both my trainers had been dashed off into the heath somewhere. My socks were wet and my jeans were torn.

I was crying on my back, hugging my knackered ribs when Gedge found me. He'd staggered through the bracken following the long scar of my landing, he told me later that night, a crazy line drawn into the undergrowth. He had my sneaks with him. He assessed my twisted frame and yanked my dislocated shoulder back into position. I must have lost consciousness.

Kallie came later, not much more than a dancing outline from where I lay. The train had ground to a halt over by Kirknewton station, she explained, and now the track was spotlit and crawling with cops who'd disembarked and counted every passenger. She'd legged it before seeing what had become of Ruiz and Gonzalez. Kallie estimated six cop cars, maybe twenty officers. A dog van had been the last to arrive.

'Coke was furious with me for bailing,' she finished. 'Still. Didn't have much choice, did I? At least they'll get him to a hospital.' She wiped her face, grinned and said, 'Hey! We jumped out of a train!'

Gedge was looking off into the dark. 'There's a town down there. That's Kirknewton, right?' He leant over me, clicking his fingers all up in my face. 'Hey Rendall. You OK to move?' He tried lifting me. I slurred the filthiest swear words I could.

Kallie said, 'That's a no then. Whoa. What happened to

his tooth?'

I tried to get up unaided but ended up spitting blood and wiping my face in the bracken before making it to all fours. My mouth ached, my shoulders felt black and blue, my legs pummelled to jelly. Gedge helped me to my feet. I sagged like a newborn foal. Eventually I made it a few steps. The night air was chilly, the sky clear and star-peppered. We stopped for a rest and set off again. I made it another three metres before I had to call a halt. Gedge held me upright while I got my breath back.

They were limitlessly patient with me over the course of that journey, like family, like parents. I was so grateful it took all I had to keep from weeping. Soon I could walk alone, shivering and staggering through the heathland one shaky step after the next. Half an hour later we'd made it on to an estate of houses on the outskirts of town and found a farmhouse and clapboard barn where we rested on bales of late summer hay.

I might have slept or I might have passed out. I was still slammed into a half-consciousness that made it difficult to distinguish between hallucination and reality. I guess that goes some way to explaining what I heard in the barn.

I came around on my back, stomach churning. Nearby they were talking. I kept my eyes closed. To begin with I thought it was a dream.

'He's safe now,' Gedge said.

'He's not going to die or anything,' I heard Kallie agree. They might have been discussing Coke. Or maybe me. They resumed talking, sharing complaints – skinned knees, bruised elbows, torn clothes. There was a closeness to their whispers.

'We wrap him up, keep him warm. By dawn they'll have him in hospital.' This was Gedge.

Kallie said something in reply. I heard 'laptop', 'money', nothing else. Gedge grunted something that sounded like a disagreement.

'You know how that's going to look?' hissed Kallie.

Gedge offered: 'He's a good talker, though. He'll keep them occupied.'

Kallie didn't seem so sure. 'What if I take it?'

'No way.' I was drifting. I didn't hear the next bit. 'Last in, first out,' Gedge said.

I don't know how it went after that. Sometime later Kallie shook me back to consciousness and warmed me with a hug.

'Gedge has a plan,' she said. 'Follow me.'

This time, standing was easier. I swung my bag over my shoulders, wincing. I was so weak it felt heavy. Around the back of the barn was the oldest Land Rover I'd ever seen and Gedge was inside under the steering column putting his criminal education to good use. Eventually the old thing shuddered into life. He jumped behind the wheel. Kallie and I climbed into the passenger seat. We pulled out carefully, only one headlamp working. The ride rattled and smelt of silage. There was an estate of new-build houses on our left and then a junction. Beyond was the darkness of fields and the hills silhouetted against a purple sky.

We turned left, heading away from Kirknewton into open countryside.

37
The End of the Road

I'm not great with dark empty spaces. In a city it's like getting a hug, right? Houses, shops, tower blocks, all in a scrum around you, a friendly huddle. The night's less dark in a city, it feels warm and sheltered, the wind never blows as hard.

Out on that road above Kirknewton though – that was lonely. Now the lit streets of the outskirts of the little town were behind us and shrinking to dwindling points, we were climbing into wild nothingness. Kallie put on the interior light and rifled the glove compartment for food, maps, anything. The light inside the Land Rover made the night outside doubly dark. Trees rushed by on our left. The headlights caught twisted roots clawing the banks along the road.

I tried to replay that weird conversation that happened in the barn but it slipped beyond my grasp like a dissolving dream.

We ducked down as best we could as a cop car flashed past, blues on and siren blaring, heading for the train tracks. Kallie and me didn't come up again until it was long gone. Curling up was agony.

'Dammit. That cop got a good look at me as we passed,'

Gedge said, flicking the interior light off with a grunt.

Soon we were out in the open. The air smelt of farmland. Years of wind had hammered trees into bent shapes that hung low over the road. We slowed for a junction, took a left then a right. Soon we were down to a single track, gravel under the wheels. Then the headlights illuminated a sign. PENTLAND HILLS REGIONAL PARK. THREIPMUIR. We were in a car park pitted with puddles. Gedge pulled up, left the engine running.

We'd reached the end of the road.

The night was cooling fast so we left the blowers on full. The old Land Rover smelt of burnt batteries and petrol. In the valley below we could pick out cop cars and ambulances arranged along a line of lights that must have been the train.

Kallie was distracted, eyes on the rear-view. 'Is it me,' she asked, 'or are those cop cars closing in?'

We all turned. Craning my neck was like swallowing glass. There was a posse of red-and-blue lights leaving the trackside disaster and snaking through the distant town. Looked like they were heading our way.

Gedge glared at Kallie and she held his gaze for a silent second. One thing was for sure: those hissed whispers back and forth as I slept in the barn had been an argument and no agreement had been reached. They'd been debating what to do with me. I was a liability.

Gedge put his forehead on the steering wheel and took a breath. Then he straightened up and spoke fast and quiet as he examined the valley. 'They must have seen us when they passed earlier. How many roads out of here, Rendall?'

I prodded my phone. I didn't have much power left. 'The one we came in on.'

'Yeah. Figured. Let's leave the car and make a run for it. We need to memorize Rendall's map.'

That was a laugh. We hunched around the phone, zooming in, but there was nothing to memorize; a small building at the edge of the car park, a track across the reservoir, a distant farmhouse. The rest – empty whiteness like tundra.

'Turn right at the nothingness and proceed through the nothingness,' Kallie said with a groan as she opened the passenger door. 'C'mon then.' I swung the bag over my shoulder, feeling the weight of its contents against the small of my back. Gedge wiped down the steering wheel with a grubby rag he found.

'We only need to stay out of sight for a few hours. Until they scope out the Land Rover and realize we've legged it,' Gedge said. 'Then we gather back here.' He put his arms across our shoulders and pulled us together so we stood for a moment, heads touching. 'Then we hitch a ride home and I buy the beers. Stay strong. We can do this.'

We could hear sirens now. Gedge looked up. 'Let's get out into the dark. Hide until they've gone.'

We left the Land Rover and moved through a screen of shrubs. On the other side the wind whipped across a field. We were halfway across it when a cloud swallowed the moon. Having had an almost entirely urban childhood, I'd never experienced anything like the blackness in which I stood on the edge of that Scottish reservoir. The dark was so complete I had to stumble forward with a hand in front of my face as if that would somehow help if I crashed into the side of a cow or something. Kallie must've been the same – she gave a cry and went down and I only knew she was OK because I could hear her make it to her feet and resume walking. Above, the sky was starless and I realized clouds had gathered over us. The air had that feel of impending rain and the springy grass held the smell of it.

Behind us the horizon glowed blue-red and I heard the crunch of tyres on gravel.

We began running, following the edge of the trees. I was living pretty well with the pain by then. I actually scrambled over a drystone wall unaided and made it across a second field of rough grass. The single gravel track that crossed the reservoir seemed to catch moonlight from somewhere. I could follow it across the water like a line of thread in black velvet. Behind us, the car park was a firework display of red and blue as more vans and cars pulled up. There were voices calling.

'If we cross,' Gedge panted, 'we could split up and find shelter somewhere on the other side. Don't go too far. Spread out, lie low.'

'I dunno,' Kallie whispered. 'That's a long track. Once we start we can't turn around . . .'

'They'll find us if we stay on this side,' I said. 'Jesus, there's hundreds of them.'

The fear was all up in my throat. There were so many lights over by our stolen Land Rover it looked as if the whole damn force was out. Ruiz could be very persuasive – the cops had clearly bought his version of events. I'd never been so scared. I only held it together because I didn't want Kallie to see me cry.

The track was easier going. I couldn't see its surface so to start with I ran gingerly, expecting potholes to dash me face-first into the gravel but after a few minutes of steady progress, we sped up and ran fast and blind. My body was hot with pain. I could tell we were out on the water because the air went cold. The path was low, a metre above the surface of the water at most, and only a car's width across. It felt as if we were running across the reservoir itself. The water was a big black thing that licked at our heels. Ahead a hill rose high and rugged.

I don't know how far across we were when the headlights appeared. Somehow the cops had got a van on to the track behind us. They were driving our way. We watched, breathing hard and hopeless. I figured it could only be a few minutes before we were illuminated.

Gedge said, 'Rendall, keep the bag dry for God's sake.' He broke from the path, hopped over the fence that lined it and hunkered own.

I chose the fence at the other side of the road.

38
Into the Water

Beyond was a greyscale tangle of undergrowth. I heard the clatter of stones and the sucking of water as Gedge slipped and stumbled his way into the shallows. I guessed it would quickly drop off and get deep.

The van was closer now. I lowered myself, wincing, on to my belly. I was in the water up to my waist and its icy bite made me quiver. I tucked myself beneath something thorny and lay in rotting leaves, my upper body hidden. There was a plastic bottle and a broken torch right up in my face. My bag scraped as I moved. The lights whitewashed the track above me. Tyres spat gravel and the van skidded as they hit the brakes.

'Come out!' a voice said, broad Scottish. 'I see you. Come out now!' My heart leapt and thundered and I shook with a terror so real it felt like I'd had it permanently transplanted into my chest; stitched in there under a closed wound.

Then I heard rough and tumble. There were torches and a dog, I could smell it. Branches tore and snapped and there was a great sloshing struggle. Something was pushed hard against the fence nearby. There was a grunt. 'All right,' I heard Gedge hiss. He coughed and spat. 'OK, OK. You got me.'

The dog barked and I heard its leash strain.

I pulled myself along on my stomach. The tangle of growth above me jumped and tugged. I may as well have had a neon sign saying LOOK HERE over my head. There was nothing for it. I shrugged the bag off my shoulders, held it aloft and moved backwards over the stones, deeper into the water.

I'd been right about the drop away. My breath came in quick and shallow gasps as the black ice of the reservoir swallowed me up. I was chest deep now, my arms aching with the bag over my head. From this vantage point, I could see there were two cops: a woman with a dog and a torch, a guy with Gedge.

My feet slipped as I started moving and I went under, resting the bag on my head, icy water in my nose and ears. I began a shivering combination of swimming, walking and wading, following the track and cutting a straight line through the liquid blackness. The van didn't move but the PC with the dog was maybe ten metres behind me. She made methodical progress, sweeping the undergrowth with her torch and letting the dog push its muzzle through the gaps in the fence. I went on, slipping and stumbling, swallowing water and sobbing as quietly as I could. I wanted Mum.

It began to rain.

In a weird way it was a relief. I needed something to wash the snot and tears away.

By the time I made it out of the icy water, the van and the dog were still crossing the causeway, torch beams sweeping the bushes. I had a small start on them at least. I climbed the fence and started running, my feet sloshing inside my trainers, rain plastering my T-shirt to my chest. In a way the numbness was a blessing. The less I could feel the better I ran.

The track led to a farm. The owners had left an outside light on and I saw a puddled yard, a barn, a mud-caked Toyota and, beyond a pile of rusting equipment, a series of low buildings. Turned out they were brick pigsties, stinking and foul, straw-lined and clotted with kitchen scrapings but covered and dry. The pigs were asleep and the last sty was empty. I crawled under the pitched roof, pulled straw over me and lay panting in the foetal position, listening to the rain drum the roof. *Who knew a reservoir could be that damn cold in August*, I thought.

I wondered where Kallie might be and what the hell I should do next. Exhaustion must have pulled me down because I woke thinking I was drowning, coughing and heaving. I guessed I'd only been asleep twenty minutes or so, it was still raining, still dark. The pigs were moving. Out in the night I could see the lights of the police van coming up the road towards the farm.

I hauled myself out into the rain again, cursing. I'd lost my advantage for nothing. Still cold and wet and battered to bits but now with bonus straw and crap, I shouldered the bag and began running. The track petered out around the back of the farm and turned to churned mud as lethal as an ice rink. I found myself dumped on my arse twice as I slithered across it, heading for a five-bar gate. Beyond I crossed a couple of fields and found myself on a path that hugged the foot of the huge fell. My trainers were rubbing like crazy. After twenty minutes I collapsed in the shelter of a drystone wall and got my breath back. The farm lights were alive now, making a line of bright glitter on the field's edge. I could see the cop van's full-beams.

That farm was the end of the road, I reassured myself. If

they were to follow further they'd need officers on foot.

I steeled myself and set off at a wincing jog. My luck, thank God, was in. Half an hour later the path turned white. Chalk. The rain had churned it to a claggy putty that coated my ankles and calves but at least I could see chalk in the dark. Soon grey-white scree slopes rose either side. I was heading through a valley which meant I didn't have to climb. After an hour or so the hills opened up and I found I'd jogged my way into a broader valley. One fell was behind me now and the next rose on my right as the track curved left, down towards a building, a road and another black body of water beyond.

My heart heaved and dropped.

There were cars in the road by the reservoir. A line of five.

They didn't have their lights on so it was hard to figure them out. A sign indicated a trout fishery which explained the building down there at the water's edge. Could the cars belong to overnight anglers? I'd seen guys in tents before wearing army fatigues and sleeping with their nets and boxed maggots. Maybe the cars were genuine fisher-types parked up and dozing, dreaming of sticklebacks. I needed a break in the clouds and a little moonlight to see but the weather was filthy. As I watched, another thought came: if I was the cops, looking for a place to ambush a fleeing kid, here's where I'd park. And what's more, I'd switch my lights off, slide down in my seat and watch the path between the hills. Maybe listen to some country music, eat pistachios, polish my badge.

In the end, the thought of shelter was too strong. If I could rest up and get warm, I figured, I'd be able to follow the road down beyond the fishery, maybe flag down a lift to Edinburgh and, once there, beg a train fare and get my ass back home. I must have stumbled and slid halfway towards the squat shadow of the building before I stopped and dropped to my knees.

The place had some sort of reception area on its lake-facing side and there was a light on; not searchlight-bright but something to work with. Watching the line of five cars from this new perspective, listening to the rain drumming on my backpack, it was pretty obvious there was someone in the first car. As I studied the shape I thought I saw it move. Binoculars.

I turned and ran.

The lane beneath me exploded into life. Headlights blazed, an engine roared. Something screeched and skidded forward and I heard the doors of a van slide open. Then there were dogs. Lots of dogs – volleys of barks, boots on the ground, shouted instructions. There was a whole frickin' constabulary on the move down there.

I ran back the way I came, lungs bursting, blood like iron in my mouth. They'd close the valley path off with a line of cops. My only option was the fell to my left, a towering scree-scarred climb up through heather and boulders.

I started climbing, hauling myself upwards through tangled grass, putting one aching leg in front of the other, heart burning. I was all out of tears, it seemed.

Below me the dogs followed.

39
Lost

I was being sick halfway up the mountain when I noticed it had stopped raining. I'd done plenty of gruelling school cross-country runs where I'd come close to woofing my cookies, but real-life super-knackered upchucking was a new experience. I spat bile and carried on blind climbing. Below it was dogs, dogs, dogs. I couldn't see them but I could hear; I think their handlers had spread out into a line and were panting their way up after me, eager animals pulling at their leashes.

That climb was as close as I've come to hell.

I don't know how long I'd been going when the ground began to level out but by then my pursuers were close behind. At the top the ground was spongy and tangled and if the clouds hadn't cleared I'd have broken a leg up there. Tussocks, ditches, deep sucking puddles; I weaved my way between them looking for a path.

My feet hurt so much I had to stop. I nestled myself against a bus-sized boulder, yanked my trainers off then pulled off my socks and squeezed the water out of them. I was radiating pain. If I could wrap my feet up – bandage them somehow – and replace my trainers, I might be able to travel faster.

The dogs were closer. I could hear a copper on a radio. One officer was ahead of the others and was closing in; I caught his grunts as he sloshed his way across the moor towards my hiding place.

I peeled my jeans and boxers off, trembling and naked for only a second, thank God, put the jeans back on and tore my boxers down the seams until I had two pieces of cotton. Crazy embarrassing stuff, I know, but I was actually *made* of desperate by this point. I wrapped my makeshift bandages around my feet, pulled my socks over them and laced up my filthy trainers.

I don't know what I'd become on that wild, sightless hill-top. I'd lost my way and I'd lost myself. As I tried to stand I collapsed backwards and rolled into a peaty puddle gathered in the shelter of the boulder.

I don't like to think of this bit. I'll just tell it. As the cop approached I painted my skin in stinking mud. I smothered it like soap across my forehead, into my hair; shut my mouth against it and doused my chin and neck, ran it up and down my arms. In the puddle was a fist-sized rock and I clawed it clear. The water gave it up with a sucking sound and I wiped it on my T-shirt to get a better grip.

I could hear the cop's breath and the slobbering dog. The creature could smell me. I gathered all my strength. It gave a wild bark. It was right on top of me, its wet breath stinking as it came in close.

'Hey!' I heard the cop say, a black bulk in the dark. I swung the stone and clattered him across the knees. He stumbled and roared. The dog was barking so close I could hear its mashing teeth and tongue. I shouldered my way up and into the staggering cop with all the strength in my legs and he went down on his back. I ran, a painted savage with my pants wrapped round my feet.

There was a lot of noise. Torches, dogs, shouting. Once they'd rescued their colleague my advancing line of pursuers picked up pace. But my feet were feeling better and I'd found some purpose and energy from somewhere. Once I stumbled across a rambler's path the going became easier and I opened the gap again. When the ground began to drop I nearly shouted with joy. I'd crossed the fell.

By the moonlight I could see a village below. I set off towards it.

The lower slopes were soft with springy heather and stands of bracken. I slithered through it, losing my footing and ending up sledging on the arse of my jeans, following the line of a bubbling brook that tumbled down with me. Thirty metres or so above the village I stopped for breath and drank from the stream. Looking upwards I could see the net of persistent lights descending towards me. Below the little place slumbered, a patchwork of roofs and pools of golden streetlight maybe half a mile away.

There was a road between me and the village, walled on the moor side. As I watched a set of headlights broke the blackness. I'd been feeling a small seed of hope but the sight of that car crushed it. It was black and sleek, travelling slowly. The speed was weird. Knowing these roads well, local drivers would take the route at forty or fifty, especially at this time of night. Unmarked cops would hunt in packs, surely. If this was the law, there'd be a festival of blues and twos down there.

Instead I had a single black Audi at a crawl.

I had to keep moving. I made my way down slowly, eyes on the car. It had drawn level with me now, and stopped. The driver's-side door opened and a man got out and stood, one hand on the door, elbow on the roof, looking up at the fell.

It was Gonzalez watching the line of cops and dogs.

I bit my lip until it bled. Just as I'd feared, they'd told their story about being attacked by a bunch of kids on the train and the cops had believed them. Then they'd used our cash to get themselves a car and come to find their laptop. Ruiz would be in the passenger seat, waiting for me to walk into his trap.

Cops behind, Ruiz ahead.

But I had two advantages over the guys in the car down there. They hadn't yet seen me. And I was transformed with warpaint. Maybe I could slip past them like a muddy shadow. It was plan enough. I slithered downwards, trying not to disturb the undergrowth, and made it to the wall without being spotted. The brook had become a stream and its tumbling splash disguised my movement. Now for crossing the road. I checked the hill. I had a couple of minutes, maybe, before the police had me cornered. But if I climbed the wall, I'd be spotted by both parties. The cops would call out, Gonzalez would turn. I'd be slugged, robbed and arrested. I found myself thinking whether it was somehow possible to tunnel under the road. Crazy and hopeless unless . . .

Suddenly I saw the stream with new eyes. Water has to go somewhere, right?

40
The Wrong Side of the Line

It bubbled down a knee-deep shaft, pooled, then headed into a pipe. The space was a nasty tangle of smashed branches. I clawed a gap open, dropped my feet in and tried to kick the rest clear as I lowered myself. There wasn't enough room. I'd have to go head first and squirm into the pipe that way. On the hillside, torches were fanning the heather yellow. Four dogs followed my scent on long leashes, heads dipped in the undergrowth. They'd reached my previous stopping point up by the brook. I slipped the backpack off and put my head in the hole. It was stinking and swollen by the storm. I slithered in. My head went under and my hands sank into sludge. I broke the surface, reached for the bag, then crawled forwards into the pipe holding it over my head.

Once I found the curved concrete of the pipe floor I could move on all fours holding the bag aloft against the roof. There was enough light to see the space was choked with branches. I had to heave and drag and snap to make space to move on.

A faint illumination showed a knot of thick twine attached to a fence post, a pair of rotting snow boots and, caught up in a mesh of branches, the carcass of some creature that had dragged itself in there to die.

All around was the guttering churn of icy water.

Somehow I made it to the mouth of the pipe and took a great gasp of clean night air. The stream rushed between my arms and legs, plunging glassily and disintegrating into a cloud of cold spray. I couldn't see how big the drop was but I'd emerged on the other side of the road, in the face of a high stone wall that supported it. Directly ahead was a plantation of pines and judging from my position just beneath the trees' canopies, the drop down had to be getting on for ten metres. I watched the water funnel down into the gloom. There was a river down there. If I could get down and across it I'd be a couple of fields away from the village.

I explored the stone wall, wondering whether I could climb down. There were decent-sized gaps between stones – Kallie would glide it – but my fingers kept slipping as I investigated the handholds. I went back for the knotted twine. My fingers were so unresponsive I couldn't untie it. I had to use the twine to haul the fence post back with me, one arm still holding the damned backpack over my head. The post got caught in a smashed skeleton of broken tree and wouldn't come free. I yanked and hauled but couldn't shift it.

I was crazed by this time. Whatever the fence post had jammed itself against, I figured, might be strong enough to hold me. I unravelled as much slippery twine as I could and threw it over the pipe edge. It hung right in the centre of the falling column of water.

I began the terrifying process of turning my back to the drop and lowering myself out against the face of the wall, the twine lashed to the handle of the backpack and then wrapped around my wrist. Above me the backup team had arrived. I could hear a senior officer braying fresh orders. Eager new coppers would be joining the search party. Maybe Ruiz had been forced to move on rather than answer any awkward questions. Every cloud, right?

The descent was like taking a shower in the world's foulest meltwater. The stuff crashed over me as I tried to find grips on the wall. I went slowly, *arms straight, three points of contact*, just like Ben told me. I'd made it halfway when my super-taut twine suddenly lurched and I dropped swiftly, pulling a plug of wet wood out of the pipe as I fell.

I crashed feet-first into the stream below, shortly before a great twisted mass of branches smashed into the rocks next to me. The fence post was last to arrive, tumbling into the tangle a second later. I hauled myself to my feet, feeling for broken bones before wading the stream and plunging into the woods.

I jumped a fence and slumped exhausted against a tree, hugging the backpack against me, trying to get some warmth going. I don't know how long I was there. That little golden village must be near, I thought. I prayed for dawn.

Instead, I got a gun in my face.

'Get up.' A jowly guy in mud-caked desert boots was pointing a shooting rifle at me. He wore a New York Knicks beanie over a greying mullet. His Barbour jacket was unzipped over a novelty sweatshirt with 'To the pub!' written across the front. 'You're trespassing, lad.'

Somehow I found the energy to build a smile. 'Och, thank goodness!' I said. For the record: there's a fine line between acting and lying in a bad Scottish accent and I was a few frickin' miles the wrong side of the line. 'Jings!' I exclaimed. 'I've had a bad time of it!' The barrel of the gun didn't drop. The guy's eyes wrinkled suspiciously. I needed a cover story but nothing was coming. 'I'm lost, sir,' I said, rolling my 'r' like an extra from *Skyfall*.

'That so?'

'Aye,' I said.

'There's a stramash in the lane. Lots of police. You look as if you're mixed up in the business.' He indicated the backpack.

'No,' I stammered. I tried to zip it open and show him the contents but my fingers were too numb to work and I gave up. 'It's just my laptop,' I said, and began improvising a terrible story about my missing drone. He didn't listen to more than a few words before gesturing to my face and skin. 'This?' I laughed. 'I'm undercover.' I felt my story coming together. 'Barn owls,' I barked, suddenly inspired. 'If you're going to get really great photographs of barn owls, you need to stay undetected. I managed some incredible shots earlier but now I've lost my drone and I don't know where I am.'

'Barn owls,' the bloke said. He surveyed the woods then examined me. 'Your drone camouflaged as well, is it?'

'No, I . . .'

His gun twitched upwards. 'What's your name, sonny?'

As I climbed to my feet the fatigue of the last few hours caught up with me. I tottered, gripped a trunk to stay upright. He watched me with wry amusement. 'Brendan,' I said in my crapola accent. The guy raised a world-weary eyebrow as I scrabbled for a surname. In my defence, there was nothing in my exhausted head except barn owls and somehow the two words got tangled. 'B – owels.' I stammered.

There was a ridiculous, suspended silence. The guy said slowly, 'You're Brendan Bowels and you're filming owls?'

I threw every atom of energy at keeping a straight face. 'Aye.'

He turned and began to pick his way through the wood, the gun at his side beckoning me. 'Real name?' he asked over his shoulder as I fell into line behind him.

'Tom Rendall.'

'And while you're at it, real story?'

I dropped the accent. 'You wouldn't believe me.'

'Wouldn't I?'

'Well,' I said as we picked our way through the darkness, 'it's like this. I've stolen a laptop on behalf of Greater Manchester Police. But no one here knows that so I'm being chased by a bunch of Scottish coppers. And there's a couple of guys in a black Audi – persuasive guys – who the police are going to believe before they listen to me so I can't turn myself in. It's bad.'

The man nodded and said nothing. I wasn't ready for actual acceptance but the fella seemed to have genuinely suspended judgement. I found myself telling him everything. By the time he'd led me to the edge of the wood he was up to speed with the politics of wealth redistribution, Payback's frantic summer, portfolio recovery specialists, student loans and the charms of Kalima Shah. Listening, the guy parted the undergrowth. Turns out we were nowhere near the village. Beyond the trees was an open space of neatly mown grass and in the centre, a huge mansion, its moonlit walls washed a pale grey.

'That's an interesting tale,' he said as I drew up beside him. 'John Campbell.' We shook hands. I felt hope kindle in me;

for some reason Campbell didn't seem inclined to shop me to the cops. He removed his beanie and ran a hand through a shaggy mane of hair. 'I'm the groundsman here at Penny-crook,' he said, turning to face the house. We'd emerged side-on so I couldn't see the grandeur of the whole facade but it was a huge mansion, three floors of wide, empty windows. I could see the night sky through the gaps in the structure. It was a skeleton; a shell. One section was screened with scaffolding and plastic sheeting. 'Destroyed by fire in 1899,' Campbell explained, 'but the restoration project is preserving what's left. Round the front, you'll see the steps rise to a wonderful elevated central portico.' I nodded, wondering what an elevated central portico might be and whether I could hide from lunatic bad guys in one.

'Mr Campbell, does this mean you actually believe me?'

John Campbell didn't hesitate. 'Yes.'

'Why?'

'I have two items of what a lawyer might call corroborating evidence,' said Campbell, examining his rifle. 'One, I suspect, will be good news and one bad.'

'Good first.'

Campbell grinned at my desperation. 'I think I saw your friend Kalima hereabouts maybe twenty minutes ago. That's why I'm stalking the woods.'

I tightened both fists in relief. *She got away!* Tiny victories feel giant when you're desperate. This one was short-lived though. 'What about the bad news?'

Campbell looked out into the dark. 'There are two men in a black Audi parked halfway down the drive.'

41
Eaten by the Dark

'Wait here,' Campbell said.

'You can't be serious. They'll kill you.'

'Sonny, this estate is my responsibility.'

I grabbed his arm as he tried to move off. 'No way! It's not worth it!'

There was something in his eyes at that moment – a fleeting realization that I might be talking sense – but he dismissed it with a brisk grin. 'Wait here.'

Campbell stalked into the night following the line of the drive, a pale path between black trees. Beyond the Pennycrook estate I could see cop cars lining the road beneath the fell, lights aglow. The sky was a moving map of cloud. I smelt rain in the air again and I spent that last moment of silence and safety watching the groundsman's dwindling silhouette get eaten by the dark.

I waited maybe ten minutes, praying for the sound of Campbell putting his intruders down. Nothing. Instead, the steady crunch of gravel as a car moved towards the turning circle at the front of the house. There were no headlights – Gonzalez was too careful to redirect search parties up here. I was trapped. The chilly realization felt like slipping below the

228

water of that reservoir beyond the hill. My lungs flooded with fear. I was going to die hundreds of miles from home.

Going around the front wasn't an option unless I fancied getting shot. What else? I could leave them the bag and retreat; head for the line of coppers. It was tempting, until I thought about Gedge. He was hours from a new life. So, could I trade with them somehow? Ridiculous. They didn't have time for discussion. They needed to be out of here, laptop secure, before the cops came. They'd shoot me as I made my opening offer. And then there was Kallie. I owed it to Kallie to stick around. If Campbell was right, she was still out there somewhere.

I began a run towards the back of the house. My body had stiffened and it took gritted teeth and a long grunt of pain to get my limbs going.

I made my way along the dark side of the mansion, shivering and babbling a desperate *thinkthinkthink* under my breath. Destroyed by fire, Campbell had said. The long line of lower windows were like the empty eyeholes in a row of sightless masks. They were too high to reach.

Around the front I heard the car slow and stop. I pictured Gonzalez taking the safety off his gun, Ruiz brushing down his coat, looking up at the pale face of Pennycrook.

I kept moving. Further along a set of steps ended at a door bolted shut with a pair of three-barrel combination padlocks. (I thought of Coke saying, '*Three barrels. That's a thousand possible combinations. I'll do it in three. Any takers?*' and wished he was here. I wondered where he was now: hospital, cop shop or morgue?)

There was no way I was using the door but the raised steps

meant I might jump and grab the barred window nearby. I readied myself, held my breath and went for it. I clattered against the fencing and hung on. My legs spun as I found my footing on a ledge then rolled over the fence top and into the house. I spent a moment in a heap as the pain took hold then made it to my feet, swallowed a sob and hobbled into the centre of the room, crookbacked.

I was inside a three-storey shell. The floors and walls had been sand-blasted, cemented and braced, making the large open rooms like moonlit echo chambers. I could see the sky beyond the missing roof.

Ruiz and Gonzalez were outside somewhere, their position marked by torchlight panning through the bars of windows or glowing through plastic sheeting pulled across the scaffolded sections. The thought of them closing in gave me a bladderful of ice-water.

I made my way along a passage and out into what had once been a stately room.

Someone was in there. I froze.

It was Campbell, gun raised.

He padded over, put a hand on my shoulder. 'Your friends in the Audi are here,' he whispered. 'And I reckon they're armed.' *Jesus, you think? I told you that before you went skipping off to check them out, you spaceface.* 'Can you draw them here?' he asked. I stammered vaguely in reply. 'I'll hide,' he breathed in explanation, 'and when they arrive I'll disable them.'

It seemed a crazy plan to me. Gonzalez was big and ruthless. But Campbell seemed pretty handy with his rifle so I agreed. The groundsman tucked himself in beyond the fireplace, back against the wall, and gave me a nod. This would only work if Ruiz entered the room from the same empty doorway I had. I moved into the centre of the space and checked the angles.

I swung the bag off my shoulder.

There were noises in the house. I needed a pee so badly I figured I might have to just wet myself. A torch flashed somewhere in the passageways beyond. It began to rain. I dropped to my knees.

I raised my voice and called, 'Over here Mr Ruiz.' It came out so choirboy I sounded like that cartoon kid who holds hands with a snowman and does 'Walking in the Air'. I had to clear my throat and try again. 'I have your laptop,' I said. I unzipped the bag, praying its insides weren't totally flooded.

The torch changed direction and a familiar voice echoed. 'Bellboy. It's been quite a ride. Don't move.'

Staying on my knees, I explored the bag. There was something heavy and wet in there. But whatever I'd been carrying around . . . *wasn't a laptop*. My chest almost exploded. In the passageway the torch expanded into a bright fan of light and two figures grew in stature as they approached. I hauled the thing clear. It was a hardback book, the perfect size and shape for a switch. My hands shook so violently it was a struggle to inspect the cover. 'Land Rover Series II', it said. 'Owner's Workshop Manual'. Ruiz stepped into the room. I jammed the book back in the bag, every pore thumping with panic. I felt a rivulet of mud roll between my shoulder blades.

It had to be Gedge. The discussion in the barn. I was a liability, I wasn't meant to get this far, I'd talk my way out of trouble. He'd found the manual in the Land Rover, completed the switch while I slept. He'd sold me out.

'Bellboy.' Ruiz entered the room, a gun in his hand,

eyebrows raised at the sight of the mud-caked savage I'd become. Gonzalez pinned me in torchlight and raised his weapon. I was spotlit and cacking it, pretty much the story of my life. 'You know what I'm expecting at this point?' Ruiz said calmly. 'Some foolish switch. So if you don't mind I'll ask you to lift my laptop from your bag, open it, turn the screen to me and hit the power button.'

Somewhere the wind tugged and flapped at loose plastic. I was going to get a bullet in the head. Not only would the pain be bad, the knock-on effect – the whole death thing – was probably no picnic either. Even then, on my knees, Gonzalez's gun in my face, I tried a second search of the bag in case I'd missed the laptop in an interior pocket or something. I hadn't. I blinked away tears, grabbed the book and readied myself, terrified.

Ruiz's eyes widened and his gun went up.

Campbell saved me. He emerged from his hiding spot, rifle raised and drew breath to speak. Gonzalez swung his gun and torch from me to Campbell and pulled the trigger. The muffled thud of a silencer echoed. The groundsman folded over and fell. I stood transfixed, watching black liquid bloom in a pool across the front of Campbell's stupid sweatshirt as he wheezed.

Ruiz trembled with anger. 'You just got that man killed. Give me the goddamn laptop now.' I couldn't move. 'Jesus!' roared the old man. He beckoned with his gun. 'Throw me the bag.' He gave Gonzalez a nod of instruction and the bodyguard raised the gun towards me. I somehow managed to put the bag on its back, ready to skim it across to him.

There was a shot and the world went dark.

Except this time the shot was loud and it came from

Campbell's direction. There was an explosion of plastic and a roar of pain. Gonzalez's torch had burst into a cloud of bloody shrapnel; I felt it pepper my face. He collapsed, cradling the shattered remains of his fingers. I leapt towards the doorway beyond the fireplace and fell over poor Mr Campbell. I heard his rifle skitter somewhere.

Gonzalez was bellowing, 'My hand!'

I looped my useless bag over a shoulder and heard Campbell whimper as I rolled across his body, scrabbling for the butt of the rifle. I dragged it with me, spinning out into the starlit space next door and running.

42
Left for Dead

That damned house was a maze.

I blundered through room after room trying to shake off Ruiz. I could hear him following but footfalls echoed in unreadable directions. I weaved through triple-height ink-black passageways into a set of smaller rooms. Movement was the thing. Stay mobile, stay alive.

The laptop switch, I kept thinking. *Gedge had left me for dead.* My scalp crawled and wet lines of mud oozed through my hair. I had Campbell's rifle in an iron grip despite my hands being slippery with muck and sweat. Gonzalez had stopped swearing but I'd hear the determined grunts of pain as he moved. Soon after that I heard the rip of fabric and figured a makeshift bandage was under construction some-where. There were other noises as well, the clatter of a stone dislodged, a creeping figure adjusting position. I was so strung out it felt like Ruiz might have a whole bunch of backup, their positions hidden under a drumroll of echoes.

One thing was for sure: poor brave John Campbell was silent.

Surely the cops had heard the shot, though. The grounds-man's rifle, trembling in my hands, didn't have a silencer. It had given off a mighty crack . . .

That was it.

I figured my best chance was getting the law up here; if Pennycrook was overrun with coppers Ruiz would have to retreat. I found an open space near the back of the house, pointed the gun to the sky and pulled the trigger. There was a sharp boom and a vicious kickback that hammered my arm. I yelped with pain – it was the one Gedge had wrenched back into its socket after the train jump – and spent a moment on my knees, gagging. As soon as I could, I moved. Ruiz and Gonzalez would be heading for the source of the shot. I needed to be gone. Time went weird. I'd been ducking and weaving for what felt like half the damn night and I could still hear my patient pursuers.

Eventually, signs of life in the lane below the house.

I risked a quick glance from a window then retreated into what might have been the entrance hall. I don't know why getting some height hadn't occurred to me earlier. There was a set of smooth stone stairs leading up from the hall. They ended in a wide landing that would have been the first floor, edged with an iron fence. Still, they suddenly seemed the safest option. I headed up.

Most of the first floor must've been destroyed in the fire; the landing was safe enough but the fringe of fencing prevented further access. DANGER, a sign said. NO ENTRY. UNSAFE STRUCTURE. I could hear the snap and tug of plastic somewhere beyond. The restoration team hadn't got this far. Around me the walls of Pennycrook rose smoothly and wind whipped gusts of rain through higher windows.

The landing gave me a decent view of the driveway, a gravelled curve cut through the black bulk of the woods. A car had pulled up at the front. A single car. 'Are you kidding me?' I hissed to myself. *Where was the stream of flashing lights? The gun-toting posse coming to save my sorry ass? Maybe gunshots aren't that uncommon on a Scottish moor.* It got worse. Through the mist of raindrops on the windscreen I could see the outline of two cops. Two.

Way down in the village another group of cars was waiting. I'm not the brightest but even I could see the tactics – they'd sent a single vehicle up to scope out the lie of the land.

I didn't have a chance for further assessment of my crappy situation. A sound sent me ducking down. Someone just below me moving through the hall. It was Gonzalez, wounded hand cradled against his chest, gun outstretched. He had his back to me. A horrible thought occurred: maybe I should shoot him. I raised the rifle and pointed it down between the struts of the metal barrier.

I aimed at the head of the figure to begin with but it felt too wrong so I dropped my sights. The upper back or the shoulder would do. The gun was jumping in my hands and I couldn't get it still. *Gonzalez wouldn't hesitate, right?* He moved away towards the windows to check the sound of the cop car doors slamming – the two officers must be out now – and I had to withdraw the gun from between the iron struts of the fence and reposition it. I clattered the barrel against the metal accidentally.

Gonzalez spun, gun raised. 'Don't move,' he hissed. He padded across to the base of the stairs, pistol steady. 'Put the rifle down, kid.' I placed it on the stone balcony, weirdly relieved, and raised my arms above my head like in the movies. He mounted the steps. I saw him wince and press his broken hand against his chest below the raised arm holding the gun. 'Stand up and back away from the weapon.' I stood. He was going to kill me. Again. This time he wasn't taking any chances, he wanted a clean quiet shot before the cops made their way into Pennycrook and things got complicated. I backed away and he took the steps upwards, holding the gun level.

He stopped halfway, steadied himself, and his finger tightened on the trigger.

Then something fell on him. It was too dark for details; I saw a silent liquid shape. It came down on to his shoulders and head, swung something down into him and he buckled beneath it. His temple smashed the edge of a step, the gun clattered to the ground as he rolled back and downwards. He came to a stop in a twisted pile on the floor of the entrance hall and groaned.

The shape crouched on the steps, catlike. It turned towards me. Kalima Shah, breathing hard, hair wild, eyes bright. She held a broomstick tight in her hands.

'You owe me, Rendall,' she whispered, then clocked my whole wild-hermit-of-the-Highlands look and said, 'Whoa. Who do you think *you* are? Bear Grylls?'

43
Being Deathtrap Boy

We hugged fiercely.

'Ruiz is still . . .' I began, whispering into her ear but she just nodded. Guess she'd been tracking us all the while from some lofty perch. I hadn't been paranoid, I realized, it'd been Kallie I'd heard moving up on the exposed tops of the house walls, waiting for a chance to take one of them out.

'Gedge switched the laptop,' she whispered, breaking the hug. She picked at a knot. Lashed around her waist was Gedge's money belt. It held Ruiz's laptop close to her stomach. 'I let him talk me into it. I shouldn't have. I'm sorry.' The sudden comfort of having her close burnt in me. I figured kissing her would be good, but never got that far.

'You stink,' she said and pulled back, wrinkling her nose.

'Thanks.' I rammed the laptop into my damp backpack and reached for Campbell's rifle.

'There's two cops,' she whispered. 'The guy stayed outside, the woman came in through the windows at the back.'

A crazy thought occurred. 'Is the woman old with short hair and the guy black, tall, younger?'

'Yeah.'

'Sinclair and Cooper,' I whispered.

I didn't have chance to answer. The single car made sudden sense. The DCI had talked her way into the operation. This was her mess and she was going to clean it up. She'd be calling the cavalry just as soon as she'd established how badly things had gone wrong. This gave us a chance to get out alive.

The clatter of the fallen gun had drawn footsteps. We both froze. Gonzalez gave a strangled groan. The steps halted in response, shifted, came again. Ruiz.

Kallie placed a finger to her lips and raised her eyes. 'I'll track him from above,' she whispered. In a moment she was gone again, leaping from the fencing up to a windowsill and slipping away on to the network of walls. Her shadow vanished and I was alone. I hoped to high hellfire she'd be ready to drop down again at a moment's notice.

I needed to think fast. Ruiz was going to find Gonzalez and rouse him, right? Cooper had stayed outside and only Sinclair was in here with us. I couldn't keep sneaking from room to room waiting to be rescued. I had to take control. I didn't have much in the way of trap-setting skills but I knew suddenly what I had to do.

The house could be my weapon. I yanked the gate's warning sign free, slipped it into my bag alongside the laptop, pulled the bolt back and moved out into the darkness of the first floor. I left the gate open behind me like an invitation.

In this incomplete section of Pennycrook the floorboards were uneven, the walls rough. The passageway turned right. I stepped over a large roll of waterproof sheeting. A corridor was stacked with workbenches, a saw, a set of ladders, hard hats. Three rooms beyond. I scoped out each and chose the one that looked most dilapidated. In the corridor I pulled down another couple of warning signs and bagged them too. The wind snagged scaffold sheeting. I watched the pale rain curl and drift.

My corner room was a mess. Sections of the ancient roofing still sagged, brickwork leaning and blackened struts standing exposed. One of its exterior walls was braced by thick wooden poles standing at angles. There was a tumbled pile of bricks in a corner. The upper sections of the house looked as if they were ready to collapse. For my desperate purposes, though, the room would work well. This was the perfect place to build a deathtrap. All I had to do was rush through this next bit by pretending it was a stupid Buzzcuts video.

I assembled my props and staged my scene in a panic, terrified they'd find me halfway through the job. First I had to heft the roll of industrial plastic from the corridor into my corner room. It was thin, translucent stuff that I could cut into huge curtains – a knife would've been handy but the saw was all I had – and drape over the most damaged sections of the walls. If I could hang enough of it, the room wouldn't look danger- ous. I was strung out and worked fast, only dimly aware of the pain in my body. The rain drew muddy rivulets down my face as my disguise dissolved.

I was tortured by distant noises; sometimes birds in the skull of the house, sometimes imagined footsteps. Once I thought a shout echoed nearby. The wind kept lifting my plastic sheets as I hung them so they flapped and shifted. I quickly hid the worst of the damage, the wall-props protrud- ing between my big semi-transparent curtains that gathered in folds. Then I finished with the floor, rolling out a carpet of plastic that hid the rotten boards. In a few desperate minutes

I'd created a big plastic-coated space. Walking in for the first time you might assume it was safe. Just what I wanted.

I tucked the laptop under one of my drapes in what looked like the sturdiest section of the room, flung the bag down beneath the wooden struts and positioned myself at the furthest strut. I gave it a quick check. If I kicked the prop free and nothing happened, I'd have more than just looking a total spaceface to worry about.

I hefted a few of the bricks, scattered them around me, threw Campbell's rifle clear as a convincing detail, then quickly lay face down, one foot against the prop. I balanced a couple of bricks on my shoulders, one in the crook of my neck. In the moonlight I'd look as if I'd fallen and dashed my brains out as I tried a risky escape.

I was ready. I checked everything one more time. Then I raised my head, gave a pretty convincing wail, and waited.

Here's what I know. Once your performance is in motion there's not a lot you can do to. It gets a life of its own. Take *The Sound of Music*. We all knew it was going to be a car crash from the first line of scene one but the tickets were sold, the place was a quarter full, the lights had dimmed and that gorgeous velvet hush had fallen over the meagre crowd. Once that's happened you can't stand front and centre, raise a hand and say, 'Hang on. Maybe we should just call this whole thing off.'

You push forward and then keep going even as the whole disaster falls apart around your ears.

I tell you that because when Ruiz and Gonzalez tracked me down and entered the room, they weren't alone. They had Kallie at gunpoint.

44
Curtain Line

Suddenly those earlier noises made sense and my scheme looked big-time foolish. I'd drawn the old man up to the most dangerous part of the house but I'd drawn Kallie – cursing me filthily I bet – up there too.

She'd taken a fall. I could see she was unsteady. Her arms were scraped and bleeding, her T-shirt torn. There was going to be a trade. Ruiz was standing just behind Kallie and she was arching her back away from the barrel of his gun.

Rather than going for unconscious I was lying in a heap doing wide-eyed disorientation, groaning like Gonzalez at the bottom of the stairs. That way, even doing my unfocused mad blinking thing, I could check what I was up against. I'd seen Ruiz clock the fallen rifle. I'd noticed with some satisfaction that Gonzalez was a mess, his forehead bruised and bleeding, his busted hand tucked in his armpit. He leant against the door and wore the same expression as Ruiz, a sort of guarded surprise which told me the whole set-up looked pretty convincing. They were expecting something, though.

When Ruiz talked it wasn't with his previous unflappable control. He was breathing hard and he was angry. 'Very careless,' he observed. 'Looks like you've both had unfortunate accidents. Let's make this easy. Mr Gonzalez will check the laptop and we'll be on our way. Any nonsense and Miss Shah will be leaving with us.'

I groaned, played at shaking my head clear, spat dust from my mouth. I steadied my foot against the wooden strut ready to push hard against it, praying only a section of the wall would collapse. Gonzalez moved into the room. I could tell by his sure-footed steps that my carpets and curtains of plastic had done their job. He didn't walk carefully. He couldn't see the extent of the danger.

But rather than go straight for the bag Gonzalez approached me. Not part of the plan. I wasn't expecting it – I was still playing at being concussed when he pistol-whipped me across the face. My left cheek exploded. I curled up, arms over my head, the agony impossible. I thought I'd lost an eye but I blinked it open, realized with sweet relief I could still see and rolled away, dizzy with pain. I'd lost my footing against the wall prop.

Gonzalez squatted casually by the bag and placed his gun on the plastic. He winced as he wrestled with the zip and tore it open. My muscles were rigid and my face a ball of fire.

'Don't move!'

I emerged from my huddle, made it to my knees. DCI Sinclair in the doorway with a gun. Gonzalez, without looking round, raised his good arm over his head. The other hand – the bloody bandage – remained lifeless against his hip.

'You too, Ruiz.' Sinclair had taken a step inside. She prowled, knees bent, gun hand steady. Edison Ruiz backed off. Kallie was looking at me with wincing sympathy. I spat blood.

The next bit happened very quickly.

Sinclair said, 'Both hands Mr Gonzalez.' Gonzalez, back to her, tried to raise his ruined hand and grunted. His shoulders shuddered. 'Both hands now!' The DCI took a step towards him and lost focus. Unwatched, Ruiz extended an arm and hooked it around Kallie's neck. He held his gun against her temple. She closed her eyes, falling still.

'I have Miss Shah. Drop the gun.'

Sinclair spun, eyes wide. She swept her weapon back and forth, trying to pin both men, thinking. Her mouth went tight. She placed the gun carefully on the floor. I was almost rigid with fear for Kallie but somehow managed to make a show of slumping sideways and on to my back with a groan. I stretched a leg, shifted position, closing in on my wall prop. Ruiz was saying something. Sinclair was still. Kallie was looking at the sky, the gun at her head. Gonzalez dropped his good hand inside my bag.

I kicked as hard as I could.

The heavy strut fell with a crash and the floor shifted, throwing Ruiz off balance. I watched as the outside wall of Pennycrook House folded inwards, its plastic curtain coming with it. I pedalled my legs madly, trying to roll clear. There was a huge crash and a spray of shattered mortar. The sound of chipped brick drifting against plastic. Sinclair steadied herself. Ruiz stared. Gonzalez coughed as we watched the dust settle.

That was it. Nothing else. My trick was a dud.

Gonzalez began a dry laugh as he stood up.

Then he vanished.

The floor had gone. Gonzalez and the bag disappeared into a plug of plastic and my whole set unfurled into a yawning hole, tugging Ruiz and Kallie off their feet. Ruiz went down, Kallie screamed. Sinclair threw herself clear, scrabbling back into the safety of the passageway. Campbell's rifle bounced end over end into the abyss and I followed as the rest of the floor gave with a roar and the world plunged downwards. Another wall went next. I barely saw but I felt the brick and splintered wood exploding around me. I scrabbled for purchase on anything but felt myself slip. There was a boom of collapse. Ruiz slithered past me and fell.

Kallie threw an arm towards me. 'Take my hand!' she screamed. I tried to reach her. But I was swallowed by the hole.

I rolled backwards, struck my head, saw fierce fizzing stars. I was on my back on the stone floor of the room below in a fog of bitter dust. I pushed clear of the wreckage and found myself sitting on a gun so I pulled it from under me and held it out, grip jumping. A length of wood that looked like it might be an ancient floorboard fell through clouds of debris. Another tumble of bricks. I backed off again pushing myself along on my back, gun up.

After a minute the chaos stopped. Rain was falling in moonlit lines through the clearing fog. In the centre of the room was a pile of shattered masonry and slate. I could see someone's foot protruding from beneath it, the leg twisted at a weird angle.

I pointed the gun at the heap of smashed stuff and waited for that indestructible old man to push his way clear, praying Kallie wasn't under there with him. But nothing happened.

Then from somewhere above me I heard a cough and a small voice say, 'Whoa!' Looking up I saw a corner of that upper room remained, stubbornly clinging to the wall. And here's the thing: it was the corner where I'd stowed the laptop.

Sinclair appeared at a doorway somewhere across the chasm looking down gingerly. 'Thomas?'

But I was thinking of someone else when I called up, 'You OK?'

'Nice performance, Rendall,' came Kallie's voice in response. I couldn't see her but I could hear her grin as she added, 'You brought the house down.'

45
Four Conversations

I saw Patrick Gedge once more before the end of that summer. It was the last day of August.

I'd been keeping Coke company at the hospital while he tried to teach me about cricket. He wouldn't be playing again himself, he noted, hobbling about the ward on his crutches. He'd bought some silk pyjamas and wore them neatly buttoned under his hospital smock. His slippers had gold piping around the seams. Despite his standard dandying about, he seemed changed by that night on the train and for a few visits I couldn't put my finger on how. Later I realized: he never brought up Payback. I let him talk, and he chose other topics – the upcoming term at school, the Ashes, hospital food, terrible daytime TV and some weird podcast he was geeking out about. We were never going to be close friends, I'd known that long ago, but there was at least tolerance by the end of that last visit. He wished me luck as we said goodbye.

The rest of my time was spent up at Greenheys, the biggest of the city-centre police stations, where I wasted long hours kicking my heels in hot waiting rooms, drinking vending-machine tea and reading the papers. A front-page article in the *Guardian* soon after the Scotland madness read: PAYBACK MELTDOWN. *Police interrogate multiple members of Robin Hood group, but identities remain a secret.* Sinclair had been as good as her word; we were kept out of it. She handled everything. She even sorted Yate who apparently put in a claim for unpaid earnings. He never did get to break Gedge's legs but when Arch 17 had it assets stripped, Yate was given a small share and made to sign a confidentiality agreement. For a while in late August I pored over the details of Ruiz's trial. Each day the papers would summarize court proceedings and accompany them with disconcerting pastel drawings of Ruiz, Gonzalez and a stern-looking QC. They looked like illustrations from some dystopian kids' book. I didn't like being reminded of that night in Pennycrook. Sometimes I woke seeing Gonzalez falling through a hole in the floor, or saw again those crushed limbs under a mountain of broken stone. Sometimes I dreamt about John Campbell. Once I saw an off-duty police officer wearing the same damn sweatshirt – the one with 'To the pub!' cheerfully plastered across its front. So in the end, I stopped checking the papers. As it turned out, we made it through the rest of the summer with no publication of names, no media interviews and no paparazzi circus at the gates of our schools that September. Clean records.

When I wasn't trying to ignore the media coverage, I was signing statements and endlessly reviewing every move I made from the moment that Edinburgh train had departed York. Aside from the hospital visits, they kept us all apart for the duration.

That particular afternoon though, I'd managed to slip away and stretch my legs.

Gedge was in a DCI's office on the third floor sitting at an empty desk washed in dishwater sunlight strained through the grime of the window. There was a signed statement before him. The tall chair opposite was awaiting the return of its owner.

I was too mad to stop and think; when he turned I went for it. 'You sacrificed me!' I spat. 'You switched the laptop and you knew I'd end up being chased down for it! You know what I went through? I spent a night out on the moors tracked by cops and dogs!' I cursed and raved along these lines while the big lad rubbed his face with the open palms of both hands.

He adjusted that stupid cap. 'Listen. Listen, Rendall. I needed that laptop in the hands of the police or I was screwed. It was my one chance of freedom. I had to try and clear my record.'

I slammed a hand against the office door. 'So we could've stuck together and handed ourselves in up by the reservoir before it all went crazy!' I knew what he was about. I pointed a trembling finger. 'The groundsman at that house *died* because of what you did! All because you had to be the one to strike a deal. Playing the reasonable, principled guy who'd got mixed up with a bunch of young criminals.'

Gedge took a long breath. 'It wasn't like that.'

'It was! You needed to be the helpful one even if that meant making the rest of us look like lunatics. What was all that cooperation designed to get you? What made it worth sacrificing me? Abandoning Coke?'

'I needed to act alone,' Gedge said. 'I didn't want you involved. You know how my background looks to a copper? Theft, firearms, illegal substances? I swear, you don't want to be associated. I had to play it like we weren't closely connected.'

'Everyone knows about Payback for God's sake. Everyone knows we're connected.'

'It was for your own good.'

'That night up in the hills *was for my own good*? Gedge, I nearly got shot. *Twice.*'

'Oh come on. How was I to know Ruiz would follow?'

'You knew.'

Gedge shrugged. 'I went through every possible outcome. There was a chance, I figured that much.'

'You sold me out.'

'C'mon. Kallie took it anyway in the end. I just need my history erased. More than anything. It's not the same for you. You've only been doing this for a summer. Me? I've lived a pretty bad life up to now and my record tells that story. If I want to start afresh—'

I got it. 'Oh that's what this is about. Starting over. Going back to Ireland.'

'It's not about me, Rendall. My mam needs me. I'm all she's got left. Who'll help her if I'm in prison?'

'*At least you've got a mum!*' It came out so loud I shocked myself. I got myself together. 'Last in, first out,' I said, remembering those words from the night in that barn outside Kirknewton. I stared him down and said, 'Don't ever speak to me again.'

Chris showed up a week into the whole process. His hair had gone blond, his skin golden brown. He had a Cribs tee and cheap plastic sunglasses. The receptionist called me down from the interview room where'd I'd been kicking rocks for the last few millennia.

In the entrance hall Chris bellowed, 'Hey, Buckaroo!' and attempted a moonwalk across the reception area but got into difficulties on account of his flip-flops. 'Fives!' he boomed when he eventually made it to me.

I felt a million years older and tireder than the kid I'd been when we parted. I left him hanging.

'Listen,' he sat down. 'Dad's on his way. Not a happy chappy. Just wanted to make sure we were tight about the whole Croatia thing, yeah?'

I mentally rehearsed my story. It was doable. 'We're tight,' I said.

Graham Anthony Rendall made it to Greenheys an hour later. Tall, straight-backed, with a parted wave of silver hair, wearing a dark Hugo Boss suit over a white shirt with no tie – his man-of-the-people look. I saw him charm the receptionist. They laughed together over something I couldn't hear.

The pretence was dropped once he'd crossed to me. His pale blue eyes seemed steely grey by the time he sat and spoke. No *missed you son* or, *Well done on your results*. Instead he genuinely opened with this: 'I hope there isn't anything here which might compromise the company.'

Yeah. *My dad, folks.*

'Relax. No charges are being pressed.'

He worked his jaw in furious silence. 'Since when have you been interested in politics? Every time I've tried to make you watch the news you've slunk upstairs.'

That riled me. 'It was something that came up recently. I met some people.'

'These protesters the police told me about.' He rolled his

wedding ring with his thumb. 'Direct action. Pressure groups. God, Tom, that stuff's for slackers and activists. What next? You're going to be growing some dreadlocks? Piercing your eyebrows?'

He could be such an idiot. It was a total embarrassment. 'Before you go off on one Dad, it wasn't environmental. I won't be criticizing your precious fracking programmes.'

'Here we go again. Have you *any* idea who pays your bills?'

'It was money. Distribution of money.'

'Oh, right. The *life's so unfair* stuff. Well if you've turned into a bleeding-heart leftie, Tom, why not start by giving away yours. Shall we discuss your trust fund?'

'Yeah. Let's do that. I don't want a damn penny of it.'

Dad laughed bitterly. 'Better get a job then. Like the rest of us.' I scuffed the floor. 'Stop that petulance, Tom. You're not in a playground. Moving forward, I want a full explanation of what's been happening and we're going to be looking at future arrangements when I have to work abroad.'

Moving forward. I hated the way he said that. 'Whatever.'

'You haven't grasped this, have you? You're in serious trouble.' Dad made to prod my chest but I backed off.

An idea had occurred just that second. A plan. I nurtured it.

Two weeks into the new term, I came home from college, let myself in, kicked off my shoes. Then I began the routine that had developed since Dad took me out of boarding school: make some toast at the kitchen island, fire up the coffee maker, take a pee and stare out of the window watching the September rain. It was the *doing* I missed. Payback were always doing. Now term had started at college we were just discussing, relating, complaining. And the people. I couldn't be friends with those people – most of them were into Snapchat face-filters, celebrity dance shows, haircuts and – in a way, worst of all – bake sales for Amnesty. *Bake sales.*

Dad wouldn't be back from work for ages. I took out my tablet, punched in my bank details and checked my dwindling balance. That thought I'd had – the one Dad had planted about the trust fund back in the summer – had been growing steadily since. I wouldn't get the dough until I was eighteen. There was a few thousand in there, I was pretty sure. Just over a year away. I'd need some funds in the meantime. And there was this new way of doing things I'd been considering too. Franchising. I mooched through the house, thinking. That was when I saw the package on the mat. It must have been there all along.

It had an Irish postmark and an unfamiliar stamp.

I took it upstairs, lay on my bed and tore at the edges of the little bubble-wrapped parcel. Inside was a brown envelope sealed shut and folded into a wad. I unrolled it and tore it open.

Five pearls fell out. I stared at them. I checked the package inside and out. There was no note, nothing. For a long time I lay on my bed staring at those perfect little marbles. After I got myself together I collected them carefully together in my left hand and called Kallie.

'Rendall,' she said when she picked up. She sounded bored. 'How's tricks?'

We talked for a bit and she brightened. She was hitting the books for her Chemistry course. Her brother was being an overbearing ass as usual. Her parents were back from Pakistan. I told her about Chris and Sofia – it was going really well for them – he was over in Croatia again before the university term restarted. Then, for a while we talked about Ferg. Jay had told her parents everything and she'd been grounded indefinitely. It had all gone quiet. But Kallie had got in touch and now they were messaging. (Ferg had gone white hat, apparently. I had to ask what it meant. 'Ethical hacking,' Kallie explained. 'Basically, she's working for a group of charities, improving their computer systems by trying to break into them. Penetration testing it's called. Did you know you can get qualifications? She's studying for some certificates. And you know she's applied to Cal Tech, right?') When we ran out of news to swap I described my bedroom and the view from the window. She described hers. There was a pause.

I thought *here we go* and then I said it. 'What if we started again?' I began. 'I think we could do things differently. Better.'

There was silence on the line until she said, 'Go on.'

'There's nothing happening at college I swear. Everyone's so pampered and comfortable and passive. It's like torture. We could keep Payback going. We'd need a new leader of course, maybe a whole new crew, that'd be the first challenge . . .' There was a crackle on the line and an awkward gap. I wasn't surprised to find my heart was hammering.

'OK,' Kallie said. 'Yeah. I'm in.'

And that was it. I couldn't keep the grin off my face. 'Excellent! That's . . . *excellent*!' I smiled. I think I said excellent a few more times. I may have used swear words for emphasis just in case she hadn't got the message.

'The leader thing,' she said when I'd calmed down. 'I think that's you.' I'm not the brightest. I lay stunned on my bed as she continued. 'You've got something. You jumped out of a train.' She laughed. 'But like you said – new crew as well. And a new place, of course. Oh, and here's the thing: we'll need decent cash reserves to get us up and running.' I heard her stretch and shift position. 'Which is going to be harder than it seems. Gedge was the guy with the talent for finding funds. We wouldn't need much, though. A few grand max, if we really wanted to make it happen. But that's a *big* problem right?'

I was thinking about the trust fund, locked up until I was eighteen, and doing some cack-handed maths. Also I was thinking about franchising – about how we might set up three or four organizations to start with: interview leaders, assign territory, control it all centrally.

'Rendall? You there? I was saying it's a big problem. We haven't got any money.'

I uncurled my palm to examine the five pearls again and found myself wondering whether I might track down Yate. When I spoke, my voice felt suddenly steady. 'Kallie listen,' I said. 'About that . . .'

THE END

A Note on the Setting

Payback is partly set in a parallel version of Manchester, UK –
a weird half-cousin of the city called Dark Manchester. The
two places share so many similarities that residents of Dark
Manchester think they live in real Manchester. But the
good people of real Manchester expecting this mirror city to
operate in the same way as theirs might find themselves
taking issue with the positions or characteristics of streets,
squares, parks, gardens and buildings in this story. In Dark
Manchester the Midland Hotel is different. St Peter's Square
is different, the columns of the Central Library are different.
Real Manchester has no Maxi's AutoService and no chain of
smokin' hot pizza takeaways called Donnie's. The arches are
in different places, trams and trains run at different times,
cops work different shifts and 'Carjack' by New Sedition
hasn't been a hit – it's almost as if everything's been conjured
up to serve the purposes of a plot.

The same goes for Halfpike Abbey, the Westwater Mall,
Blackhouse Langley, Pennycrook House and others, all of
which you'll struggle to find on a map. Whenever there's been
a conflict between story and reality, I've chosen story – for
better or for worse.

I point all this out in case, fired up with revolutionary zeal,
you head for the arches under Victoria looking for a secret
hideout tucked away beyond the shutters of Maxi Johnson's
workshop . . .

Acknowledgements

This book began with a sketchily summarized heist story called *Takeback*; nothing more than a couple of paragraphs I shared with my publishers one sunny afternoon in a caff in Bristol. It was Chicken House's Editorial Director Rachel Leyshon who initially championed it. Barry Cunningham and Kesia Lupo were quickly on board to bring it to life. Without their astute observations, guidance and direction, *Payback* would never have taken off. I am immensely grateful to all three. A special additional mention goes to Rachel who agreed to take the project on as editor, which meant living with it for eighteen long months . . . during which she provided thoughtful and incisive feedback as the manuscript grew. *Payback* is a vastly better book for her careful and considered input. It's no wonder Rachel's a prizewinning editor. Big thanks also go to Ben Illis for representing me and providing constant encouragement, support and freewheeling discussion of ideas, character, voice and plot as the story developed.

Others have been invaluable in helping it along. Thanks to Fraser Crichton for his input, and to Victoria Walters for hers. Esther Waller did a blinding job pulling it all together. Thanks so much to Jazz Bartlett and Laura Smythe for spreading the word. A big *woohoo!* for everyone at Chicken House, a special place crewed with inspiring people.

Thanks to Tony Morrin (*il miglior fabbro*) for all his insight and feedback. Thanks to Yogita Patel for her measured and thoughtful suggestions. Special thanks and love to my wife Jo for her tireless rereading and annotating. And for being so brilliant in every other regard of course. Thanks and love to Aggie for calling me a writer. Thanks and love to Mum and Dad and my brothers and sisters for all the support.

Sometimes when I'm visiting schools and speaking with pupils I ask for help with plot problems and we end up discussing solutions. That was certainly the case as *Payback* came together during the autumn of 2016 and the spring of 2017. I got smart answers from clever young people who stayed at the end of sessions to chat. I'd like to thank the pupils of Windsor Academy in Halesowen, St Paul's in Wythenshawe, Allestree Woodlands School in Derby, St Edmund Arrowsmith in Wigan and of course the pupils of Ellesmere Park High School in Salford (where I'm lucky enough to be the Patron of Reading) for all their help.

Others have provided the spirit and soundtrack without ever knowing *Payback* existed. So final thanks go to Chuck D, Mos Def, M.I.A., Aesop Rock, Posdnuos, Common, Brother Ali, Gil Scott-Heron, Q-Tip, Talib Kweli, The Roots and Nas.

And if you've enjoyed this story – special thanks to you too!

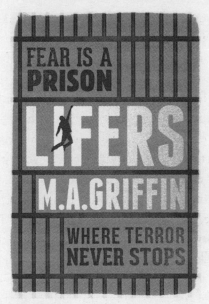

LIFERS by M.A. GRIFFIN

Fear haunts the streets of Manchester: a schoolgirl has disappeared.

Preston is drawn to investigate, exploring the city in the hunt for his missing friend. Deep in the bowels of a secret scientific institute, he discovers a sinister machine, used to banish criminal teenagers for their offences. Captured and condemned to the cavernous dimension, Preston is determined to escape – but this is no ordinary jail.

Friendships are forged and lives lost in a reckless battle for freedom, revenge – and revolution.

Set partly in the grim backstreets of Manchester, this dystopian YA thriller will appeal to fans of The Hunger Games, Maze Runner and The Fayz . . . The plot is fast paced, and the dialogue gritty and authentic.
THE SCHOOL LIBRARIAN

Paperback, ISBN 978-1-910002-25-4, £7.99 • ebook, ISBN 978-1-910002-26-1, £7.99

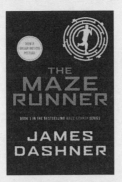

THE MAZE RUNNER by JAMES DASHNER

When the doors of the lift crank open, the only thing Thomas can remember is his first name. But he's not alone. He's surrounded by boys who welcome him to the Glade, an encampment at the centre of a bizarre maze.

Like Thomas, the Gladers don't know why or how they came to be there, or what's happened to the world outside. All they know is that every morning when the walls slide back, they will risk everything to find out . . .

A dark and gripping tale of survival set in a world where teenagers fight for their lives on a daily basis.
PUBLISHERS WEEKLY

Paperback, ISBN 978-1-909489-40-0, £7.99 • ebook, ISBN 978-1-908435-48-4, £7.99

ALSO AVAILABLE:

THE SCORCH TRIALS
Paperback, ISBN 978-1-909489-41-7, £7.99 • ebook, ISBN 978-1-908435-49-1, £7.99

THE DEATH CURE
Paperback, ISBN 978-1-909489-42-4, £7.99 • ebook, ISBN 978-1-908435-35-4, £7.99

THE KILL ORDER
Paperback, ISBN 978-1-909489-43-1, £7.99 • ebook, ISBN 978-1-908435-69-9, £7.99

THE FEVER CODE
Paperback, ISBN 978-1-911077-03-9, £7.99 • ebook, ISBN 978-1-910655-66-5, £7.99